MARIËTTE WHITCOMB

ORCA

Copyright © 2020 Mariëtte Whitcomb

ISBN Paperback: 978-1-990988-59-2
ISBN eBook: 978-1-990988-60-8

This novel is dedicated to every person who has been trafficked or held captive.
To the survivors, those who were murdered, and the ones who still suffer at the hands of their captors.

Also, to the brave men and women who have dedicated their lives to hunt these predators and fight for justice for the victims.

We see you.

One

War. Rage and anguish bumped into each other in the mosh pit which had become my inner being. The constant throbbing left me nauseated and broken.

Coming home had always been bittersweet. The day I returned from my last tour – more bitter than sweet. As I stepped off the aircraft, I realised my mouth was parched. The ever-present taste of sand.

I stood motionless on the tarmac watching as people rushed past. They had somewhere to go, loved ones to embrace, lives to live. I closed my eyes and inhaled a mixture of city air and salty ocean breeze.

The darkness of the night enveloped me as if shielding me from the reality that only daylight can bring. I had made it home. *Home?* Those who had made this place home were no longer here. I tried exhaling the brokenness of my reality. Mustering my strength, I lifted my head as high as possible. In the dark corner of a bunker, my soul lay covered in blood and tears. Not tears for myself – never tears for me.

Soldiers don't cry.

Our eyes met across the bustling arrivals hall. She sank to her knees, crushing the last piece of heart I had left. Her relentless sobs filled the terminal, overshadowing the happiness of those around us. I rushed to her and dropped to the floor beside her. As I wrapped my arms around her, I didn't know if I clung to her for her sake, or for my own.

"I'm sorry," I continued reiterating, stroking her golden hair the same way she stroked mine when we were children.

She faced me, her green eyes piercing, tears flowing down her flawless face. Her eyes widened with shock. "What did they do to you?" A breathless murmur.

I willed a smile, the scar less visible as I did so. Irony at its best. "We will pull through this. Hell, if we could get through Mom's cooking, we can make it through anything." Laughter took over, in equal measure to her sorrow.

"Let's head home." She wiped her eyes, careful not to smudge her mascara.

Home she said. Beautiful Lizzie. The accomplished CEO, the perfect daughter, my sister.

A car honked next to us and I held my breath, needing to remind myself of my whereabouts. *You're no longer captive, you're free.* An internal argument ensued, one of those where your heart says one thing and your mind says something different, and you, in order to find sanity in the mush of your inner being, try to figure out if your gut has anything to add to the debate.

If it was a backfire or something resembling an explosion or gunshot you would be less insane. So, man up and soldier on. My mind reprimanded my body, the last part my father's voice. My sister stared at me with a perplexed expression. Did I see concern or fear in her eyes? Too exhausted to care, I turned my focus on the early evening traffic ahead of us as commuters made their way across the city of Marcel.

We arrived at Lizzie's soon thereafter and I asked if I could take a shower and go straight to bed, telling her we would catch up in the morning. Lizzie offered me some food, but I lied and said I had eaten on the flight. I don't know if it was the sleep deprivation or the unnecessary emotions creeping out of me, but I couldn't recall when last I ate.

To my astonishment, sleep came that night.

"How long? Grow a pair and tell me how long!" I yelled at the startled nurse. She looked like a cross between a child getting caught with her hand in the cookie jar and someone who is staring at a monster. "How long?"

"Four months, Sergeant." I heard my father's voice.

Tears stung my face as it gravitated towards the pillow. I turned my head hoping to see him standing there, that he had come to take me home with the promise of everything being all right. I had hoped he would tell me their deaths had been a cruel joke and that he was still proud of me. Instead my father stood in the door, blood dripping from his lacerated face, his head contorted on his broken neck. I cried.

Not the muffled cry you might expect from someone who had seen and done much worse. No, a deep bellowing cry from a place of fury, brokenness, and a profound yearning to have been there with my parents before death ripped them from our lives. To have attended their funeral. To not have been tortured, to not have been raped, to not have seen my squad tortured and killed in front of me as I watched, powerless to save them. To have been rescued sooner, the first time the general knew where we were being held. To not have been a pawn in a political game; to not have killed innocent civilians carrying suicide vests; to not have seen children used as human shields, playing real-life soldier. To not have needed to defend ourselves against children. Their faces will forever haunt me.

"Wake up, Finley. It's only a dream. Please wake up," Lizzie whispered, her voice riddled with fear. Was this how she would treat me now? With whispers and stares?

"A dream? What do you know except your perfect life? Go back to your unicorn, bunny and butterfly-filled medicated dreams. Get out!" Resentment pulsing with every word.

Sleep didn't return – perhaps I willed it not to. I stared out the bedroom window, across the park from Lizzie's house all the way to the ocean. She had done well for herself, being envious of her life was nothing new.

In darkness I stood, my subconscious picking at the scabs of memories, thoughts, and emotions I fought to repress. My subconscious proved itself stronger than a decorated soldier.

Soldier. Prisoner of war. Hero. Victim. Labels.

A blind rage filled me. How does one dull-witted military-appointed psychiatrist who has never been in any real danger have the balls to diagnose me with moral injury, survivor's guilt, and post-traumatic stress disorder? The rage that simmered within me made me lash out at the little man, his concerned expression and calm voice the tipping point. Everything about him irritated me. His tiny spectacles, his tiny pull-over jersey, his ridiculous little bow tie. I left his office slamming the door behind me, but not before yelling a number of superb profanity combinations at him. Not the kind of language my mother would approve of. The tension in my jaw eased at the memory of her, my mouth may have even attempted a smile. *I miss them.*

My father had spent years moulding Lizzie to take over his company, the reasonable thing to do as she had played with chemistry sets from her diaper days and was passionate about medicating the world into a pain-free, healthy, antipsychotic status quo. To her colleagues and employees, she was Elizabeth Williams. To me, she would always be my Fizzie-Lizzie. How that girl could throw a tantrum for a Fizzer was equivalent to politicians throwing punches in parliament. My older sister, the person I wanted to be growing up.

I am my father's wished-for-a-son daughter. He taught me to hunt, fish, shoot, and tamper with anything and everything electrical. During our family holidays, he always found something for us to build, alter, or kill. Not only did I inherit his love of cars – both big and fast – and guns, but also his name. If he was to remain without a son, I would carry on his name and had to promise a million times, in the event I ever got married, I would hyphenate my surname. They christened me Finley D. Williams, to be Williams-Whatever in a different life. Alpha. Bravo. Charlie. Duncan.

Duncan! Not something I advertise as my father could've been less of a donkey's behind for bestowing such masculine names on a little girl who had to beg her teachers not to say both her names in class. *Children can be so cruel.* So are mother's who compromised as she had the right to name her first born after her favourite queen. The first. The Virgin Queen. That my sister wasn't, but my parents preferred to believe in her innocence. Elizabeth Williams, too, is a rock which bends to no wind.

With a fair complexion and warrior spirit, I embraced Finley. Fin to my friends and family.

Sergeant Williams no more.

Two

The sun rimmed the horizon, in a warm orangey-red contrasting the dark blue of the ocean. I was back. For the time being, I would leave the word *home* in a corner and dust it off once I was ready to use it again. I tiptoed out of Lizzie's world-renowned interior decorator-inspired (whose name I can't remember but which always made me laugh as it reminded me of an improper, below-the-belt, pre-teen joke) living quarter. No, not ready for home yet.

That morning I didn't jog, I ran. Ran from screams, ran from men speaking a foreign language, their bodies doing a universally spoken horror. *Four months.*

I ran until my legs ached as much as my being did. The sight of a little form being pulled out of the water grounded my feet.

Waves crashed; an eerie silence filled the already hot morning air. I made my way over to where a crowd had gathered, hearing someone whisper, "How many is it now?"

"Seven," a whispered reply.

All I saw – the wet, white hair of a little girl. She couldn't have been much older than nine when someone stole a lifetime away from her, and those who loved her. For weeks her parents had lived in hell, not knowing her location, who took her, or what their baby had to endure. Their thoughts gnawing at them like a rat gnawing itself into a corpse.

"In the ocean? Best estimate, a week." A towering, dark man answered. His enormous back covered with the words, *Police: Homicide.* I recognized his voice but couldn't place it.

My palms itched; no amount of rubbing them together eased it. I needed to leave, get away from the victim of a war in front of me. War followed me home. Or did it never occur

6

to me it was always there, surrounding me? An invisible, unspoken reality we consciously choose to ignore because the truth about this world is much too dark for our liking.

I ran until my legs no longer wanted to move and I collapsed onto Lizzie's lawn, retching. Lizzie, dressed in perfect Saturday, my-sister-has-returned clothes, came rushing through the front door. Her gentle arms surrounded me, her voice a symphony of calm, peace, and love. Lizzie rocked me until my stomach emptied itself. She's a safe zone, a comfortable, familiar environment, and I allowed myself to shift the image of the wet, white hair from my thoughts.

"I feel terrible about this morning, Liz." My voice rattled with remorse, doused in pain. I offered her a smile to hide the hideous scar, trying to make myself look familiar. To soothe her.

"Let's get you cleaned up and fed," she said, pulling me to my feet.

I ravished the plate of Eggs Benedict she placed in front of me with the fervour of long-lost lovers. At long last my appetite also returned.

"Uncle Tom will be over in an hour to discuss the will," she said with hesitation.

The will? I had no desire to discuss what our parents left us when we needed nothing more than them. A great bond existed between us, the glue, as in most happy families, had been unconditional love. Mutual respect and a need to see each other grow to our fullest potential covering it all like one of the snug blankets at the lake house.

Many things come to mind when one thinks of Thomas Anderson, punctual being at the top of the list. Not our uncle by relation, but a constant pillar of strength throughout our lives as one of our parents' dearest friends, and our godfather. He had lost his wife to cancer, a short while before. *Four months.*

In a matter of four months, all of our lives were shred to pieces. A shark snuck up on the pod of seals that were my loved ones, shredding at will. It tore my soul out and didn't even have the decency to devour it. The ones who survived barely did so.

I thought of the little girl with the wet, white hair. A different shark breached, rows and rows of deadly teeth exposed, ripping the life from seven little girls, destroying the lives of their families forever.

Uncle Tom smiled his warm, familiar smile as he walked out on to the patio where I sat contemplating sharks, not the cold-blooded aquatic kind.

"Welcome home, soldier." The same greeting he always gave when I returned from war.

Home? Soldier? I no longer had a home, and I was no soldier. I smiled and hugged him, veiling the truth in my eyes.

Uncle Tom is a real-life lie detector, often sent by my parents to pick us up from school or visit us at the University of Marcel to find out the truth if we were reluctant to talk to them. Lizzie and I often strategised how we wouldn't allow him to pull the truth out of us, but alas, he has a way about him. No matter how strong our youthful resilience, he remains a bloodhound for the truth. This made him a very successful detective and state prosecutor in his later life. A run in with a gang-banger's sawed-off shotgun cost him not only his right leg, but also the career which had been his life. Unlikely circumstances.

Lizzie placed a tray with coffee in front of us and took a seat next to me. Her hand reached for mine. The tremble of her hand made me realise: Lizzie was just as damaged as me. Since waking up in the hospital, I never once considered the effect everything that had happened had on her. In my mind, she's the unmovable rock. How painful it must have been for her to have an enlisted sister, knowing I never feared being the first one through the door or out the armoured vehicle, that I preferred it that way. To know about my abduction. Being subjected to the videos sent by our captors, being both glad and horrified when seeing it. Glad I was alive, sickened at the sight of me broken and disfigured.

Lizzie had identified our parents' bodies. She saw them mangled up, cold, their lives gone.

Three

"Finley. Where are you?" Uncle Tom's voice brought me back to the porch, to them, to the warm ocean breeze. Seagulls in the distance.

"Sorry, Uncle Tom. It's hard for both of us and I guess for you, too."

Lizzie squeezed my hand. A simple squeeze when she was too afraid to hug me as she hated showing emotion in front of others. *Don't we all?*

"May I continue? To Finley Duncan Williams." He cleared his throat, trying to hide the grin. "We leave our penthouse in the city, Williams Manor, including the surrounding properties which make up the total of the Williams Estate. Your father's gun collection, his prized collection of vintage cars, and sufficient funds for you to live a comfortable life, set up in a trust fund. A twenty-five percent share in Williams Pharmaceuticals."

Uncle Tom turned his focus to Lizzie. "To Elizabeth Williams, we leave a seventy-five percent share in Williams Pharmaceuticals. The beach house in Wild Bay. Our art collection, and sufficient funds for you to live a comfortable life, set up in a trust fund." He waited for it to sink in before he continued. "All other shares and stocks to be sold, if so requested by Elizabeth and Finley. The proceeds to go to both equally. Elizabeth, you are to continue with the work your mother started by donating medicine to inner-city clinics and head the foundation, Medicine For All. Finley, you are to be the head of Tabula Rasa. You are their protector now."

Starting from nothing, my father had built an empire, my mother by his side, encouraging and inspiring many of his greatest ideas. They raised two daughters, whom they loved and were proud of. They wished only the best for us. Always hoping we would one day find the love they had in each other, and when the time was right that we would have families of our own. They reminded me to carry on the family name and hyphenate Williams-Whatever as I had promised, and the agreement to such I had signed when I was twenty-one years old. *Oh, to be twenty-one again.* What I wouldn't do differently if I got a second chance. Sure as it would rain that afternoon, not have fought someone else's war.

In an instant, I was a protector.

Again.

Four

Tabula Rasa. The name I first proposed to my mother when she had decided to do something about and for the many victims of violence in our city. Her guests, as she liked to call them, came from various backgrounds. Domestic violence, prostitution, and a remarkable number of guests who either escaped, on the odd chance they were able to, or were rescued from traffickers. Women and children, some only babies.

I was sitting on my bed studying for a Biology examination when my mother had burst into my room at Williams Manor. Why my parents had decided on such a formal name for the lake house, I will never know. My mother's face had beamed, her voice elated and hurried like a schoolgirl with the gossip of the year, saying she knew what she wanted to do. She plonked down onto my bed and had spoken with such passion, I couldn't help but admire her strength, her heart, her bravery.

That bravery I saw in action the day my mother and I were attacked outside Tabula Rasa Manor. *What is it with them and manors?* She fought off the attackers and shot one, injuring another. The latter died a block down the street, on the filthy pavement like the piece of trash he was. She shared my father's belief in carrying a weapon at all times. The police informed us they were traffickers who wanted to scare my mother into closing down the manor, as a warning to her guests, a reminder they would never be safe or out of reach. My mother employed around the clock armed security and spoke without restraint about the attack with the guests of Tabby Manor, as everyone would come to refer to it. They all drew strength from her bravery, and I realised I may have my father's names, but I have her courage.

The trash who died down the street didn't succumb to the

gunshot wound my mother had inflicted on him. I chased him down and found him lying in a pool of blood. He pleaded for mercy. I smiled at the irony, drew my flick knife, and slit his throat. A warm breeze stirred my hair. The scent of the ocean tainted by a faint copper smell.

I finished my degree in Psychology and Criminology and enrolled in the army. To serve and protect. No charges were ever filed against me. Money can do a lot of things. To protect.

"Finley Duncan Williams. Welcome home. So lovely to have you back home with us." The soft voice of the manager of Tabby Manor greeted me as I got out of my car. A survivor of trafficking herself, Ashley had all the heart it took to create a safe haven for the guests and the determination to get every single guest to a place of self-love and hope. With reckless abandon for her own safety, she made her sweet escape at the age of sixteen. She saved the lives of the young girls being held with her, the youngest only four. Sheer willpower made her wait for the perfect moment, not stopping when they shot at her, or threatened to burn the others alive. Running until she stumbled onto Uncle Tom, literally. *Unlikely circumstances.*

"I missed you, Ash." We hugged, not a normal friend's hug, but a survivor's hug. A hug reserved for people who have shared similar horrors. Yet, I was a soldier, not a scared, ten-year-old little girl. I often thought of Ashley after they were done with me and wondered when I would have that perfect moment where I, too, could escape.

As if she read my mind, she held me tighter and whispered, "You survived. No matter how you got away, you did, and you survived. You're safe now."

Wet, white hair. I willed the sight out of my mind and focused on being in the moment with my best friend.

We sat in her office and spoke about Tabby Manor, the guests and what had been going on in the city. I told her about the little blonde girl and how I couldn't get the image of her tiny broken body out of my mind. Ashley told me everything she knew about the predator the media referred to as Angel Taker. Not a term they coined, no, he was taunting the police and families of his victims with letters and photos. A shark came to mind. Bumping, circling, going in for the kill.

Ashley is not only a survivor, she's an acclaimed psychiatrist. In true psychiatrist fashion, she asked about my own dreams and thoughts, and I tried to hold it in but failed miserably. It all came out. Every detail, every horrific sight, sound, everything. Ashley looked at me, a knowing behind the wall of tears she held back.

"Thank you for not crying." Not realising I said it aloud.

She smiled, nodded, and I knew it was her turn to talk. "I agree with the observations of the military psychiatrist. The only way you will get through it all, and I mean all of it, is to get through it. There's no other way. Helping others helped me and I know you. You're a protector and your mother knew what you needed when she left you to run this place. Don't even think it; not once did she give up hope that you would survive and return to all of us. Long before they took you hostage, she told me you would need to come and work here once you got back. You are and always will be a protector. It's who you are, it courses through your veins. Most people need oxygen, water, and food, to survive. You, my friend, you need a purpose, you need to protect. It's right there at the top of your hierarchy of needs, if not in equal measure on all five tiers. It's who God made you."

We spoke about many things, like friends do, including her upcoming wedding. How far had she not come? Ashley introduced me to all the guests. A baby cried and I rushed in the direction of the cries.

"Finley, meet Hope. Hope, meet Finley." Ashley introduced us as I reached for the little wriggling girl, rocking her and holding her so close I was afraid I might hurt her. I kissed her cooing face, not wanting to think of what had brought her to us. I would protect her. I might not be a soldier anymore, but I was my mother's daughter and I would make her proud. I would be the warrior God had made me to be. Hope lay in my arms, her body trusting a complete stranger not to hurt her. To give her the life she deserved. Hope survived, her future a clean slate.

Five

The sun cast an orange light over the city streets as I drove to Lizzie's. It made one final attempt at offering warmth before darkness would envelop the remainder of the day. The approaching darkness echoed in the void which formed in me. Pouring myself out to Ashley had left me drained, tired, and empty. Before leaving Tabby Manor, I had deemed it wise to drive back with the top down, thinking the warm summer wind in my hair might soothe me.

A ridiculous idea, but worth a try.

Hope's soft cooing and babbling sounds filled my mind as I turned towards the promenade, in the opposite direction of where I intended to go. I parked the sleek German convertible and stared over the ocean, not seeing water. Something stirred in my subconscious, it tried to climb out of the dark pit that had become my mind. Whether a thought or a notion I didn't know, but it was desperate for air.

I closed my eyes and focused on my breathing, something Ashley proposed before she told me to stand up, put on a brave face and meet the guests. She informed me Tabby Manor had reached capacity over the preceding months and we needed to discuss either starting a second facility or buying the property next door and expanding. The police, she told me, had started a task force to fight the surge in human trafficking. They hoped to turn the tide on a tsunami which was crushing not only our city, but the surrounding areas. It was, in fact, a pandemic, reaching across the globe, obliterating everyone in its path. This I knew but never gave much consideration to. Most people don't.

I met the victims over the years. I heard their stories, yet they weren't stories. They were memories of nightmares come true. None of it ever affected me, as strange as that sounds.

A frantic, panicked, scream yanked me back to reality.

I jumped out of the car and ran to where the screams were coming from. Gun drawn. Instinct.

Wet, white hair. Two little girls had washed ashore, their broken bodies for the world to see. Two small bodies bound with yellow nylon rope. The site of the rope yanked at the notion in my subconscious to try harder at surfacing. My feet refused to move; I yelled for someone to call the police. The custom-made grip of my SIG left an imprint in my palm.

The police arrived at the scene. Again, the tall, dark figure was there. Still, I couldn't place him. I gave my statement to the first responder and left.

The sound of the convertible's roof going up blocked out the crashing waves. I cried. Not for myself, but for the millions of victims and survivors suffering at the hands of men and women; not monsters, but real-life predators.

As children, our parents protected us from the bleak reality of the world. They told us there were monsters out there, far from us, who did terrible things. More often not, they're closer than we think.

I wept for nine little girls as I drove, seeing only blots of red, yellow, and blue as the tears wouldn't stop.

Lizzie's house smelled of comfort and warmth. I found her in the kitchen, busy cooking one of her signature dishes. A yearning for normality crept over me and I rushed myself to the shower. As water and tears mixed, I thought of nine little girls, the faces and smiles at Tabby Manor. Smiles in different stages of acceptance, grief, recovery, and resurrection. I wondered what others saw in my smile?

Water covered me and I let it, hoping somehow it would help the something in my mind come out and into the light where I could face it.

Lizzie and I ate on the patio, the air humid, thunder cracking in the distance as the trees stirred. We barely finished our dinner before heaven opened. Storms were common at that time of the year, but this one was louder than most. Thunder bellowed as the city skyline turned blue in irregular flashes.

I wondered whether God was mourning the lives of these nine little girls and making His presence known through the storm. When I was a child, my parents would tell me thunder was God's voice, telling the clouds where to rain. A comforting idea as a child.

God hates hands that shed innocent blood.

Does God hate my hands? I wondered, as I lay my drained body down on the bed. Sleep came easy that night, a welcome relief.

Wet, white hair pulled me down into dark, icy water. Beady eyes surrounded me. Every cell, every part of my being screamed for air. Out of the dark, shapes appear. Circling me, bumping me. A dark figure heading straight for me, nine large bloodstained teeth exposed in a grimace. Beady eyes focused on its prey. Its large body swaying from side to side, coming closer. Millions of years had allowed it to evolve into a cunning predator, rivalled by none. Wet, white hair held my throat, pulling tighter as I desperately tried to free myself. Hope screams and slips out of my hands into the gaping mouth of a predator, watching, waiting below for a moment such as this. Nine bloodstained teeth tear into my body, ripping, gnawing, laughing.

Sweat streaming from my body, I jerked upright, still trying to get the wet, white hair to loosen its grip on my neck. *Breathe.*

Six

I got up and made some coffee. The images of Hope slipping out of my hands, beady eyes, nine teeth ripping at me, remained ingrained in my mind's eye. If not for the sound of Lizzie's voice behind me jolting me back to reality, I could've sworn I was still dreaming.

"Why are you up so early?" Her yawning voice filled the kitchen.

In those precious moments where she was just my sister and not the fierce CEO, she reminded me of the times we had snuck out of my parents' house to some party to get drunk and see who could bag the hottest guy. The next morning, we would survive our hangovers by greasing our arteries with the fattiest food imaginable, reminiscing about the previous night's adventure. Lizzie and I often got into a heated debate as to whose guy was, in fact, the hottest. Or guys, some very interesting evenings.

Being Irish twins often led to competition between the two of us. Lizzie was a year ahead of me in school, a fact she often brought up when trying to win an argument or persuading our parents not to give me permission to attend the same parties she did. She hated competition, still does.

Lizzie is the academic star; I'm the athletic 'twin'. She was by far the most beautiful girl in school and at university, her beauty only rivalled by my own. The opinion of others, not mine.

For years Lizzie and I were very much at war, but blood is thicker than water and we have a bond shared only by other *twins*. We had an unspoken language growing up, infuriating my parents, as we could have lengthy discussions and they were none the wiser to what was being said. Uncle Tom always came by for a visit the next day to spend time with us, his excuse being he missed his girls, followed by the most charming smile plastered across his face. As we got older, we wised up to his and our parents' antics.

Uncle Tom and Aunt Kelly were permanent fixtures in our lives. Never having children of their own until they adopted Ashley, they put all their parental affection and energy into us. *Aunt Kelly. Gone.* Ripped from us by a predator that struck with such voracity, she died within a week of being diagnosed. Invisible to the naked eye, no one saw it before it leapt up and devoured such a magnificent creature.

"I'm going to the lake house for a week or two," I said with a subtle sternness, knowing Lizzie would refuse, yet again turning into the rock.

"I understand. Perhaps I can drive through on Friday evening and spend the weekend with you? Like old times," she said. I had to will my jaw not to drop.

"Don't get me wrong, I love staying with you, but I need to clear my head. Find my rhythm again, if that makes sense. I'm sure you would welcome some undisturbed sleep." I smiled and covered the scar she was staring at with my hair.

Lizzie sipped her coffee, shifting her gaze at something else, maybe nothing, and turned to me, sighing as she did so. A telltale sign what she was about to say would be both important and difficult for her. "Fin, I'm concerned about you. It's understandable you would be different. I mean, uhm..." She gathered her thoughts, her foot tapping on the cool tile beneath. I thought it might be her attempt at setting a beat to the conversation or perhaps hiding her vulnerability.

"You know I don't mean it like that. But what you went through is unspeakable. And coming home to this? I don't know how you get yourself out of bed every morning." The corners of her mouth lifted. "Without being medicated."

To be honest, neither did I, but I kept this to myself. "I love you Fizzie-Lizzie." I waited for my words to nuzzle into her being. "It will only be for a few days and I can be back here in forty-five minutes if you need me."

She watched me with a firmness in her beautiful face. "I love you more, Duncan." Her laughter streamed across the patio.

I contemplated changing my name, my father no longer around for it to break his heart. I resolved to change my face – remove the scar. Reclaim who I was before. No visible reminder of what I had to endure for four long months in that intolerable heat.

People have watched me my whole life, so much so that I had to work much harder at getting and staying in the army.

Beautiful girls are dumb, fragile, whores. The voice of my would-be attacker rung in my ears as I pinned him to the ground and beat him until I had no strength left. He never again thought of forcing himself on any other girl; worth the scar on my knuckle.

A small part of me rejoiced when he got killed in combat. Briefly happy then, now glad one less predator prowled around searching for dumb, fragile whores. His words, not mine.

I drove to Williams Manor in the comfort of my Mercedes-AMG G 65. As I turned from the main road onto the dirt road leading to the lake, a thought came to mind. *Are all people inherently predators? Do we all have it in us to take as we please, hurting others, ripping at their being, to destroy their souls? Or try to at least.*

The guests at Tabby Manor have shown what willpower and a need for survival is, coming out of the worst pits of hell. Stoic. That's what they are. *I can be stoic!*

I turned the music louder as one of my favourite heavy-metal singers shouted at me. A fitting song about embracing who you are at your core.

Seven

Williams Manor came into view. A storm was forming behind it, to the south. Not a manor, but a grandiose house none the less. Our home away from home. *Mine*.

Its original owners built it as a weekend retreat, our parents had explained to us when they first took us to view their newest acquisition. A splendid addition to their growing property portfolio. As they got older and my father became more sucked into his work, they sold most of the other properties, but this house, this place, was dear to them and to me.

With rock walls and a slate roof, it appeared ominous, but I found comfort in it. It blended with the surrounding woods. A simple two-storey building, with a jetty to the left, fireplaces in the main living areas and each of the four bedrooms. Perfect for a family getaway, complete with a soundproof wine cellar.

A lifetime ago, I found myself procrastinating, not wanting to do an assignment for Criminology. I can't recall the topic. Either serial killers, juvenile delinquency, or forensics. So, in my desire to be productive while being unproductive, I did a Google search on the origins of the property. My father was hiding something. After half an hour of searching, I found it. The original owner, none other than the infamous Anthony Andretti – Tony, to his few confidants. A ruthless Don who struck fear into, and life out of, anyone he pleased.

"The bolted down chair in the wine cellar, I know what it was used for!" I shouted at my father as I raced down the stairs, taking two steps at a time. I almost broke my ankle, but the pain had been well worth the look on his face.

How I loved outsmarting him. I still miss him, my heart aching to hear his words of wisdom. If only he had been there to guide the notion, still trying to claw its way out of the pit of my subconscious. *Who will I best now?* My father is my hero, mentor, teacher of so many things a girl shouldn't be taught but a son should.

"Was, Fin! Was!" I screamed as I parked the car in front of the garage door closest to the house, sorry, manor. My hands clenched the steering wheel, knuckles turning white. I sat breathing hard, wondering when, if ever, I could have a normal driving experience again. *Normal.*

I smiled and got out of the vehicle, holstering my SIG Sauer P226. Only the best for daddy's not-a-son-girl on her twenty-first birthday. The hairs on the back of my neck stirred as I unlocked the front door and carried my belongings into the house. *Someone is watching me.*

The notion tried harder to claw its way out.

Rain poured down as if the heavens tried to wash away the sins of that house. Past and future.

The storm raged for hours. Had it been tornado country, I might have been in the wine cellar tied to that chair. My father told me it had been a safety precaution as the previous owner broke his arm when he fell asleep in a loose standing chair and toppled over in a drunken stupor.

"A terrible drunkard," my father had said, shaking his head to make the story more believable. Now I knew better. Scuff marks from where hands and feet were once bound still visible.

I stared at the chair for a long time, looking around the soundproof room, two big vault doors separating it from the house. The room was built into the foundation of the house. Mr Andretti had been specific in his requirements. His architect disappeared after construction commenced. The room never appeared in any filed building plans. *Architect in the lake.*

A switch between the two doors controlled the flow of oxygen into the room. The perfect place to keep prized bottles of wine and whiskey for connoisseurs like my parents.

A love for whiskey was something else I shared with my father. I removed a bottle of Johnnie Walker Blue Label from the shelf. Sanity, as my father referred to it, enough to get me through the week. I poured myself a glass, seeing my mother shake her head as she always had.

"Soldier or not, you're still a lady, Finley. Ladies have a sip, not a glass."

I drank it in one guzzle, grateful I drank it neat as it burned my throat, my stomach, warming me. I do love a good Walker.

Pouring myself another, I sat on the sofa facing the lake, contemplating sharks. Beady-eyed little sharks. White, wet hair pulling me down into the abyss. The following morning the tenth little girl would be found.

I tried to shake the sight from my mind and pulled one of the family albums closer. The top album held photos of our best family holiday, in Resurrection Bay, Alaska. It was a dream of my parents to go there and see the whales. They took us along on this adventure of theirs. My father had thought the clean air and unspoiled nature would calm his daughters' raging teen antics and hormones. On the last two days of our trip, we saw orcas.

A pod of orcas made their way past us, breaching for air and gracefully disappearing again. An older calf played, its mother nearby.

I looked out on the darkened lake. Night had come, visions of dark shapes under the water filled my mind. Apex predators. At the top of their food chain. I glanced back at the photo, at our happy faces, orcas visible in the background.

That night I had the best sleep I had had in months. Again, wet, white hair pulled me down, dark figures circled and bumped into me as I descended into the dark. Every cell in my body screamed for air. From the corner of my eye, I saw an enormous figure moving. Gracefully gliding through the water, up and down. Not swerving. The enormous figure fixed its sights on the sharks, coming closer with tremendous speed and accuracy, ripping at the sharks leaving carcasses in its wake. The wet, white hair loosened its grip and I swam towards the surface. Sunlight hit my face and I breathed, the air sweet and warm. It smelled like home.

I slept for fourteen hours that night and woke up with a smile. Sharks are not at the top of the food chain, there's something higher than them. Bigger. More gracious. Warm-blooded.

Black and white, not grey.

Orcas.

The notion had made its way out of the pit, stretching its supple body as it took deep, long breaths. It was out.

Eight

I went running, as had become my routine each morning since I returned, but this day I was simply running. The air fresh with the scent of pine trees and moist earth. My heart light.

I had a purpose again, now I needed a plan. A fair warrior I was yet again, no longer a victim, but a survivor. A protector. Deep, long breaths.

A strategy pulsated through me: Rapid Decisive Operations.

I would start with my face, blend into society, look like me again, no visible scars. My sight fixed on a visible enemy, lurking, watching, waiting. I would find them one by one and rip them out of this world, leaving carcasses in my wake.

Dr Schmidt's receptionist picked up on the second ring. *Efficient.* You better be when you work for the most renowned plastic surgeon this side of the hemisphere. Dr Schmidt's receptionist was bending over backwards, and telling me so, to accommodate me by booking surgery for the following week Tuesday. She put me on hold for a few minutes while she was talking to the good doctor, leaving me to listen to the most awful elevator music, and then she was back on the line to make the final arrangements. No, it wasn't necessary for me to come in for a consultation first, the doctor knew my family so well. *Money opens doors.*

"About a month, but it depends on the extent of the damage to your face. The doctor will give you a better indication after surgery. See you next week, Miss Williams," she said, before she ended the call. *A month.*

"Perfect," I said to myself as sunlight filled the house. Enough time to get everything ready and to learn the art of hunting a different kind of prey. Being prepared for the hunt and the subsequent kill is all in the details. Patiently waiting until you know your prey's life is in your hands, my father had taught me.

If you can't kill it, you don't hunt it.

Nine

I wanted to spend time with Lizzie before I went for surgery and started executing my mission. I invited her and Uncle Tom to the lake house for the weekend. Uncle Tom was keen to discuss his job as he knew I shared his passion for justice. He had hoped I would become a criminal profiler, as was the plan when I finished high school. I completed my degree and then enlisted in the army, a sense of duty I had explained to my parents. It was, I felt at the time, the right thing to do. Perhaps in hindsight, not.

My years in the army, and all the years spent in an active war zone, taught me much more than any police academy ever could. War had been my life for so long, it coursed through my veins. I was born for it. A warrior. A protector. A weapon.

Could I have more blood on my hands no matter how putrid it is?

There are ways of keeping one's hands clean. I grinned.

The notion created a home for itself in my being. I took out my handguns and cleaned each one with meticulous care. This is what one does before hunting, or going to war.

All I had to do – identify my prey's habitat.

Lizzie and Uncle Tom arrived late on Friday afternoon; Lizzie had left work early and Uncle Tom's trial had not taken as long as he had thought – the killer had confessed. Less for me to worry about, I thought, as I poured drinks. Johnnie Blue for everyone. I grilled meat while Lizzie made a salad. Uncle Tom kept me company, knowing better than to give commentary on my grilling skills.

"What's going on with the Angel Taker case? Any leads?" I cannonballed in. Why waste time with dipping your toes?

"You know I can't give details about an ongoing investigation, but I wish I could get your opinion. Even as a child you understood the psyche of these monsters. You need to consider going back to university and qualifying as a profiler."

"Uncle Tom, I want to help in any way I can to bring closure to the victims' families. I've seen three of the little girls the ocean gave back."

He looked away from me and fixed his eyes on the darkness hanging over the lake and surrounding woods, his voice heavy with anger. "They haven't located all the families yet. The girls are not all local, only three have been so far. He has sent fifteen letters, we have only found ten bodies. Fifteen photos. Where are the other five?"

I closed my eyes, letting what he said sink in. "Well if the others aren't local, where are they from? Are they in any missing children databases?"

"This is off-the-record, Fin. You are not to repeat this to anyone," his focus still on something across the lake. "They are from all over the country. We don't know yet how he gets them, or why he brings them here. Travelling with an abducted child is extremely high-risk."

Before I could censor my thoughts, I uttered, "Also, high reward and lucrative."

He jerked his head to face me, his eyes filled with questions.

"We received intel on a trafficker in the region where I was stationed who was abducting children and forcing them into God-only-knows what. He sold them to the highest bidder – on the dark web. We were closing in on him, but he fled before we arrived at his compound. We found the bodies of some of the children. A bomb ended their lives, maybe an act of mercy. Perhaps he didn't want them slowing down his escape or, I don't know."

Uncle Tom stood motionless, the wheels of his brilliant mind turning almost audibly. "This is how he is finding the girls, Fin. He is buying them online. The sonofabitch could be anyone, anywhere. If he is doing this on the dark web, which he probably is, there is no way for us to find him. If we don't catch him dumping a body, or a routine traffic stop, or receive a tip from the public, he can, and will, keep on doing this for as long as he pleases."

He returned his gaze over the lake. "The forensic pathologist told me some of the girls' hair had been dyed blonde. Either he is doing it himself or whoever is supplying him is meeting his requirements."

Bile rose in my throat.

"I need to make a call." Uncle Tom walked towards the jetty.

The notion tried to get my attention. "Wait. How sure are you he isn't part of the task force?" Uncle Tom almost lost his balance as he spun around to face me. "I mean, the taunting letters, he sends this even when a body hasn't yet been found. Always a step ahead. Cunning, cruel and he has some big balls showing his hand like this. He must be in a position where he believes it's impossible he will ever be caught. He won't be the first serial killer to have been a policeman. Has there been anyone who signed up for this specific case, anyone who inserted themselves into the investigation?"

A sound tore through the silence that hung between us.

"Anderson," Uncle Tom answered his mobile phone. "That is impossible. We can't even get the one we know of and have been tracking, or trying to, for months. Now there are two? Shit!"

Uncle Tom never swore, not in front of us at least, always a gentleman. My stomach twisted itself into an untenable knot. *This is bad.*

He shook his head. "Send me what you have, and I will look it over. We need to discuss the Angel Taker case. I think I know how he is finding them," he paused and cleared his throat, "this has to stay between the two of us until we can discuss it first thing Monday morning. I suspect he might be part of the task force." His face drained of colour, he looked right through me as he hung up on whoever he was talking to.

"We have another one. Sniper. Three kills confirmed so far."

Sharks swam through my mind, the notion swam for its life.

We spent the rest of the weekend in a blur, a dark cloud hung over all of us, and I kept wondering why Lizzie also looked haunted.

The two of us drove back to the city together on Sunday afternoon and it was my chance to get her to talk. "Lizzie, what's eating at you?" My eyes steady on the winding road ahead of us.

She focused on her hands, repeatedly stretching her fingers. "What if I don't make them proud? What if I fail and lose everything they spent their lives building?"

"That's the most preposterous thing I have heard in a long time, most surely coming out of your mouth. You have *never* doubted your ability at being the best in whatever you put your mind to. What is it you're not telling me?"

Lizzie focused on the rhythmic movement of her hands. "What if I lose you? I will be alone, with no one to confide in, no one to go home to, no one to love or be loved by." Tears dropped on her trousers, reminding me of an inkblot test, as she hunched over placing her head in her hands. "The irony is I don't have time to meet someone, or the time needed to build a relationship. All I do is work. I have to. The weight of the success of Williams Pharmaceuticals is on my shoulders, all those people depend on me for their livelihood."

With reservation, I put my hand on her back, gathering my thoughts as I did so. Only my thoughts didn't seem in the mood to be gathered, rather running around like deer when the first shot cracks through the air.

"Stop being so bloody dramatic." I didn't understand where that came from, but before I could stop myself, I blurted out, "You know what you need? You need to get laid."

She turned to face me, drying her face as she did so. "Pardon me?" Indignation dripping from both words.

"Sorry, but you do. You need to get out of your head and have fun. It doesn't have to mean anything, a one-night stand would suffice with your busy schedule."

"Where, pray tell, must I find a man? Standing on a street corner holding up a sign emblazoned with the words – *Not a whore, just horny.* Should I ask for money upfront or after we're done?" The corners of her mouth edged into what would become a smile.

"What happened to your friend Sam? Remember the night we went out to celebrate her divorce from that abusive nincompoop before I left for my last deployment?" The events of my last tour rushed through me, leaving my mouth dry. "Sam mentioned she wanted to open a singles bar where people could hook-up for a good old-fashioned romp and be on their merry way the next morning. No strings attached. No real names. Only pleasure – if he knows what he's doing."

We laughed until our stomachs ached, much like thirteen-year-old girls do when they are in that ridiculous giggling-phase. *My poor parents, poor any parents.*

"Sam did open a bar – Alias. It's close to the business district, so people can stop by after work."

"Well then, call her and get some. What do you have to lose?"

If I knew then what she would lose I would never have pushed her. Instead, I would've burned the place to the ground.

"What indeed? Except for my morals?" Lizzie rolled her eyes at me.

"You, dear sister, lost all your morals that night on the beach in Wild Bay. Now tell me, was it called *wild* before or only after that night?"

Lizzie smiled, a triumphant memory of that night. "I'm not twenty anymore. I have responsibilities. I'm a respected member of the community."

"So what!" It came out louder than I intended. "You're

beautiful, could still pass as a young woman, you deserve to cut loose and have fun. Phone Sam. Do what you need to do to get in."

A very vulgar sentence tried to escape from my mouth, I held my tongue, laughed on my own.

Ten

Tuesday came, and the reconstructive surgery of the scar on my face Dr Schmidt proclaimed 'a tremendous success'. I would be as good as new, he told me when he signed my discharge papers. *On the outside at least.*

After being discharged, I stayed with Lizzie for a few days as I needed to take it easy and rest for at least a month. With a repaired face, I was eager to move into my parents' penthouse. *My penthouse.*

The penthouse was situated on the top floor of one of the new high-rise buildings on the beach. Residents had access to a private beach. The view and location were well worth the money. Large windows all around, offering uninterrupted views across the city. On a clear day, you were able to see all the way to the island.

From this vantage point I could see if someone signalled in distress and I could swoop down and save the city, just like Batman. No doubt about it now, the pain medication did a number on me.

As I placed my bags down on the white-tiled floor, I took in my new surroundings. My mother had a keen eye for decorating and could create something stylish out of a cardboard box. It was too blue and white for my taste, but I spent the next few weeks changing it to fit my style. Create my space. Not ready to call anywhere home yet. What I no longer needed I gave to Tabby Manor, as we were expanding. Lizzie arranged the removal of the priceless art collection she inherited. *Minimalism is key.*

A Walker made its way into my body as I sat in the infinity pool making sure not to get the gauze on the left side of my face wet. The day I officially moved in, the temperatures soared. With the rise in temperature, so does the crime rate. The sniper brought his body count to four, the last being killed while I was still in hospital. At that point, he had slain a prostitute, a pimp and two drug addicts.

I closed my eyes and felt the whiskey warm me while the water cooled me, a strange feeling crept around inside me as the two mixed. *Why target these people? Why do they make you go boom?*

Uncle Tom came to visit me while I was staying at Lizzie's, to make sure I had what I needed. *A real dad.*

We spoke at length about both killers. The head of the task force agreed with my theory of Angel Taker's MO. Captain Taylor outsourced the bit of information to an old acquaintance of his in the Cybercrimes unit, in case the monster lurked amongst them.

The sniper, however, proved to be a more difficult profile for both of us. I had surmised that he was not a psychopath but that something traumatic happened that triggered his need to kill. Multiple studies have concluded snipers select victims at random, but still, I knew the Marcel sniper didn't choose his victims at random. To him it was personal.

Prostitutes spend hours on the streets, and he had ample time to take them out, but he waited until she returned from a trick. Witnesses claimed she had spent at least half an hour on the street before the first John arrived, giving him plenty of time. *Patient.*

"Why did you wait?" I caught myself asking him as if he was with me. "Was it the power of knowing you held their lives in your hands? Do you think you're God?" Uncle Tom waited for me to finish. "The accuracy with which he shoots shows someone with extensive training. It's possible he is or was part of an extremist group or served in the military. He might have just gotten back from a tour and is suffering from PTSD. Or he might just be an excellent marksman." Which I doubted even as the words came out of my mouth. Uncle Tom kept his gaze on me, patiently waiting for me to give him the information and insight I didn't have.

"The sniper's weapon of choice, an SVD Dragunov. He likes to get close, ensure the kill, or he needs the thrill. Based on what you told me about the bullets, I think he makes his own. This is his signature. Or perhaps a forensic countermeasure. He's intelligent and patient. You won't be able to draw him out, he's too good. And he won't stop, not until he has completed his mission."

Uncle Tom drew a deep breath and exhaled aloud. "Thank you, Finley."

I wondered if the sniper also liked doing online shopping on the dark web. There is nothing you can't find if you know the correct online directory and have the means to pay whatever the seller asks. Both our killers either had the financial resources or something to trade.

"Clever shark, aren't you?" I again said out loud, not knowing which of the two killers I directed my question to.

Uncle Tom stood, patted my shoulder and left.

The dark web. It should be called the abyss.

The darkness is overwhelming, devoid of even a sliver of light. Abyss isn't dark enough. Through my conversations with Uncle Tom, I found my hunting ground. I did a lot of research during the time I stayed at Lizzie's and continued the day after I moved into the penthouse. Total anonymity; untraceable.

I became whoever and whatever I needed to be in order to bait my prey. *But at what cost?*

I vomited so much a bucket kept me company whenever I logged on. As a soldier, you see many things, working with survivors you hear many things, but to interact with these grotesque things, these non-humans parading as humans, seeing what they do, sometimes while they do it. There are no words for the depravity of this world.

The general population choose to ignore the existence of the abyss, which in truth surrounds them in a heavy fog.

No, they prefer to remain in their happy little bubbles and refuse to acknowledge the existence of a darkness they can't comprehend. They turn a blind eye to the horrors next door, often in their own homes.

The easy part of my mission – getting into the dark web. I downloaded TOR, The Onion Project's free software, and installed it. A brilliant military idea in its origin, opened to the world to flood the stream of information, making it harder to hack military communication. I wonder if its creators created it with the sole intention for what it's being used for now.

Covered by a very thin veil, you only have to peek inside, take your first step into the darkness, and wait for it to consume you. You don't realise the moment it lays claim to your soul. It's simple to get in if you have a computer, laptop, smartphone, tablet, or any device that connects to the internet.

Welcome to hell.

It took me weeks to find the correct online shopping directories. Yes, plural. Whatever you need, someone is ready to supply you. *Ah, depraved capitalism.*

Late one night, I stalked prey in a paedophile chat room. They didn't call it that and it took me weeks to find. The conversations are extremely descriptive and heinous. The members felt the need to post photos in an attempt to stake their claim as the biggest in the food chain. As usual, I spent most of the evening with my face in the bucket.

A faint flicker entered my right eye as that night's dinner left me. Someone had hacked my laptop. Someone accessed my webcam. *Shit! Who, how, why?*

Adrenaline rushed through me, my heart pounding in my ears. I grabbed my Glock 42, holstered around my ankle. The closest of the guns on me, both always a part of me.

Instinct.

The bile covered butterflies in my stomach scurried around with the same frenzy as a shoal of fish being lunged at by a predator.

My right hand released its grip on the Glock and I reached

for the screen to cover the webcam. I gripped the screen so hard I heard a faint crack just before I slammed the screen shut. As if it was possible for someone to see through a closed computer, I stood on the other side of the dining room table gripping the wooden edge so hard my nails left indentations.

As my breathing calmed, rationale returned. *If this is how you want to play, let's play.* Sanity had returned. Not yet ready to have my presence known, hiding behind an account name: Cerberus. A man with a dark, lustful appetite for everything and anything. The persona I created. A persona which left a putrid taste in my mouth. The persona they saw not knowing the reason I chose Cerberus.

My little secret in this world where everything is a secret, except the faces, bodies, and terrified screams of the victims. Maybe the darkness was sucking me in. I needed to take a few days off and regain my composure. Would it not create suspicion as I had been active for so many hours each day the preceding weeks? *Think Fin, think!*

My unpacked boxes in the spare bedroom held many wonderful things, reminders of a once happy, promising life. I dug through it, ripping and tossing as I searched. Motionless, I stood and traced my fingers across the face. A face which filled many of my peers with fear when we were growing up in a time synonymous with slasher films.

The mask I had bought for a friend's eighteenth dress-up birthday party, the theme being 'favourite movie genre'. The prankster of our close-knit group of friends, often scaring my friends when we watched these movies. It had brought me great joy to torment them.

Now I knew it as a tactical military skull balaclava. My ghost face, as I liked to call it. This is the face people would see if they hacked my webcam again. *Total anonymity.* Something funny, nostalgic, to cover the disgust I couldn't hide.

I resumed my position behind my laptop and with trepidation, lifted the screen. It took time for my laptop to register it was supposed to be wide awake at this dreadful hour, the horizon turning a fiery orange. "Let's play," I said to myself, to my laptop's webcam, at whoever watched me from their own dark corner. Ghost face stared back at me.

The webcam's flickering light, a dragon's eye. *Red. Danger.*

"He who fights with monsters might take care lest he thereby become a monster. And if you gaze for long into an abyss, the abyss gazes also into you." Friedrich Nietzsche's famous quote ingrained in me since the first time I had read it.

For the first time, I truly understood the meaning.

Eleven

Dr Schmidt gave me the all-clear after my check-up on the Monday afternoon, one day short of four weeks after surgery.

Everything was going according to plan and I found myself almost ready for the hunt. First, I had to prepare my workspace and fill my arsenal with what I needed.

I drove to Lizzie's house for dinner after my appointment with Dr Schmidt. He wrote me another prescription for painkillers, I explained I had an intense burning, more of a stinging, sensation in my jaw. I lied, but was grateful he prescribed a revolutionary tablet by none other than Williams Pharmaceuticals. I simultaneously contributed to Lizzie's salary and my own income. The pills held just enough codeine to numb the pain and I left his office with a smile. No longer smiling to hide an unsightly scar. Still smiling to hide a sweaty, foreign-speaking man-inflicted scar no surgeon could ever remove.

I parked my Mercedes-Benz SLS AMG next to Uncle Tom's silver sedan in Lizzie's driveway. Although I prefer the robustness of an SUV, I love the slim lines, the craftsmanship, the visionary design of a car as fine as this one. The incredible power of its engine. The way it did whatever I told it to do with my hands wrapped around the soft leather of its firm, round steering wheel. Fast. Vigorous. The roar of the engine as I increased the pressure of my foot. *Maybe I need to get laid.* I shook my head, slipped out of the car and made my way to the front door.

Before I got to the door, Lizzie threw it wide open, champagne in hand. "Shipwrecked champagne." She explained with great enthusiasm. "It's over two hundred years old, stumbled upon by divers in the Baltic Sea a few years ago.

Costs a fortune, but only the best for you, Finley. This is your night."

It was my night. A dinner party, similar to those my parents threw for me before I left for another tour, another round with the boxer named War I didn't pick a fight with. The war zone I was on the verge of entering was again not a fight I started, but I would be damned if I didn't stop it. Or at the very least, take out as many of the enemy as possible.

Yet again I found myself on a mission, a fight to fight, a war to win. One assault at a time.

Lizzie looked more relaxed than on the way back from the lake house. She was her talkative self. *What's up with her?*

The doorbell rang, and Lizzie hurried to get it, her Manolo Blahnik's clicking on the original hardwood floor. Ashley and her fiancé Kyle, an accountant who transferred to his company's east coast office two years before, joined us for dinner. Hope came along for her first dinner party.

Ashley and Kyle had met through online dating, something which at the time I deemed risky for her to do. I asked Uncle Tom to use his law enforcement contacts to do a full background check on Kyle the first time she spoke about him. It turned out he was a run of the mill good guy, came from a good family, passed his degree Cum Laude. On paper, there seemed nothing wrong with him. Forever being protective of her, I followed them on their first ten dates. Something I have never told her and never will. I violated her privacy. I had no choice, not after what happened to her while we were studying at UM.

Hope had grown so much since the last time I saw her, full of little sounds that only Ashley understood. I couldn't look at anyone or anything else. Two people brought together by the most atrocious circumstances.

"Kyle and I are adopting Hope," she said with so much excitement I waited for Hope to scream at the sudden outburst coming out of Ashley who was busy giving Hope her liquid meal. "Once we get married. We have spoken to an adoption lawyer – thank you again, Dad. The paperwork is in place and we can't wait. Kyle has already prepared a room for her as we will move in with him as soon as we're awarded temporary guardianship. We can't wait to be her parents. We love her so much, she's perfect."

I watched Ashley, waiting for her to faint, not stopping for air as she rambled through their life-changing decision. "That's wonderful, Ashley. Hope is the luckiest girl in the world to have you both as her parents." A sliver of light in the darkness of the world.

If things didn't work out for Lizzie with Williams Pharmaceuticals, she could be a chef, her culinary skills were remarkable. The screaming chefs on those ridiculous television shows can learn more than a thing or two from her.

After dinner, Ashley, Kyle and Hope left. I walked them out and helped put sleepy, yawning Hope into her car seat.

As their taillights rounded the corner, I thought of the millions of children being kept against their will. They, too, deserved happiness, to have what Hope has and will have.

An idea came to me and the notion shook its head at my stupidity for not realising it sooner.

If I take out the predator, what happens to the captive prey? The bile-covered butterflies panicked again. *Think Fin, think!* The answer was right in front of me. *Come on notion, give me a hint.* I forced a smile and walked back into the house, consumed by whatever the notion was trying to tell me.

"Your favourite." Uncle Tom held the tumbler out towards me. A nightcap. My poison. I love a good Walker.

"On a beautiful night like this, we have to sit outside. Come on, shoes off. Now the real party can start." Lizzie led us outside. Red indentations visible on the top of her feet.

New shoes. New Lizzie. *What is up with her?* I followed her outside, intrigue pushed me out the door.

"There has been another attack by the sniper," Uncle Tom said, shifting in his chair.

Something about these killings ate at him, more so than

the usual serial cases that came across his desk.

"I heard. It will escalate if you don't catch him soon. You must limit what's being released to the media, he's following the reports. He wants to know what you know, the city knows. Has the story gone national?"

"No. If I have things my way, it won't. The last thing we need is a copycat. It's much easier to kill people from a distance, who knows who he might inspire. The Angel Taker has been sending new letters, egomaniac that he is. He changed his MO – he is now telling us before, not after, as he used to. Explaining in great detail what he planned to do to them. He is including photos. Their eyes wide with fear, a dreadful mixture of...how should I put into words what is in the minds of these petrified girls?" Uncle Tom's shoulders sagged. The knowledge of what was still to come pressing hard on him.

These were not the first serial offenders to cross his path, both as a detective and a state prosecutor. For reasons unknown, these two haunted him. A child killer, brutalising innocent little girls. An elusive sniper on a mission. Neither leaving a discerning pattern to anticipate when and where they would strike next.

I was unable to tell Uncle Tom I found a certain 'Baalares' whom I believed to be Angel Taker.

During my second year at university, I took a course in Ancient Cultures for extra credit. Greek mythology intrigued me the most. This is where I got the idea for Cerberus. The three-headed guardian of Hades. His job: ensuring the dead never leave. I, too, wanted to keep the demons where they should be – in hell. I wouldn't have given Baalares a second thought, given the weird, creative, and often disturbing names some of these predators came up with.

Baalares had to bring up the Angel Taker killings in each of the chat rooms I bumped into him virtually. Every day he said something to draw everyone's attention back to it. I put him down as a fan at first. Just a sick fan who idolised his hero. But late one night just before I logged off, when I couldn't vomit anymore, when dry heaving was the only thing left to do, Baalares referred to the yellow nylon rope that bound two little girls together.

'Not alone in death', he typed, with a smiley face emoticon. The notion kicked me in the head. It was him. Somewhere on the other side of a computer screen. It was him. A clever little piece of excrement. Baalares.

Baal Ares. Baal the god of rain, thunder, and lightning. I researched Baal and found papers mentioning that his worshippers offered children as sacrifices to him, to appease him. Ares, the god of war, representing the violent and untamed physical side of war. It was him. I had him in my sights, now to lure him out into the open.

Uncle Tom and I spoke a while longer, taking sips of our whiskey. Lifting our arms in unison, the same whiskey in our glasses, both drinking it neat. Different thoughts running through our minds. He left with the burdens of the world weighing him down like an anchor.

"I thought he was never going to leave," Lizzie sighed and walked back out on to the patio, unclipping her hair. Golden strands fell carefree.

"What's going on with you Liz, what is it you haven't told me? It's not as if we don't speak to each other every day." My curiosity, or the whiskey and painkiller combination, loosened my tongue.

"I took your advice; I joined Alias two weeks ago."

"Joined? You make it sound like a club or a gym. I always had the idea it was just a singles bar." Trying to comprehend that my sister had signed up for one-night stands.

"Alias is a singles bar, at face value. Sam does interviews with everyone before she allows them to join. She even has background checks done. Has her own PI and everything. She even subjects prospective members to a lie-detector test." A rumble of laughter burst out from deep within her. I couldn't remember the last time I had seen Lizzie elated.

"She can save herself a heck of a lot of money and ask Uncle

Tom to join, maybe give him half price on drinks as payment. The way he looked tonight, perhaps he also needs company."

Lizzie looked at me and burst into another fit of laughter, as if the idea I had put forward of Uncle Tom being lonely was so silly.

Aren't we all? Even in relationships, in marriages. We are born alone and die alone, no one can do either for us. A mother can push, or a doctor can pull, but the baby breathes, it has to breathe.

Lizzie looked at me, wiping happy tears from her eyes. I waited for her laughter to fizzle down.

"So, tell me, was it worth signing up? Are you getting what you paid for?"

"You don't understand. It's so liberating, exciting, different. I'm so glad you proposed I join. You must join; you must." Golden specks flickered in her eyes.

Apart from earlier that night, I had not even considered having sex again, never mind making small talk with someone only to get them to drop their pants. What would I say?

"Hello, my name is Lauren, Jennifer, Kate, or whatever alias I wanted to use. I stalk perverts on the dark web in my spare time. During the day, I run a safe haven for victims of violent crimes. A real superhero I am. I have a plan in motion to get rid of them, not in a pretty, please-leave-our-world-and-go-sit-on-a-deserted-island-somewhere way. No, more in a leaving them rotting in a ditch, their limbs scattered, removed-with-no-sedation kind of way, or I might burn them alive. I haven't decided. I can be so indecisive when it comes to these big life decisions. I also like old movies, nature, and long walks on the beach. But the thing I love most is a good whiskey, I have a thing for a good Walker. Do you want to have sex with me?"

Out of the corner of my eye, I watched her. Whatever this lifestyle was doing for her, it worked, in the there and then. Lizzie was always too trusting of men and I didn't want her to get hurt, no matter how good Sam's PI might be.

"Lizzie, I'm not ready yet. The idea of a man touching me

makes me want to pull out my gun and shoot the first thing I see."

Silence.

"I hope you're still carrying yours, you know you can't take any chances. A gorgeous, single woman such as yourself can never be too careful." I included gorgeous as she had a way of listening with greater intent whenever there was a compliment directed at her.

No woman can ever be careful enough. Not even a decorated soldier. Assault rifle, handgun, grenades, Kevlar vest, and her squad with her.

"I'm glad this lifestyle is working for you. I've been meaning to tell you, I want to do renovations around the lake house, beef up security. I will spend more time there in the coming weeks and with everything going on around here the past few months, one can never be too careful. Please understand, being at the lake house reminds me of who I am."

"I wondered when you would tell me you're leaving. I got used to having you close by and now you're going away again." The sorrow in her voice bit into me.

"Just to the lake house, Liz, I'm not leaving the country. The past few weeks have been amazing, but it's not far to drive and I will still spend time in the city. I need to oversee the remodelling of the new property. Ashley is a fantastic manager, but with the upcoming wedding, and now with her being an instant mother to Hope, she needs to focus on giving herself and her life her full attention. She deserves it."

I thought of the new property, a second building for Tabula Rasa. It was both exciting and heartbreaking. We had to expand. More survivors needed a home. More people saved, more people needing saving.

I got up, kissed her head and walked to the front door. How many things would I have to do before I would see her again, things we would never be able to discuss?

I had no choice.

It was war.

Twelve

One does not walk out on to the battlefield guns-a-blazing. No, you do recon, or as it's called in non-military circles, reconnaissance. You study your enemy and if you have balls of lonsdaleite, you infiltrate. You need to be stronger than a diamond in this war. Diamond balls are not this girl's best friend, it has to be lonsdaleite.

Once on the inside, you get to see the enemy's weaknesses, that little something that makes them tick, and where they are most vulnerable to attack. I became a mimic, never one of them, I just talked – well typed – like them. Hours and hours of brutal training prepares the body and helps focus the mind. In the moments where your body is screaming at you to stop, your resolve has to be greater, you have to keep your focus on the mission.

Faces, screams, and wet, white hair.

A quick online search – for a change, on the normal internet I hoped most of the world still used – yielded the perfect result, only two blocks from my penthouse.

During my time in the military, we did extensive hand-to-hand combat training, and I enjoyed Krav Maga the most. If you wish to be the best in any sport or discipline, you need the best coach. I scheduled an appointment to meet the instructor, Ari, to do a bit of civilised interrogation. It was the only way to make sure he was the right person to train me.

The second I entered the building I knew something was wrong. The deafening quiet was my first indication. As always, I arrived fifteen minutes early. My mother had taught me that if you are on time, you are late. I wondered if I should wait or call out. The hairs on the back of my neck stood up. A faint sound somewhere, I couldn't establish its origin. My body lunged into what others call fight mode, adrenaline pumped through me in droves. Flight is not in my DNA.

Motionless, I stood trying to figure out what shook my cage. My hand reached for my SIG, holstered on the right side of my lower back, not reaching it in time.

Big, strong hands grabbed me in a chokehold. Instinct took over, and I fought as I haven't fought since the day we got ambushed.

I leaned forward. My right hand struck a knee and my elbow connected with a chin. Blind rage and fear mixed inside me like oil and water. I spun around and jabbed, ducked, kicked and finished him with a crescent kick. None of his punches or blocks registered. Survival my only sight, I grabbed my gun, always carrying it one-up. The barrel stared at his smiling face.

"Excellent," the smiling man said with a distinct Israeli accent.

"Stay down!" I yelled, wiping the blood from my mouth with my free hand, grateful the scar on my face had healed enough since the operation.

He did a kick up and came to his full length in front of me, still smiling. He was taller than I expected but my punches landed where I intended. From our skirmish, I had gathered he was strong. His body glistened with sweat, his pecks moved as he, too, was catching his breath. Muscles strained against his shirt. *Veins galore.*

"Finley, I'm Ari. I'm looking forward to training you. You're good. Military?"

"Yes." I holstered my SIG. "What the hell was that?" I was supposed to screen him. This was not going according to my plan.

With Ari, I would learn nothing went as I planned.

"I knew you were military from the way you spoke on the phone."

Would he ever stop smiling? *Intoxicating.* His dark eyes held mine.

"Ex-military." I corrected him. "I served and now I want

to keep training. You should understand, once a soldier always a soldier. This makes more sense than joining the gym across the street for spinning classes and Zumba – not my scene."

"I also struggled to return to civilian life. Sometimes one must leave the war and start new. People who return to a family sometimes have it easier than the rest of us. We need to find our own direction on our own after being a part of a unit, a family, for so long."

What was it he knew or sensed about me? It made me feel both understood and vulnerable. Something no man had made me feel in a very long time.

"Do you want to join a group class or private lessons?" His voice pulled me back into the room.

"Private lessons. Four days a week?"

"We can start now, but first go put your SIG in the safe in the changing room. Don't want to take it from you and use it on you."

"I would like to see you try." I turned and made my way towards the changing room sign on the other side of the building. My words, and walk, a little more flirtatious than intended.

Ari and I trained for the next four weeks and he was the best instructor I ever trained with. I often wondered what brought him to Marcel, what was he running or hiding from. We often spoke after my training sessions, discussing life and fitting back into normal society. Some days our conversations turned into lunch. Other days we lay side by side on the floor, staring at the corrugated iron roof, talking. He once let slip that he had been part of Sayeret Matkal. The moment he uttered the words his eyes lifted to meet mine.

"I never heard that," I said, and continued talking as if he had said he liked bacon and being Jewish, that would be a sin.

On my way back to the penthouse I thought about his little Freudian slip. Did he want me to know, did he trust me or was it an honest mistake? It didn't matter. I gathered as much from our interactions as I could, both verbal and physical. Something drew me to Ari. A dark, dangerous, and manly in all the right ways, down to the stubble on his face, flame.

The day I told Lizzie I was to leave for the lake house was the day I informed Ari I could no longer commit to four lessons a week. I committed to two days a week and trained by myself while at the lake house. I had remodelled the downstairs guest bedroom into a home gym of sorts.

The security system needed an upgrade, I explained to him. My sister and I were spending a lot of time there and something bothered me. I hated leaving her there on her own when I went for my early morning run. He nodded and proposed he would drive out and we could train there every Wednesday afternoon, and the woods made for more realistic training grounds. I agreed, looking forward to seeing him in a different setting.

Training with Ari had given me an outlet for the horrors I witnessed as Cerberus. As long as their depravity made me vomit, I considered myself not to be a part of them.

I hadn't become acclimated to the darkness.

The following Tuesday morning, I left to prepare my battleground to ensure I always had the upper hand and remained in control of every and any situation. A soft drizzle started before dawn as I set my dark web face down on the table next to my laptop. I used my time to stalk and shop. I found several useful sites which offered military-grade equipment for sale. Perfect for fortifying Williams Estate.

Which military it came from I could only guess but it was already stolen or sold, so I brushed away the idea of my actions being wrong. Most people might consider what I was doing as wrong, but I kept my focus on my mission.

One of the main principals of Krav Maga is to avoid conflict; if unavoidable, you do whatever you have to do to win, to survive. I didn't enter this fight by choice. No, a predator pushed me in by dumping the bodies of innocent little white-haired girls into the ocean, knowing one day it would give them back. Twice right in front of me.

Victory had to be mine.

Thirteen

The expansion of Tabula Rasa was going ahead as planned. I purchased the property next door and with the exception of a few alterations, it was in perfect condition. With the papers signed, payment made, we waited only for the title deed.

Ashley's happy screams reverberated through the main building when I told her the owner had accepted my offer without hesitation.

I offered a good fifteen percent more than the market value. Mrs Ashbrooke was close to eighty and the estate's upkeep had become a nuisance for her, and she wanted to be closer to her grandchildren. My timing couldn't have been more perfect. In less than two months we would unveil it at a special ceremony, inviting our partners and sponsors. The perfect event to unveil a third property I had acquired, on a drive to the lake house.

Six properties from Williams Estate there lay a farm. The owner had been trying to sell the property for years, he had told me over coffee. As the property does not lead up to the lake, prospective buyers were few. Due to the nature of my business I couldn't elaborate on the reasons for my purchase of his property. I implied it would form part of my non-profit organisation but kept the truth to myself. The farm, as we had come to call it, had a big barn and the property itself had two houses, the main had eight bedrooms and the smaller house had four. The perfect place for the guests at Tabby Manor to spend their weekends.

As I drove to the lake house I went over my strategy in excruciating detail when a question dawned on me. Had I thought of every detail and purchased all the equipment I would need?

Packages got delivered to the empty apartment I rented

in an area known for trouble, the landlord only too happy to receive an upfront cash payment. Anonymity in the real world. The young boy with the absent father and alcoholic mother was eager when I spoke to him one day, telling him I would pay him a handsome amount for taking the packages and delivering them to another empty apartment. From there I collected it without being noticed as the building fell in the heart of Fangs territory. The people who lived there knew how to stay alive – keep your head down, and your mouth shut.

The question bugged me for a good five minutes until I saw the barn. *Perfect.*

I drove to the house and got out of my SUV. I almost reached the steps leading to the porch when the owner stood in the doorway. Reluctant at first, eager once I wrote a number on a piece of paper and signed below it to show him I was serious.

Williams Manor had remained as we had left it, although the surrounding landscape had changed, preparing for winter. Leaves had turned an orangey-red, and a few overachievers had left the comfort of the branches that had nourished them since before spring. Ready to give back to the earth from which they came.

Under the staircase was a hidden door. The two vault doors led to the wine cellar- my soon-to-be soundproof workspace. The only point of entry; the no-door-here-door under the staircase.

I stared at the bolted down chair just as I had done countless times before.

"Thank you, Mr Andretti," I said as if his ghost remained there, reminiscing about the good old days when he tormented the living. Now it was my turn to instil fear and angst into those who deserved nothing less. I believe Mr Andretti's guests were not of the same calibre as my intended guests.

With great care, I unpacked everything I had bought in the abyss, stood back and looked at it with excitement so tangible goosebumps appeared all over my body. I thought of Ari and wondered if I could ask him in his previous professional capacity to approve of my work or make suggestions when he came over the following Wednesday. He would of course come the following day. I had work to do.

I started with the basics. I wouldn't tell him about the motion sensor cameras being set up around Williams Estate, the new property for Tabula Rasa or the neighbouring estates.

"Always be vigilant. Never let your guard down," I said to the glass in my hand before taking a sip of my Walker and switching on the television.

"Two bodies washed ashore this morning in close proximity to where an unlucky jogger had stumbled upon the previous two." The unemotional, robotic voice of the news anchor cut into me. "Police suspect they are victims of the Angel Taker. Please contact the hotline if you have any information." She rambled off the number, even though it appeared at the bottom of the screen.

I drank the rest of my whiskey in one swig and phoned uncle Tom.

"Anderson," he answered with a tired voice.

"Two more?" No good morning, to the point. My mood turned fast.

"Fin, as always, keep this to yourself. There have been three others, but we blocked the media from releasing any details. We are trying to make him come out of hiding. Deny him the recognition he craves."

"By infuriating him? Whose bright idea is that?" I barked.

"The captain enlisted the help of a profiler who said this would be the best chance of getting him to make a mistake. To use his need for admiration against him."

"That's the dumbest thing I have ever heard." Clenching my jaw as I wanted to enhance my sentence with creative wordplay which would have made my mother shake her head and have her remind me, yet again, that I'm a lady.

"What do you want me to do? I have no say in the matter at

this stage. Once they arrest him, the squirrel is mine."

He will never see the inside of a courtroom. "Has the Cybercrimes unit not had any luck finding him?"

"No, not him, but they found five others. We haven't released this information to the media as we don't want to scare him off. This, this—"

He didn't finish his sentence before I interrupted. "This is bullshit. That's what this is. To deny him another fifteen seconds of fame will infuriate him and who will take the burden of that brunt? The little girl, or girls, he has now." No longer controlling the rage that escalated inside me as the notion tried to duck for cover. "When this is over, you need to prosecute the profiler and whoever agreed to this idiotic idea."

"I agree with you, but my hands are tied."

Your hands might be, but not mine.

Someone called in the background for Anderson and he said goodbye and hung up on me. Rage entered my hand and my mobile phone was treated to an aerial view of the living room before coming to a bumpy landing on the couch to my left.

The time had come. No more planning – only action. I pulled my laptop out of my bag and nausea pushed up and out of me. I made it to the kitchen sink just in time. I wiped my mouth and stared out of the window as the rain ceased its earth-drenching crusade. Ironic, as mine was about to start.

I put on my face and got to work.

Too easy. It shouldn't be this easy to buy and sell living human beings. Similar to most online shopping sites. Photos of merchandise for sale and basic selling points listed. Eye and hair colour, build, age, location. The basics someone would need to consider before making such a big, or too often small, purchase. It operates as a cash-only system, electronic transfers are easy to trace. Anonymity is key.

A circle, a bump, and then my first tug on my virtually-created bait. John, a blonde ten-year-old boy who looked petrified in the photo millions of predators might have been circling at that precise moment. *My creation.*

Peter and I had dated for almost a year during my first year at university. We were complete opposites. When I told my family about him, I described him as gentle and creative. He did, however, have a strong side that drew me to him from the first night we met at a party. Peter introduced me to kickboxing, and I took to it like a hound to a rabbit hunt. Ours was my first serious relationship. My first for many, many things. *Thank you, Peter.*

He studied sound engineering and graphic design, in complete opposite to my world of Sigmund Freud, Abraham Maslow, Carl Jung, Ted Bundy, Andrei Chikatilo, and Theodore Kaczynski. Peter taught me how to use Adobe Photoshop and I often made funny faces of our friends, even making a composite of what our child would one day look like. Young, naïve, and in love.

I welcomed his patience and was eager to learn whatever he wanted to teach me, not knowing it would one day be this useful. Our relationship had ended on amicable terms, it took its natural course. When the darkness overwhelmed me, I thought of Peter and what might have been in another life. He always supported my dream to become a profiler. He played the biggest part in my decision to switch from law. Peter was my rock during a time when I learned what it meant to be no longer living with my parents and finding my budding adult feet in a world that can be so daunting.

His life now filled with a wife, a dog, and two point five children.

The predator grabbed the bait. *Sold* appeared across John's face in bold red letters. I smiled. Nothing the buyer fantasised about would happen to John or any other boy ever again. *Now what?* The owners of the farm would only move out at the end of the week, I needed to think fast. This had happened a bit

sooner than I expected. I took another sip of the whiskey I poured whilst thinking of Peter. *Game time.* Thursday night my room would see its first guest. The buyer was not Baalares, but this one had to be stopped just as much as any other.
My other bait was still being circled, bumped and stalked by beady eyes.

Behind beady eyes, unspeakable things had already been done to them.

Ari arrived on time, punctual as always. I told him when we spoke over the phone that we needed to up my training that day. Whatever he hasn't taught me yet, this was the time for him to do so. Confusion sounded in his voice, but he agreed to two sessions, one during the afternoon, the other at night. I must learn to listen and see in the darkness. I didn't tell him it was all I had done the preceding weeks.

"Beautiful place, Fin." He climbed out of his SUV, big and dark like him. His intoxicating smile took my breath away. Was this nothing more than an adolescent feeling of being in love with your teacher or was it more?

He, too, had been a soldier and his warrior spirit showed its gorgeous face when we were locked in combat. Never once did he hold back with his punches or kicks, often leaving me bruised and sore for days. The generous prescription Dr Schmidt gave me for the still sore scar had been a life saver.

"Thank you, Ari. Welcome to Williams Manor." Helping him take his belongings out of the back of the SUV. *A lot for training,* I thought and a part of me hoped he had brought an overnight bag.

He was not joking when he said this would be the hardest training I have ever been through.

"Why now? Is someone bothering you?" He only asked once.

I wanted to tell him, tell someone what I planned to do, my mission, crusade, whatever you want to call it.

"The time has come for me to learn the rest, you know,

from you and not what I was taught in the army. It didn't help me jack before." He knew, only because I told him one day after training. My tired and horror-exposed soul spilled my secret in front of him like a dump truck unloading a ton of bricks. For reasons unknown to me, I trusted him. He listened and nodded, his jawline tensed as he did so.

He never saw me as a victim, only a broken warrior. *His own reflection perhaps?* Something made him move across the world, away from the country which was in his blood, his life, as he told me one day over lunch. Never so much as hinting to the real reason he left it behind.

It was possible for me to get used to having a man around, especially one that cooks, I thought, as Ari prepared lunch.

"Dinner is on you." Smiling that intoxicating smile, his dark, broody eyes always fixed on mine. He held my gaze a while longer before returning his attention to the aromatic sauce. The house filled with the scent of basil, thyme, and garlic.

"Pasta for lunch. What does he have planned for tonight?" I said out loud. These ought to be unspoken thoughts being aired became a problem.

He turned his broad, well defined – even through a shirt – back, no longer offering it as an art piece to admire and undress with my eyes.

"Wouldn't you like to know?" His heavy accent made my stomach turn.

Lunch was delicious. I had better bring my A-game for dinner. When Ari stepped outside onto the deck, I grabbed the chance to send Lizzie a text listing the ingredients I had in the fridge and pantry. I asked what amazing dish I could conjure up from it.

Five seconds later she replied. Question after question but no recipe. *Waste of time.*

I promised to tell her everything over the weekend when we scheduled to go out and celebrate our birthdays. Just the two of us, a night on the town like the old days.

She sent a recipe just as I had resolved to send Ari to bed hungry. Again pasta, but I needed to carbo-load for the following night. An easy to make Vodka-pasta he will devour before devouring me. Her words, not mine. The *Alias* lifestyle agreed with Lizzie. Two emotions played tug of war in my stomach. Happiness for her, and worry.

I sat contemplating this, not realising Ari had turned on the radio. *Sniper.*

The sniper had struck in daylight, two hours earlier.

"You changed your MO," I said out loud. A growing problem, maybe a mild case of Tourette syndrome. "Why now? Today? Why a lawyer?"

"Who are you talking to?" Ari stared at me for a change.

"No one. The sniper. It's silly. I've always done it whenever I try to get into someone's head." I looked away from him, knowing how ridiculous I sounded.

"Why do you want to get into his head? Ley, you're not planning on going after this guy? A task force has been set up to catch him. Also, the other one." I loved it when he called me Ley.

"The other one calls himself Angel Taker." The door leading to the deck always a good place to escape to, and I did so in a desperate attempt to end the conversation.

He walked over to where I stood and cupped my face in his hands, lifting my head so I had nowhere else to look but into his black eyes. The heat of his body woke mine. Ari's touch soft and warm on my skin. This strong man, who punched harder than anyone has ever punched me whilst sparring tenderly held my face and gently stroked my cheeks with his thumbs.

"There are people out there who can take care of this. It's not your responsibility to do anything. This is not your war."

The Angel Taker made it my war when I saw what he, the ocean and its creatures, did to three little girls. For once my words stayed where they should.

I held his stare, reached for his face and pulled his mouth

hard onto mine. His hands slid down my back and settled on my bum. Ari lifted me, slamming me on to the counter next to the brick pizza oven. The coolness of the marble counter didn't register. He bit my lower lip, and I moaned into his mouth. My lungs forgot what they were made for.

He pulled away, gave that intoxicating smile of his and let his lips find mine again with the same earnestness. As his hands slid down my body, I tried to pull his shirt off. My brain had no idea what my hands were trying to accomplish and gave no assistance whatsoever. Not once did I consider where this kiss might lead. A hungry longing took control of me. I wanted to be with him. Ari would have my full consent.

He laughed as I struggled with his shirt. The first time I heard him laugh, it was contagious. 'Exhilarating, liberating,' Lizzie's words filled my mind.

His eyes held mine as we both tried to regain control of our breathing. The heat of his hands teased the skin of my thighs as he allowed his fingers to wonder higher. I didn't tell him to stop.

"You need to rest before tonight's training." He leaned closer and licked my top lip.

I don't want to rest, I want you. Now. My thoughts again not verbalising themselves. Something was wrong with me. Words slipping out when they shouldn't, holding on to the neurons of my brain like passengers of a sinking ship when they should just let go and embrace the plunge.

I nodded and released my grip on his shirt which I should've ripped off. He turned around and walked back into the kitchen to make us coffee. I realised I liked having this man in my life. In my home.

Didn't see that coming.

Ari had not lied when he said I needed to rest for that night's training. We played what he called killer cat and mouse. The objective was simple – we walked into the woods in different directions and after five minutes, counted to ten and then hunted each other. He brought paintball guns along because 'using real guns wouldn't be as much fun,' smiling his ever-intoxicating smile. There is no other word to describe it.

Before he turned away from me, he said I had to sense my opponent as if blindfolded and I needed to rely on my other senses. *Blindfolded.* A part of me hoped that would be part of a scenario in our near future, a little less cold than the autumn wind trying to remove the last leaves clinging in desperation. We set off, Ari headed west, I headed east.

To find him proved more difficult than I expected. It took me an hour before I spotted him hunched down behind a boulder. I had to either surprise him or wait for him to show himself. The latter I knew he would never do.

I considered my options, running a handful of best outcome scenarios through my mind. A twig snapped a stone's throw away to my right. I listened and waited. Eyes closed, I breathed in the smell of wet earth, a footstep followed by a searing pain in my left arm. Ari had broken cover without me realising.

I swung my gun around in the direction from where the ball of frozen burning hell had come. Hastened footsteps behind me. My pulse raced, and I jumped up running towards the boulder. I had to get to the top to have an advantage. Any advantage over this man, a trained killer. One hell of a kisser, wondering what else he could be amazing at.

"Get out of your head, Ley! Focus. What do you hear? See? Smell? Let it guide you to where he is." Ari yelled from the dark.

Who was this man play-hunting me?

"You will never win if you are not thirty steps ahead. Focus! Anticipate his next move and make your own rules! Force him to play your game!"

I controlled my racing heart and shifted the afternoon's kiss from my mind. I thought about *him.* Self-proclaimed Angel Taker. Sharks surrounded me in the woods, circling, moving in for the kill. The sniper.

I saw a branch not too far up from me. I jumped and pulled

myself up into the tree just as I caught a glimpse of Ari down below. Without making a sound I hung the paintball gun or marker, as referred to by enthusiasts playing make-believe wars, on a higher branch. My hand removed the hunting knife strapped to my left thigh. Ari said nothing about bringing a knife to a paintball gun fight.

I waited for him to pass below me again. It felt like minutes but in reality it was only seconds and he crouched against the boulder, right below me. Ari waited for my next move.

My heart knocked against my ribs as I leapt from my position. He moved just as I descended on him. My legs buckled under the pressure of his kick. I fell to my side and the knife was knocked from my hand. The earlier ball of frozen fire didn't compare to a kick from his muscular legs. I kicked him in the stomach, he bent forward.

I kicked-up as he had taught me and pounced on him. Only when the Angel Taker begged me to stop did I cease the relentless blows of my fists. My hand reached for the other knife I had and put it to his throat.

"Enough, Finley. Enough!" Ari's screams brought me back.

"I don't know what happened." My knife-clenching hand relaxed, dropping to my side.

"Never lose focus." He backed me into a tree, his forearm to my throat. Bark cracked from the impact of my head. He stood so close his heart beat in my ears.

My knife against his throat.

"Cut," I said smiling, waiting for him to respond. Ari remained quiet, his eyes held mine. "What's wrong?" Willing my heart to calm down and adrenaline to return to dormant levels.

"You're ready." Leaning in, he kissed me until I dropped the knife and my hands found his body. I pulled him hard into me. Not feeling the hardness of the tree behind me anymore. His own being my only focus.

He pulled away from my mouth, yet his body remained. "Why didn't you shoot me when you were in the tree? You had a clear shot, and you didn't take it."

"I want to look into his eyes as he takes his last breath." In the faint moonlight, I saw sparks in Ari's eyes.

"Let's go home. I need a shower." He took my hand in his. We walked out of the woods as if we had merely enjoyed an evening stroll.

Ari led me up to the bedroom in silence. My heart thumped erratically. As he entered the room, he turned around and looked at me. Ari pulled me against him and wrapped his arms around me. Something played in his eyes, something I had not seen before.

"I want you." The words had let go of their grip and plunged into the water below.

"Say it again." His lips teased mine.

"I want you, Ari." He picked me up and threw me down on the bed. Before he lay down next to me, he took his shirt off. I was grateful I wouldn't have to struggle with it. *He should buy bigger shirts. Do they make them big enough to cover those arms.*

His touch soft as he made his way down my body. My clothes heeded the commands of his warm hands. He claimed my body as his trophy after almost besting me earlier. If I was to be his trophy, I didn't care where he landed on the roster. I wanted him.

"You keep on surprising me, Ley," he whispered as his tongue met and made friends with all the right parts of me. I moaned into the back of my hand as I bit down and let him take me places I had not known in a long time.

When I finished, I pulled him up and looked at him. Kissing him, I pushed him on to his back. It was my time to explore, and that I did. Every part of this handsome and dangerous man. I teased him enough to not end the exploration, and I grinned in triumph as he himself moaned and arched his body as I lifted my head. Our eyes locked.

I moved closer to kiss him. He reached for me and pushed me down onto the bed. I let him. I let him again that night as many times as he wanted. I stopped counting after three. *Free.*

Ari helped me reclaim what had been taken from – no, ripped from me – for four months. Every movement of his body brought healing. Mine moved with him and the burst of endorphins followed as I let go of everything that held me prisoner, long after I no longer was, watching him as he did the same.

I could enjoy a man, my own body.

For the first time I realised I had survived the aftermath. *Free Finley.*

Morning came and I awoke to Ari's warm body next to mine. I kept my eyes closed and savoured the freedom of the moment. The first day had dawned.

Ari stirred behind me and kissed my neck. "Boker tov," he whispered, kissing me again up to my ear, biting when he reached it.

I turned around to face him, to see his handsome, rugged face in the light of dawn. He kissed me and I let him do the wonderful things my body knew his to be capable of. We showered and got dressed for this day.

It had arrived for me.

After breakfast, I broke my own heart.

Fourteen

"I'm sorry, Ari, but I think it's best if we don't see each other anymore," I said, fighting to keep my resolve.

"Can you honestly tell me last night, and this morning, and all the time we have spent together means nothing to you?" Ari reached for my hand, but I stepped back.

"This, us," I gestured between us, "this is the reason why I need to take a step back and focus on all the things that need my full attention. My safe house, the expansion, and the acquisition of the farm."

"No, Ley, you're pushing me away because you're on a mission you don't want anyone to know about. Don't tell me I'm wrong."

I answered with silence.

"You can't go after the Angel Taker or the sniper by yourself. And I can't stand by and watch the woman I'm falling for go down this road. I know where it leads." His accent somehow made the words sound worse.

The notion woke up for the first time and together we tried to figure out how he knew what I was planning. *Impossible.* Perhaps my supposed to be unspoken thoughts voicing itself in front of him the day before gave it away.

"What road?" I played dumb, fighting for control of the emotions which swirled in my gut. I didn't want to push him away, but I had no alternative.

"You're not the only one. You don't have to do this alone. If you want to play lone wolf, so be it. Do what you need to do and when you're finished, come find me." He kissed me and I wished I could hold onto him. It took every ounce of my faltering strength to let go of him.

Before he reached the door, I willed my voice to respond to

the cues of my heart. "I don't want to fight this war by myself, but I can't take you or anyone down this road with me. I don't know where this ends, but I can't turn my back on it."

Ari smiled that intoxicating smile of his. "Walking away from you is the hardest thing I have ever had to do. Find me when you're done, Ley. You owe me dinner." With that, he left and closed the door behind him.

Anger filled the emptiness his words had created. *How difficult is it to just be happy?* Leave this war for someone else to fight and allow myself to live a normal life?

I sank to the floor and cried. *Ridiculous.* A part of me didn't want to face the road ahead. Not alone. I never realised before I awoke that morning, not only did I carry the weight of the deaths of my squad with me every day, but I missed the camaraderie, the sense of belonging.

I cried for myself, for what I was about to become, for what I may already have been. What Ari and I shared had been unexpected and intense. I hoped one day the hunt would be over for both of us. Until that day came, I had work to do. I wouldn't lose this man, but most importantly, myself, for no reason. The notion stretched as it had done the first time it made its way out of the pit.

I picked myself up off the floor, wiping my tears as I did so. *It's time.*

Ashley preferred Abraham Maslow's theories, I prefer those of Sigmund Freud. He is a questionable character, but his Theory of Personality is the closest explanation to grasp the darkness of humans that I have ever studied, in my opinion. Freud's theory sees the human psyche as structured into three parts – id, ego, and superego. The id is the part which represents the primitive and instinct-driven needs, sexual and aggressive. It's also the part containing hidden memories. The superego operates as the moral conscience and the poor ego tries to mediate between the other opposing parts. The id is impulsive and unaffected by logic or the reality of the everyday world.

The id operates on the pleasure principle, requiring each wishful impulse to be satisfied.

I hunted ids.

My plan had not yet been perfected; I had not been prepared for a buyer so soon. A squirming little shark in a pond of my creation. I spent the rest of the day preparing for the arrival of this id and the ids to follow. Darkness fell and I headed out to meet id. Sweetylover1977, the name behind which id hid on the dark web, had a vile taste for young boys. Id was not the man who called himself Angel Taker, but I would get to that specific id. It was only a matter of time.

Sweetylover1977 had destroyed the lives of prepubescent boys. How many, I didn't know yet. One is one too many in my book. Soon id would share the details of id's horrid acts with me. If id was reluctant at first, good. I looked forward to using the methods I had prepared to have a good old-fashioned forced conversation. Interrogation sounded too simplistic in my mind.

I decided weeks before to treat the paedophiles with a little – what should I call it? Let's call it a little extra attention. There is nothing more despicable in this world than a destroyer of children. A fitting fate should befall those who do.

During our private conversations to make arrangements for the transfer, I had set up the meeting point. Id was reluctant to drive so far out of the city, but I reminded id that doing so would be well worth id's efforts. Transfer, I came to learn, was the term used for selling human beings, animals, corpses, organs, or limbs.

Appalling things are happening around us, day and night. No rest for the wicked meant no rest for me.

I came to see ordinary people in a different light. Well, at face value they appeared ordinary. I often allowed myself to wonder what made him or her tick. What was the one thing that gave them the most pleasure? Something as normal as reading a great suspense novel? Taking part in recreational activities? Or was their ticker a dark desire shared only with others swimming in the abyss? If only it was as simple as having our sins or darkest desires appear like tattoos on our foreheads. *What would be written on mine?*

A symphony of frogs and crickets filled the cool night; nature has a way of setting the perfect atmosphere. Unspoiled and crisp. The moon was full, a cool white-blue light, watching me as if it knew. A night to remember forever, my first. You never forget your first.

Id was following my instructions to a tee. Id stopped where I told id to, and right on schedule, id's car crept around the corner, headlights off. A rage-fuelled excitement filled me as id got out, a rental I assumed. Id walked over to where I stood right in the middle of id's car and my own.

"Cerberus, I wish to enter." Id's masculine voice stirring the notion who was as excited as I. *Our first.*

"You may enter. Open it." The voice-altering device answered. Right on cue, the muffled screams of a terrified boy emerged from under the Tonneau cover. Id hurried towards the pained voice. The sparkle in id's eyes ignited a hatred inside me for this specific shark. As I lifted my hand and shot id with the tranquilliser dart, a smirk crept onto my face.

Id grabbed at id's neck and spun around to face my smirking face. An emotionless ghost face was all id saw. Id lost id's footing and fell.

"Welcome to the underworld, Sweetylover1977." I tied the cable around id, and the winch mounted on the back of the double cab Ford Ranger did the rest.

I got in behind the steering wheel and sent a text message from the burner phone.

The text read: Fetch it.

Simple and to the point. In less than fifteen minutes someone would take the car with which id had taken id's last drive into the picturesque countryside. Id wouldn't see this road again.

***

Sweetylover1977 stirred, a little disorientated from the effects of the tranquilliser. I had upped the dosage enough to take down a bull. I had no idea who I would meet until I saw id. Much like online dating, I assume.

Id had slept for about eight hours which was good considering id wouldn't be getting much, if any, sleep until id would close id's eyes for the last time. Not with Cerberus on guard.

I contemplated waking id as I was eager to start. In a few hours, I would need to drive into Marcel to spend the weekend with Lizzie for our birthday celebrations. Keep up appearances and present an outward appearing wholesome life.

I spent countless hours finding the perfect methods to extract the information I required. For a brief moment, I even considered making use of a Judas Cradle. The unhygienic element thereof made me decide against it. Perhaps if a suitable shark made its way into my pond, I would reconsider.

It excited me to test out my chosen tools. Yes, it might have been medieval in its conception, but I focused instead on its effectiveness and the reason it was shunned from use in our civilised world. A world where predators had more rights than their prey. A sick, twisted society we are. Less civilised in our treatment of the victims of these horrid beasts.

I sighed, not a sorrowful sigh, but one of anticipation. Id had no idea what was waiting for id. The thumbscrew would wake id, to meet id's end. I slid id's feet into the thumbscrew and admired my craftsmanship. I was proud of my work, knowing my father wouldn't be. Even though he had taught me how to build various things with my hands.

Twist, twist, twist. Id screamed out in pain, followed by the sound of bones crushing. Of the twenty-six bones in one foot, I estimated I obliterated eighteen in each. It was a good thing id would never need id's feet again.

Still screaming at the top of id's lungs, id looked bewildered and found me sitting at id's pulverised feet, my hands still on the device that brought an end to id's gallivanting.

"Who you? What you? Where me?" Id stumbled to find the words to make a grammatically acceptable sentence.

I stood up and faced id. Eye to beady eye. My face no longer covered as id wouldn't leave this place with the ability to tell anyone what, or who, id had seen. "Welcome to your hell, Sweetylover1977. Or should I perhaps call you by your real name?"

"Who the..." Rambling an absurd amount of profanities in one breath, "are you?"

"The last person you'll ever see. I'm the person who will make you regret giving in to your dark desires and destroying the lives of little boys. The person who will make you wish you took your own life the first time you reached out to ruin the precious gifts God had given to this world. Whose light was forever obliterated by your touch! Your desires!" I slapped id, the imprint of my hand would be visible for hours to come. A good slap across the face stirs something a little carnal in me. I spent four months on the receiving end.

Id spewed more profanities, and I grew tired of id's blasphemous words.

"Okay, you're not yet ready to talk. Let's try this again in a few days." I dabbed a needle into id's neck, waiting for the fluid to retake id's body.

This time id's sleep would be more of a nap, just long enough for me to move id to id's next and perhaps final position.

I myself needed a few hours of rest before driving to Lizzie's house. Being well rested would help my disguise. I needed to have my wits about me to continue playing Lizzie's returned sister.

On my way to Lizzie's, I would stop at Tabula Rasa to check on the remodelling of the new building and grounds.

For six glorious and uninterrupted hours, I slept. Restful sleep, and I awoke refreshed and ready. Excited to spend the weekend with my sister to celebrate our birthdays, celebrate us. I knew the weekend was about her.

Sweetylover1977 wouldn't be going anywhere. I watched

as id woke up, id's shirt covered in blood. The heretic's fork around id's neck would make sure id didn't sleep again. A crude instrument I constructed out of a meat fork and neck restraint. The chains around id's ankles and wrists would keep id in a very uncomfortable position. I wondered if id would be a little more forthcoming when I returned on Monday.

Id wouldn't die of dehydration by then, the temperature in the room comfortable. For the time being. *Only one way to find out.*

I showered and left for the city, checking my phone one last time to make sure id was awake. A bewildered look had filled id's face. I cued the playlist and left.

Driving past the vacant space where I left id's car, I thought of new-found virtual acquaintances. One hand cleaning up after the other. Ari's filled my mind, the warmness of his touch, the mere thought of him made my whole body tingle. I longed for him. A deep longing from a place of being alone in what started to consume me, bite by bite.

Should I have enjoyed torturing id as much as I did? Would God forgive me for going down this path and doing what I had to do? This was after all war, and God often sent His people into war. A small still voice told me I couldn't justify my actions. It was my hand, not God's.

Exhaling aloud, wiping away tears with the sleeve of my leather jacket, I wondered if God would forgive me.

My thoughts were still filled with questions about retribution and salvation as my hand reached for my mobile phone. Ari. I wanted to call him and tell him how well the previous night went. I picked it up, looked at the dark screen and tossed it onto the passenger seat.

Why did I want to share this part of my world with Ari? Perhaps because I had spent so many years as part of a team. Ari and I had not known each other that long. "Find me when you are done." His voice pulled at the question I had not yet considered: When would I be done? A number perhaps, say fifty, and then I would throw in the proverbial towel, realising for every head I cut off three more would appear. A never-ending war.

Or would it end when I found Angel Taker? Would my insatiable thirst to hunt predators be quenched by id's death? Followed by another and another after id?

Have the levels of the depravity of this world not yet reached maximum growth point? Would there not be new generations of little sharks growing into fierce predators who could only be stopped by something bigger than them? An orca. Me.

It's an awful life cycle that won't end, not until…? *Rhetorical question.*

Even if I, too, turned my back on this pandemic, as most people across this supposedly wonderful world do, would I ever be able to let go and turn my back on it? To not protect? No. It will never be over. But one day I would need to walk away. If I was still capable of walking or breathing by then.

Questions kept forming in my mind, unanswerable questions that plagued me for months to come. I had driven all the way to Tabby Manor and not even registered that I passed other vehicles or turned onto the correct roads. I assured myself I would have heard a thud or felt a bump had I not been focusing on the task at hand.

Leather on leather made a strange sound as my back caught the side panel getting out of my SUV. I holstered my SIG which lay on my lap like one of those yappy little lap dogs I despise. A barking rat. I love my SIG, but when it comes to dogs, I prefer bigger breeds.

As a child I had a Dogo Argentino, and my fondest childhood memories include her. I named her Texas. The perfect companion for a young girl always off on an adventure in the woods at the lake house. My parents had refused that I leave the house without her, not that I ever considered it. The adventure was always more real, more dangerous, with her by my side. Fearless, athletic, and my fierce protector. For me, she didn't kill the bull, but she did kill the snake. Not a poisonous snake, but still. With no regard for her own safety, she pounced on it the second it slithered across my shoe, shredding it to pieces as she tossed her head from side to side.

Texas and I were kindred spirits, and she, too, is a loved one I miss to this day. Should I get a dog to keep me company at the lake house while I waited for id to decide id was ready to talk?

Too focused on the construction crew next door, I didn't notice Ashley walking towards me. Did they all undergo background checks before being employed by Duvall Construction?

"Finley?" Ashley kept calling out to me.

I whipped my dart-free neck around to where the sound was coming from much the same way id had done the previous night.

"Oh, hello, Ashley darling, so very lovely to see you on this splendid and warm autumn afternoon. Isn't the sunset just bloody marvellous?" My British accent startled both of us. Binge watching episodes of Downton Abbey was the only way I could lull myself into sleep after spending too many hours in the abyss.

Ashley burst out laughing at my idiocy and I laughed with her, because it appeared to be the right thing to do.

"What brings you to my humble abode?" Her accent was absolutely ghastly, darling.

"Ash, please never use that accent near Hope, you will leave the poor child scarred for life." Not hearing my words and that poor Hope might already have scars, inflicted by the hand of horror she must never remember, and that all the love Ashley and Kyle were bestowing on her would erase every bit of whatever those pure eyes had seen and little body had felt.

"We found her. She's in jail for murder. Her mother signed the papers waiving all legal rights to Hope or Candy, as she referred to her. Can you imagine that? Candy! To think my beautiful daughter would have grown up with a stripper's name." She rambled on for a good few minutes, I stopped listening after *murder*, almost not hearing stripper.

"Murder?"

"Yes, she murdered her boyfriend. He wanted to do unspeakable things to my Hope, her Candy, and she lost it. Stabbed him. The reports said they counted fifty-six wounds. Serves him right. The piece of scum got off easy. The boyfriend wasn't Hope's father. Her father was a drug dealer who died a week after Tammy got pregnant with Hope in a drive-by shooting or something. Some turf war thing. Who knows? Anyway, so there she found herself pregnant after a one-night stand and then she met what's-his-face – well, guess it's more like, where-is-his-face after she was done with him – and he stuck around. Smacking her a good bit and then he wanted Hope. It's possible he wanted Hope all along. It makes me sick."

"Where is his face." Uncontrollable laughter erupted deep from within me. Is it not wonderful that we can find joy in these moments? Hope was safe and untouched. She had a loving mother who did everything to protect her child as every mother should. Now Hope had two.

"How long will she be in for?"

"She's awaiting sentencing. She pleaded guilty to the charges brought against her, I think she said manslaughter or something like that."

"She doesn't deserve to go to prison. I wish I had known earlier. I could've gotten her the best lawyer and gotten the charges dropped. She's a hero, not a criminal."

"Finley, she killed someone. You can't go unpunished for that."

"What she killed isn't human, Ash. They should never have arrested her in the first place. Why is she giving up Hope?"

"She loves her very much. She does, and that's why she wants the best for Hope. A better life than she had, she said. I showed her a photo, and she sat there crying, smiling, and saying thank you over and over. She isn't a bad person, she just doesn't see herself giving her little girl the best chance at the best life."

"Get me her lawyer's number. I want to visit her."

"Why do you want to see her, Fin?"

"Perhaps if she has something to look forward to during her time spent in prison, she will turn her life around and make something of herself. She deserves a second chance, to have the same life she is brave enough to want for Hope. She doesn't deserve to be in prison. Not for protecting, not for keeping evil from touching her child."

I wondered if it was the rage festering inside me or the wind stirring my hair. The old oak tree in the middle of the driveway answered me. The wind. My rage was not strong enough to rustle the last leaves on the old tree. Not yet.

"I'm worried about you."

"Don't be," I snapped. "I'm sorry. I hate how our judicial system works. This woman deserves a second chance. Just get me her lawyer's number, please."

"Finley D. Williams, your heart is both beautiful and courageous. I thank God He destined us to be friends. Sisters from different mothers." A smile made its way across her face replacing the astonished look.

"You showed me what people are capable of if given a second chance. You're the main reason I want to help. What did you say her name is?"

"Tammy. Her name is Tammy."

"Okay, Tammy. She deserves it as much as you, me, and everyone else who walks through those gates." The wrought iron gates always gave me a sense of safety from impenetrability. Tabby Manor will always be a place of safety. It was my destiny to make sure of that. And to do my utmost to bring the same safety and protection to the world beyond those gates.

"It's time we go to my office and talk. We haven't spoken about you, or how you're coping, since the last time you visited."

"I'm fine, I really am. Being busy and focused on this place is good for me."

I hated lying to my best friend, but she would never support my mission. For as strong as Ashley was, strong enough to run at only sixteen, she was a gentle soul. She wouldn't be able to stomach the image on my mobile phone's screen. Not that day or the days that lay ahead.

"Are you still training at that karate place?"

"Krav Maga, Ash. Krav Maga." Memories of Ari flooded my mind.

"What happened, Fin? And don't you dare say nothing." Ashley knew me too well, but not the version I was turning into.

Was dark, vengeful Fin after all the real me? Had years and years in active combat changed me, or had the final nail in the coffin come from months filled with torture and having unspeakable things done to me ?

Are all humans capable of this change? Do we hide it away because society tells us it's wrong to protect at any and all means necessary? Perhaps it was all and none of it. I found myself exhausted from the philosophical ideas which decided I needed to be subjected to a great and lengthy internal debate. I had to get out of my head, have normal, almost still qualifying as young-adult fun.

Early thirties is still young, isn't it? When do we become old? Is it at a specific birthday when the hands of fate push you over the wall and you land face down in the muck that is old age? Or are we... *Stop it, Fin! Stop it, other voice I am yet to name!* Was I going crazy? Perhaps the ripple effect of PTSD?

"Let's have coffee and talk like friends. I will take my psychiatrist cap off and just be your friend, as I always am. The psychobabble is a by-product, sorry."

"Okay fine, but I'm making the coffee. As brilliant as you are you can't seem to remember milk-no-sugar. How hard can it be, Doctor?"

"Have you considered it's a ploy to make you tense? When people are tense, they tend to get aggressive which leads to most lashing out and saying the very thing they are trying to hide. Show their real feelings. Anger has always been your go-to response in every situation."

"Oh, Ashley, do you still not know by now the only thing you need to do to get me to talk is a good whiskey? My weakness, a good old Johnnie Walker Blue Label, neat. Aggression isn't my go-to response."

"Day drunk is frowned upon in some places, Fin, unless you're a university student. There it's the norm. Don't you remember?" She refused to take my bait.

It was impossible to forget. Six uninhibited years of too much alcohol, too many almost-men-boys, and way too much fun all culminating in enough memories that I would sit with a constant smile on my face in a home for those waiting for death. Best everyone with tales of my youth. I made a mental note to keep the current events and those to come to myself. If people frowned on a good old day drunk, what would they do when learning I hunted hunters?

Ah, youth. A dream of becoming the best profiler in the world, staring evil in the eye, not so much as a flinch when our eyes locked. Listening to the tales of their depravity. No emotion when they tried to justify it with renditions of their troubled and violent childhood years. Just a satisfied inner glow knowing I had played a part in ending their reign of terror. I bested them in the game of cat and mouse. Not a game, but a stark reality of the demons that walk among us. Outwit them I would, and prevail as the ultimate hunter. Their little beady eyes forever circling in one little pond, watching their backs in constant fear of something bigger or bolder sneaking up on them with a shank.

I would have bested them. I would have been the ultimate apex predator. An orca.

"Coffee it is then," I said and put my arm around her as we made our way to her office. "How is our precious Hope?"

"Perfect, except she might be teething. We're not sleeping very well at the moment, but it's all part of motherhood, the joys of being a parent. Who needs sleep, right?"

"You do know I don't mind looking after her so that you can get a good night's sleep?"

"Yes, I do, but she's my responsibility, and it's my way of making up for missing out on the first months of her life. For now, let's focus on what you don't want to tell me. Let's start with the Craft Mega subject you're trying to avoid." We reached her office. No way around it now.

I told Ashley everything, every minute detail including those things I had stopped counting. Except, of course, the fact that Ari trained me for war. Relentless in his pursuit to make me a living weapon, teaching me everything he had learned over years of covert operations. Looking back, I wonder if he tried to keep me safe should a formidable opponent have presented itself. My favourite part of training had been pressure points, except for spending so much time with this man who helped me reclaim what was taken from me. His strength lay in the things he didn't say, the things he deduced. The never to be spoken about division he worked for, one of the best in the world. Ari, himself, one of the best in the world.

He spoke a language that only a few people in the world understood. War.

For a while, Ashley simply stared at me with her hand on her chest and I waited for her to say something. I waited. She reached for her mug, putting it down when she realised she had drunk the last sip ten minutes ago.

"So, let me see if I understand this correctly. He, Ari, is in all possible ways the perfect man for you. He sounds hot by the way."

"He is," I said, and my shoulders sank as the words left my mouth.

"Now, as I was trying to say, you pushed Mr Perfect, with his sexy Israeli accent, out the door without clinging on to his leg like a first grader would to their mother on the first day of school. Why, Fin? Why?" The last *why* was said so loud it could've passed for a scream.

"For the record, no man or woman is perfect. But the

timing isn't right and I still have an ounce of self-respect." I didn't respect myself all that much for sleeping with him and then pushing him away, but the feelings he ignited brought clarity. "We both need to take care of a few things and once these things are done, we might be together."

"What things, Finley? What can be more important than being with someone you are clearly smitten with? Being involved with someone physically might do you good to work through the trauma you experienced."

"No psycho-babble. I'm busy with the expansion of Tabby Manor, and I purchased a farm for the guests to spend their weekends at. It will do them good to spend time away from the city. The place needs work but you must drive out during the week and come see it for yourself. I would love your input. This will be good for everyone. The countryside, sunlight, fresh air, and all the other things plants and humans need to thrive. We can start a vegetable garden or something to keep them busy, or we can discuss putting in a swimming pool for the summer. Maybe a hot tub for winter. What day next week will suit you?"

"Nice try. You're not going to change the subject that easily. Although, a farm? It's a brilliant idea. I can't wait to see it. What if I drive out on Wednesday?"

"Wednesday is perfect, come to the lake house and we can take my car. Let's say around ten in the morning?"

"It's a date. Now getting back to Ari."

My clever little plan not so clever after all.

"What about him? I have things to do. So does he. The end. That's life. My life."

I didn't want to discuss Ari anymore. Lizzie would be furious if I ran late, I had to go. What she had planned for her big I-am-not-over-the-wall-yet weekend-long birthday celebrations remained a mystery to me. In truth, just the idea sent shivers down my spine.

"Always good at sabotaging your own life, Finley D. Williams. Too good, as a matter of fact. Overachiever as always but this time hurting yourself the most, and I suspect Ari as well."

I nearly let it slip he was ex-special ops and extremely capable of taking care of himself.

"I love you too, but I need to get going. Lizzie will try to kill me if I'm late."

Ashley laughed. "I will pay good money to see Lizzie try."

Fifteen

I pulled into Lizzie's driveway fifteen minutes ahead of our scheduled time, puzzled at the sight of the other vehicle whose owner I didn't know. Had she perhaps invited friends to join us on this ridiculous quest to prove we were still young? Witnesses or unsuspecting photographers to capture the carnival that was a night out with Lizzie? Our antics posted for the world to see because every second of every single day has to be posted for the world to see. Not on one social media platform, but multiple. People are self-involved attention whores.

I'm proud to say I only post cat memes. That's a lie. I hate memes and I'm not a cat person. My life is my own. I didn't need validation from others before the social media age. Why change now?

I checked my phone; id was still in the same uncomfortable L shape I had fastened id into. Id tried to lower id's head to ease the strain on id's neck, jerking it back when the two sharp tines pierced behind id's jaw.

It was time to change the music. I hoped id didn't enjoy the death metal mixed with screeching sounds I had downloaded to keep id company for the weekend.

I dabbed a finger at my phone's screen. Soon a never-ending red light would flicker at set intervals. I should've glued id's eyes open for this part. I made a mental note for the next one. This would continue until I decided to change id's sensory experience.

I turned up the heat in the room to a summer desert heat. This was fun. Distance torture might be a thing of the future.

"Come on, Fin, we're not getting any younger and I have a surprise for you!" Lizzie shouted from her front door dressed only in a silk robe.

I have always hated her surprises. Somehow her surprises always ended up being something someone such as myself could only consider as sibling-torture.

"I'm coming, you old hag. Don't get your grandma panties all twisted up." I was out of the SUV, holstering my SIG in the same move.

Why people drive around with a handgun holstered has always baffled me. At the moment when you need it most are you going to politely ask your assailant, for argument's sake a hijacker, to please wait while you reach for your gun to make it a fair fight? No. You will put your hand on the gun on your lap and shoot the life out of him. While he is still yanking at your locked door forgetting newer models of most vehicle manufacturers come standard with automatic locking. The idiot will go down next to your vehicle, and hopefully his intestines will have pieces of lead to digest.

The hollow points I prefer shreds its way through intestines. Digestion would be the least of id's concern. Based on the height of your vehicle, you will either hit a leg, groin, or lung. It also depends on where id landed on the growth spurt scale.

"Finley, get your ass up here now." My sister started sounding more and more like an old hag.

No. I didn't like the surprise. Not one bit. Eight-year-old Finley might have. But not this one, a year away from perhaps sounding like an old hag myself. Was it a specific number that gave you the final push over the wall?

Lizzie, in true too-early-for-a-mid-life-crisis mode, had the brilliant and utterly ridiculous idea to get her personal stylist to come dress us and doll us up for a night to reclaim her youth. I still had mine, at least for another year, I hoped.

Favio had made quite a name for himself; his flamboyancy a sight to behold. An idiot television producer had the bright idea to subject the world to Favio's shrill voice and elaborate hand gestures by giving him his own reality show. *Look out universe; a star is born.* Favio's not so catchy catch-phrase after each makeover. A middle-aged woman clawing in desperation to hold on to her youth which had run away years ago. Or a shy young woman who needs make-up plastered onto her already beautiful face just to make her think she is now, and only now, truly beautiful by society's standards. What is wrong with the world?

Is it as simple as making a terrible sex tape and suddenly your whole family is famous? Famous for what exactly? Having a slut for a sibling? If that's the case most people should be famous. Every family has one of those. Or in the case of the Williams sisters, we had two that night.

"I'm not wearing that." I shook my head. "If you try to force me, I will shoot your precious kneecaps to smithereens. Try prancing around like a show pony then."

"Just a dress, Fin. Don't be so...so butch for just one evening." Lizzie almost begged.

"Perhaps if it was black, but I'm not wearing purple. Not tonight. Not ever."

"Aren't you a lucky bitch? I have one in black. Not the same cut, but the colour you want, so you will wear it. Bitch, don't make me push you down and put it on you myself." Waving his hands around as if he was trying to show a plane where to land. Favio had a horrendous mouth, much better than the blasphemous verbal diarrhoea I had been subjected to earlier that morning.

"Let me see it first." I hoped I could stomach wearing the black option if only for one night. Favio took the dress out of its modest bag, the dress anything but modest.

"I'm going to look like a hooker. Do you want the sniper to take me out?"

"Finley, remember how Mom used to remind you that no matter how much you enjoyed playing with guns you were, in fact, a girl? Well, I'm reminding you, you're a woman. A gorgeous one. You are no longer a soldier. You need to start dressing more like a woman, dammit!"

"What's wrong with the way I dress?" 'No longer a soldier' cut deep into my soul.

Favio gave me the once-over twice, arms folded across his chest, taking in every bit of me with a disgusted look on his face. "Bitch, do you want to be a dude? Do you have a case of penis-envy or something? Or are you worried one might tear itself loose and chase your tight ass down the street?"

"Fin being chased by a penis down the street? That would be hilarious. She would shoot it or stomp the crap out of it." Roars of laughter erupted, and I rolled my eyes at their childishness.

I walked to where Favio had put the little black number down and picked it up. Giving it my own once-over. I undressed, right there in Lizzie's exquisitely decorated living room, and slipped on the dress. The laughing ended as fast as it began.

"Wow, bitch! Look at that body! Damn, bitch, you're ripped!" Favio's mouth forgot how to close.

"It's my big birthday and you will be the prettiest girl at the party. That's so not fair." Lizzie sounded eerily similar to a teenage version of herself.

"Bitch, calm thyself. Favio will make you the prettiest girl at any party. Don't you worry." Favio found a new bitch.

"I need a drink for this. Liz, any Walker around here?" Favio shook his head and ordered me to pour him champagne, reminding me ladies don't drink whiskey. This one does, and litres of it. I poured them both champagne, trying to figure out if I could strap my precious baby Glock unseen around my thigh.

After many more bitch-this and bitch-that, Favio was done with both of us and we looked like high-class hookers. So high-class only a president, oligarch, or crime lord would be able to pay for our services if he called in favours from his rich friends. But still, we looked like street walkers.

"Have fun, bitches! Be naughty; very naughty! Finley, if you see one, don't run from it." Favio said over his shoulder as he sashayed out of Lizzie's house.

Lizzie and I looked at each other and laughed, neither

remembered when last we had gotten dressed up. To my surprise, I was having fun.

Favio had done a good job and I loved my hair curled. It softened my face. The perfect disguise for a night of fun. A night where I wouldn't think about the id in my room. Not think about id's screams, wondering if id was begging for the red light to stop flickering yet. Nor the other predators in this world. Or Ari.

I readjusted the Glock around my thigh, the dress barely covering it. Again I was grateful it wasn't too tight around my hips. I never went anywhere without my gun.

"My car or yours?" I hoped she would say mine. I wanted to be able to leave when I had enough of the silliness the night was bound to be full of.

"Don't be dumb, I arranged a driver for us. Tonight we're getting trashed." The teenage girl in Lizzie was relentless. "The car will be here in five minutes, then we're going for dinner and I got us in at Rip Tide. Tonight's their official opening."

"Rip. Rip tide is a misnomer." Lizzie gave me a blank stare. Rip tide is a misnomer, so shoot me for knowing something.

"Please tell me you will not be a party pooper tonight. Please, Fin. Tonight's the first time in forever the two of us will have fun together."

I had forgotten about all the fun she was having on her own as a member of Alias. She didn't know about my very recent fun with Ari. I wouldn't tell her either, talking to Ashley about him was bad enough. No, this night was all about Liz.

"Come, the car is here. Let's get this party started." Lizzie sashayed in a similar fashion to Favio as she grabbed her coat and purse, not quite mastering the hip movement. I kept my opinion to myself. This weekend was about her.

Lizzie and I had dinner at one of those too-light-to-fill-you-up gourmet restaurants and we asked the driver to stop at the closest McDonalds and stuffed ourselves with Big Macs on the way to Rip Tide.

"I'm sorry, Fin, this place is supposed to be a culinary masterpiece."

"It's fine. Now we can both say we have been there the next time we meet up with all your pretentious friends. We will be the queen bees, again."

"That's a lifetime ago. How did everything change so much and so fast for us?" The bottle of wine she had consumed with our supposed dinner was having an effect on her. I had to do something fast or this would end up as a proper teen girl drama fest. Tears, tantrums, and the rest.

"Let's play the game we used to at UM." I hoped challenging her could yank party Lizzie back.

"What game?"

"Don't you remember bag the hottie?"

"Oh, yes." A smile filled her beautiful face, igniting a fire in her emerald eyes. "Yes, I do."

"Driver, please take us to Rip Tide."

I had the foresight to take my house keys just in case the night took an unexpected turn.

Rip Tide was housed in one of the newer buildings in the area. Old replaced new all over the city. The current recession had no effect on the construction industry. Or pharmaceuticals, Lizzie had told me over dinner. Doctors were happier than ever to prescribe anti-depressants to every person who walked through their door, even if they only had a cough. At least they wouldn't be unhappy about coughing.

The inside of Rip Tide looked as if an overzealous contemporary artist had attacked it. Various colours everywhere, not as bright and in your face as the lights were off. The only light was being emitted from the strobe lights where I suspected the DJ stood in a cage-like structure, suspended over the far end of the building. Scantily clad twenty-something bodies gyrated on the massive dance floor. The second floor looked similar with more gyrating youngsters. The music seemed different from that on the first floor. I can't explain the difference, to an almost old hag like myself it all sounds the same. Bless Lizzie for getting us VIP tickets.

The VIP floor was quite impressive, as far as these kinds of places go. Glass panels walled the area in, giving unobstructed views across this part of the city. The bar was situated to the left, with ample seating area from bar stools to lounge sets and in the middle of the area, the roof retracted over the pool. This could be fun in summer. But on a brisk autumn evening, I welcomed the bonfire and other built-in fireplaces. It created a cosy, pheromone-filled environment. Most of the patrons seemed to be single; the perfect hunting ground for Lizzie. She had her mission.

I found us a place to sit, comfortable in one of the lounge areas while she got us drinks from the bar. Lizzie refused to get me a whiskey and said she would surprise me. *Great, another one of her surprises.*

To my astonishment, she got me a decent cocktail. A frozen margarita with enough tequila to make this one of only three such drinks it would take for me to take off my shoes and jump into the pool. Clothes on. Or off, if I had a fourth. Perhaps the pool was heated, but no steam came from it, so I decided three drinks it would be.

We chatted and looked around for a suitable hottie to bag. There were a few semi-attractive candidates but not one measured up to Ari. He had set the bar high – construction crane high.

It became obvious Liz's bar was not even set as she flirted with any man that even dared look her way. In her defence, she was drunk and it was her birthday.

By the time I finished my second margarita and was just about to order another, Liz's eyes froze and the rest of her seemed to follow. Her drink froze mid-way between the table and her mouth. She eyed something or someone.

"He will most definitely do. Yum. Finley, I'm this round's winner. That right there is the fine piece of meat I'm taking home tonight. Yummy." She sounded like what I could only guess a cannibalistic teenage girl would sound like on the hunt. I turned my head to see who the unlucky winner was, and froze.

Ari. A million questions scrambled through my mind with not a single answer from any other little voice. *Why so quiet now?*

He stood at the bar laughing with a couple of people I assumed were his friends, some attractive but none compared to him. His intoxicating smile wasn't reserved only for me. Neither Liz nor I could take our eyes off him, for very different yet similar reasons. He turned to his side to pick up his beer and our eyes met. His dark eyes on me like I wished he was, and he smiled, poisoning every part of me.

"He's coming over. He's coming over. What should I say? I mean, he's so gorgeous." Teenage Lizzie continued her rambling monologue. Alcohol really does make you stupid.

His gaze stayed on mine as he made his way through the crowd. My body lifted itself up as he came closer. His warm body against mine. My lungs desperate for air. Ari touched my cheek and pushed a curly strand away. His fingers made their way through my hair and found the back of my head tilting it to meet his lips. My heart beat so loudly I was sure the gyrating bodies on the first floor thought the DJ had added base to his mix.

His lips left mine after a couple of seconds. "Wow, Ley! Wow."

My lips still warm from his, I stared at him, my fingers tingled under the heat of his chest. Ari pulled me closer but this time turned my head until his lips reached my ear. Shivers ran down my spine; a crazed herd of deer running for their lives.

"I'm working on something. I can't stay with you, but wow, you take my breath away. Watch your drinks." That sexy accent of his warming every inch of me. Ari turned around and walked away. I couldn't take my eyes off the perfect, well-defined muscles of his back so visible underneath his shirt he might have not been wearing it.

"Who. Is. That?" Liz said, her eyes bigger than usual.

"Ari." My legs gave way and lucky for me the couch broke my fall.

"Who is Ari? How do you know him and more importantly, why did he kiss you? Like that."

"He's my Krav Maga instructor." I knew she was about to open a flood gate of questions.

"Isn't that against some law or something? I understand why you're so ripped now. I would also train with him every day if it meant my reward was a kiss like that. Wait, don't tell me. No, do tell, Fin. Tell me! You have done more than just kiss! Tell me, tell me, tell me." Giddy teenage Lizzie.

"There isn't much to tell." I waived at the bartender for another round, hoping more alcohol would subdue Lizzie and perhaps subdue my wild heart.

"Oh, come on, Finley. You can't kiss someone like that, right in front of me and not tell me what's going on."

I told her the highlights of what had happened between us and that it was a one-time thing. I didn't have the energy to explain to her why I pushed him away. Too afraid the vast amount of alcohol in my system would turn me into a teenage girl who would run out of there in tears or into his arms.

"Please tell me you will hit that again. Soon. And hard. Man, that guy is...is...he's...I don't know what to say. Every word that comes to mind isn't enough to do him justice."

"I do." The waiter arrived in time for me to keep the rest of my sentence to myself.

I ordered us each another drink and a shot of whatever their house shot was. I tried my best to avoid eye contact with Lizzie as she still sat shaking her head.

Ari had rejoined his group of friends and carried on as if the kiss hadn't happened. Maybe it didn't mean as much to him as it did me, or he was working on something, the ever-professional ex-agent. *Not so ex, perhaps.*

Our shots arrived, a purple mix of something that looked dangerous. I live for dangerous.

"To you and never growing old." I raised the shot glass in the air.

"To us! To having my sister home! To being forever young!" She shouted, and we downed the vile concoction. It burned like acid all the way down.

"I'm going to the ladies room. Will be back soon." Lizzie got to her feet, took her purse and made her way towards the ladies room situated to the right of the bar. Lizzie veered off course and walked left. Heading straight for Ari was my sister, the drunken torpedo on heels.

"No Lizzie. No, inebriated Lizzie. Don't do it!" I shouted at her without a sound. My sister is an adolescent little bitch when she is drunk, to quote Favio's favourite word.

It was similar to watching an accident happen. You know it will be horrible, yet you can't will your eyes to look anywhere else. She stopped a waiter and asked for something. I assumed a pen by the way she gestured with her hand. The waiter reached into his pocket and she yanked it from him and scribbled on a napkin she found on his tray. Drunk Lizzie looked back at me, seeing two of me in all likelihood. She gave me a sly grin before spinning around on her very high, and very expensive, heels. Liz continued on her path directly towards Ari, not that torpedoes sashay. To my astonishment, she sashayed much better under the influence of alcohol.

Lizzie handed Ari the napkin, fidgeted in her purse and handed him something I couldn't make out. She looked back at me with that sly grin still plastered on her face. Lizzie turned to face Ari and said something to him. He looked at me and again that smile of his filled his whole face and he bit his lower lip.

I did the same. Stupid alcohol.

Lizzie returned from the ladies room ten minutes after her encounter with Ari. I timed her, waited for her, ready to strangle her in front of witnesses.

"What the hell did you do, Elizabeth Williams?" My voice stern as she plonked down on her couch.

"Let's just say I made sure you win tonight's round. Or maybe we both will." The corners of her mouth reached for her ears, and her eyes glistened. Someone stood behind me. I turned around to see the object of her focus and came face to crotch.

One of the men I had seen talking to Ari. His chestnut eyes glued to intoxicated Lizzie as she had walked away. Glued to her as he stood behind me.

"Please join us. I'm Elizabeth, but you can, and should, call me Lizzie. This is my sister, Finley." She waved him closer, and he obeyed, taking a seat next to her. She looked even smaller seated next to him.

A handsome man. Not as handsome as Ari of course, but still a fine male specimen. The stranger sitting next to Lizzie was either an active or ex-operative, like Ari. Everything about him said military.

Stranger danger came to mind, but the way Lizzie undressed him with her unfocused eyes, it was more a case of stranger in danger.

"It's a pleasure to meet you, Lizzie. I'm Eli." His accent heavy like Ari's. He had Lizzie from the moment he opened his kissable mouth. Hook, line, and sinker. Perhaps if I had been drunker my thoughts would have been a tad less mature, but I knew how to handle my booze. Unlike inebriated, flirtatious Liz.

"It's a pleasure to meet you as well, Finley. I hope you will come train with me now that Ari won't be giving as many lessons."

Why? Where is he going? My tipsy brain forced the words to hold on for dear life as if they were about to plunge into shark infested water.

"Sure, I will. I hoped to stop by for a lesson on Monday morning before I head back. Will my usual time suit you?" The control in my voice surprised me.

"Yes, Monday same time. Ari said you're superb, the best woman he has ever trained." *Flattering me will get you everywhere with my sister.* Liz couldn't keep her eyes off him, straining her neck to look at him. His body almost touching hers.

"Liz?"

"Yes." Not taking her eyes off him and he held her gaze.

"Let's get you some coffee and then I'm going home. I will book an Uber and will see you tomorrow afternoon for lunch."

Eli, with great reluctance, turned his focus towards me. "Ari will be waiting for you at your place."

"Ari will what?"

"Yes. Lizzie gave him your address and a key."

"Elizabeth Williams, your head is mine, but not now, I will wait for your hangover to be in full swing tomorrow and then tear you a new one."

"What's a hangover? I haven't had a hangover in years, not with all the experimental things they come up with in the lab. During research and testing, not available to the public. Not yet."

Eli looked at her intrigued. He changed his position, turning to face her. His arm stretched towards her on top of the back of the couch, his thumb exploring her shoulder. "So, tell me, Elizabeth Williams, what is that you do for a living?"

Lizzie turned to face him. She explained to him what her day job entailed. I had an idea she would much rather show him what she got up to a couple of nights each week. With that mental picture, it was time for me to leave.

"Please take care of my sister. If you hurt her in any way, I will find you, and kill you, s-l-o-w-l-y." A pleasant smile on my face, war in my eyes. To remind him what I was capable of doing to anyone who dared to hurt my sister.

"Don't worry about Liz. She's perfectly safe with me. You should know that."

I did. If Eli was anything like Ari, Liz couldn't have been safer if she was locked up in my room. That reminded me it was time to play music for id again.

***

The Uber driver arrived at Rip Tide on time but drove at the speed of a law-abiding citizen all the way to my penthouse. I considered taking my Glock out and asking him to get in the passenger seat. Old people in mobility scooters drove faster than he did.

Was Ari waiting for me? What would I say? What would I do? Well, I knew what I wanted to do. But I made the decision to push him away when every part of me was in turmoil. If he was working on something, there was a good chance he wouldn't even be at the penthouse. I prepared myself for going to bed alone.

I opted to focus on the id in the converted wine cellar for the rest of the drive. Id's shirt was stained a dark brown around the neck line, and sweat appeared to be streaming from id's face. The live-feed video quality was not movie quality but sufficient. I changed id's sensory experience. Id blinked for a few minutes after the light turned on. A bright light focused on id and the music followed. Id appeared to be screaming. Again. *Goodnight little shark, have fun.*

Sixteen

As I got out of the Uber driver's vehicle, I looked up at the top floor. A light was on in my penthouse. Either Ari was there, or someone had broken in. I got a strange feeling that someone was trespassing at that very moment.

I rushed into the building, nearly bumping into the doorman. My SIG I had left in the safe at Lizzie's but I had my Glock strapped to my thigh and rushed into the building. I pushed the button for the penthouse a few times too many.

As the elevator crept towards my floor, I wondered if taking the stairs wouldn't have been quicker. Patience is not a virtue I possess. I often ran up the stairs after training with Ari. A failed attempt to rid myself of the frustration I felt after being around him. Running up the stairs of a twenty-storey building was never enough to get him out of my mind. Cold showers didn't help either.

Maybe it was only Ari who made himself at home in a place I had not yet invited him into. How would it look if I came bursting through the door? Ridiculously expensive shoes in one hand, Glock in the other, with sweat trails down my face and chest.

I gripped the hand railing inside the elevator. My heart raced at the thought of Ari being there, waiting for me. What if it isn't Ari? That would be virtually impossible. My parents chose this building for the strict security measures. A woman can never be too careful.

I stepped out of the elevator. The doors closed behind me. I reached for my Glock. The door to the penthouse opened before my hand reached it. Stupid dress.

"Wow," he said again, and he took his bottom lip between his teeth.

I stood motionless. Breathless.

"You...I mean...you look...wow, Ley. Wow." His words teasing, his eyes filled with fire.

"What are you doing here? Don't you remember our—" I never got a chance to finish my sentence. His lips took possession of mine, of me. Not as restrained as the one at Rip Tide. His tongue decided it also wanted to play.

He carried me into my home and closed the door behind us. His arms still around me. Not once easing the pressure of his mouth on mine. *Could this never end?*

"This dress is driving me crazy." He took in every part of me, holding me at arm's length.

"My sister's idea of a surprise for her birthday. I'm sorry she walked up to you like that. Lizzie wouldn't stop badgering me after seeing you kiss me. I told her we had a one-time thing, that you were only my instructor. But there's no reasoning with her when she's drunk. Ari, I'm sorry for whatever she will do to Eli, or try to at least."

"Can you stop talking for one second? I want to kiss you, but before I do, you should know Eli is capable of taking care of your sister. She's safe with him and he won't do anything she doesn't want to. He's a good guy. I have known him for the better part of my life, and I trust him with you. That must tell you everything. Can you please stop talking and thinking about your sister and be here? With me?" He did what he wanted to do. My body ached for his. My resolve crumbled under his touch.

Ari took me in his arms and carried me to the couch. I kicked off my shoes as he made his way. He sat, making himself comfortable underneath me. His stubble was coarse under my fingertips as I dropped my mouth to his. My eyes told him what I wanted even when every cell in my body screamed for me to stop. His touch was warm as his hands ran up my thighs. He pulled away from the seduction of my mouth and lifted my dress, stopping as soon as he saw the reason for his abrupt end to our kiss. My Glock.

"That's my girl." My pulse increased. If this was a pickup line, it was a panty-dropper. *His girl.* I had to have him, right there on the couch. Desire took over and I forgot about the war surrounding us. I pulled at his clothes as his hands reached for the dress' shoulder straps. An alarm sounded on my phone.

I jumped off him and ran for my purse. Heart racing, hands trembling, not knowing whether it was from his touch or what had caused the alarm to go off. I stared at my phone while my other hand covered my mouth. It wasn't possible. It couldn't be. I turned my focus to Ari. He must have seen the horror in my eyes.

With a trembling finger, I dabbed at my phone's screen. Id still hung in the room, still moving id's head to ease the strain on id's neck. It wasn't helping, and I hoped it wouldn't. It took me two hours to make that neck restraint.

"Did he get out?" Ari stood next to me, seeing what I had done. Was doing.

"No. There must be someone else. I have to go." I headed for the door.

"You're not going alone and you're not going like that." He looked at my dress, looked at me, biting his delicious lower lip. The little cannibal was back.

"Okay, wait here. I only have my Glock. The SIG is at Liz's and I can't stop there now and ask for it. I'll get the Remington from the safe." I ran towards my room, coming to a complete stop the second I opened the door.

Candles everywhere, the flickers beckoning me to stay. A single red rose lay on my dresser. I forgot someone was roaming around my property. Trespassing.

"Finley, hurry up!"

How was it possible for him to be so at ease in my world, in my space even after I had told him we couldn't be together? Did he drive around with candles in the back of his SUV like a wannabe arsonist? Or did he consider himself a Don Juan or Casanova who was ready whenever women just looked at him?

"Finley, you need to hurry!" Ari walked up behind me and

saw the cause for my delay. "It's not what you think. I found a 24-hour convenience store on my way over here and we can discuss this later. Hurry now, Ley."

"You don't know what I'm thinking." I undressed in front of him. The dress fell at my feet. I walked towards the walk-in closet in nothing more than a small piece of black lace, covering half the roundness of my derriere. I might have sashayed.

Ari watched as I pulled my curls into a ponytail. Minutes later I walked out, covered in more material than I had been for hours. My comfortable, ready-to-kill clothes.

"Let's go." I brushed past him, heading for the front door.

"You can't do that to me."

"Do what? Can we discuss this on the way to the lake? Blow out the candles, I'm getting the rifle." I rushed to the safe behind the mirror on the wall separating the living room and kitchen.

Ari drove with the speed and precision of a Formula 1 driver. Of course, he was an excellent driver. Was there anything this warrior didn't excel in? It was exhilarating to be on the hunt with him and a part of me wished we could do it every night. I held the rifle steady between my legs and watched him in the glow of the passing streetlights. This was his hunting face. I preferred the other face I had seen a couple of times the previous night – well, two nights – before as it was close to 2 a.m.

"What were you doing at Rip Tide?" I broke the silence that hung between us. Neither of us had said a word as we rode the elevator down to the lobby or while we ran to his SUV.

"Who is in your basement?"

"Wine cellar." I corrected.

"A wine seller?"

"No, a wine cellar. A place where you store wine." I turned to face him, willing my hand not to reach out and hold on to his muscular leg. Touch the stubble on his cheek or run my hand along his arm. Touch the roundness of his bulging tricep as he gripped the steering wheel.

"You can't take your dress off in front of me like that. You make me crazy, Ley." Shaking his head, he let out a deep laboured breath.

"I'm sorry, but you were rushing me. I assumed you would turn around or leave the room." I wanted him to watch. Maybe Lizzie's adolescent behaviour had rubbed off on me.

"You're not sorry. Neither am I. When we get whoever is trespassing on your property, I'll show you what your little stunt did to me – is still doing to me. What's it about you? I can't stay away from you, no matter what you said," he sighed, changed his grip on the steering wheel and yanked it right. Tyres screeched as we turned and left the tarred road for the dirt road leading past the farm and to the lake house.

"Who is in your wine cellar?"

"A paedophile. Don't worry, he won't be there much longer."

"You can't do this. Don't you realise what this is going to do to you? Killing in combat or for survival is one thing, but this? This will change you forever. And it will kill the woman I'm in love with. Please don't do this."

"You're in love with me?"

"Yes."

A million questions bumped into each other, not a single one stepped forward to be uttered. I waited for the winner to present itself for utterance. "How is this different to what you do? As a matter of fact, we have never spoken about what you do. And we have never discussed the details of what I'm doing. Now, have we?" My heart stopped beating when he said he was in love with me.

I wondered if I was to live like a glitter-covered vampire for the rest of my life. It seems glitter helps vampires to walk around in daylight. If I was to be a vampire from this moment forward, I hoped to be a day-walker.

Then again, there is the whole blood drinking aspect. I prefer drinking my beverages from a bottle or a glass, not a squirming person's neck. The wannabes in the chat rooms I came across gave me hours of comical relief. With their stupid ideas, names and mannerisms, not to mention the way they spoke – well, typed. It's a big no for me. *Beat heart, beat!*

"I chose this life. I had no illusions about what I was getting in to." He looked at me, perhaps for the first time, through me. Our faces faintly illuminated by the glow from the displays on the dashboard.

"I didn't choose it. It chose me when the ocean pushed three little girls out right in front of me. Ari, when I close my eyes all I see is their small, broken bodies. Their wet, white hair. I can't stand by as a war is raging in front of me and do nothing. It's not who I am, I thought you understood that. Stop the car."

"What is it?"

"Here. Right here is where the camera picked up movement." I showed Ari where I installed the motion detection camera.

"I saw it on my way to your house. You did a fantastic job with everything you installed. And that little app of yours to control the wine cellar. It's disturbing how good you are at this. And sexy."

"Thank you. Now, let's go hunt."

He parked the SUV and opened the back door. Underneath the spare wheel was a compartment that didn't come standard. I suspected Ari's employer paid a little extra for a custom job on this one. It held everything you might need to overthrow a small third world country's government. This man kept on impressing me, arousing a need to know more about him, learn more from him to perfect the hunt.

"Finley, wait." He pulled me closer and kissed me, handing me a tactical flashlight before he pulled away.

"You don't perhaps have night vision goggles in there somewhere?"

"I do, was about to take it out." He turned back to remove

two, handed me one and put his own on his head, turning it up. For a moment he looked like a strange unicorn in the sparse light of the moon. He had switched off the interior light of the luggage compartment before opening the latch. It was thrilling and educational, seeing him in his world.

Before I could get the strap adjusted to fit my head, he handed me a tactical vest.

"I'm keeping the vest. That compartment is Pandora's box, but filled with the things my dreams are made of. I need one."

"You don't. You need to give this up before it destroys you."

"You're the last person in any kind of position to tell me what I need to do. We will discuss this later. Focus on finding whoever it is. I'm sure from what was visible on the still the camera captured, he was carrying something. It has been an hour since the alarm went off. He might be gone by now. This is my hunt and I'm taking lead. Any questions?"

"No. Let's get this done. Forget about everything we haven't discussed in as many words and focus on finding whoever this is."

"This is my operation, Ari. I know damn well how to run it. I might not have your training or experience but I'm an excellent soldier. I was. Now let's go have ourselves our very first hunt together."

"I have a feeling with you around it won't be the last." He kissed me and smacked my ass. "Let's make this memorable. Like our other firsts have been. Ley, that dress."

We were two combat-ready soldiers heading into the woods. Ari tracked prints. Whoever it was, this man was big. Ari estimated his shoe size to be a twelve, based on what he could see, and he was heavy, leaving deep indentations in the moist soil. Or, perhaps, whatever he was carrying was weighing him down. Side by side we hunched down, our rhythms synced. The danger and focus Ari exuded was tantalising.

The footprints lead to the lakeshore and I was grateful for the night vision goggles as it was completely dark under the canopy of the trees. It saved us a lot of time and gave us the advantage of approaching in darkness. At the end of the tree line, the last before you were out and into the clear, I held up my right arm, hand in a fist. Ari stopped.

I pushed the rifle into my right shoulder socket and scanned for movement. The night was quiet, except for the usual symphony of frogs and crickets. The moon played its part by giving us cover, hiding behind the clouds. I kept scanning and gripped the Remington 700 tighter. It was my father's; used for a different kind of hunting.

Movement to my left caught my eye.

On the opposite shore, someone pulled a canoe out of the water. At the bottom of my scope, a flicker of movement in the water. I focused in on it.

The hair on the back of my neck stood up. I ran towards the dark, cold water.

"Cover me. He's on the shore across from us to the left. Shoot, Ari! Kill him!" I shouted as I ran towards the water, dropping everything I could on the way. I had to be in time. I had to.

Ari picked up the Remington where I dropped it and steadied himself against a tree, looking towards where I last had. The figure on the other side of the shore turned around to see where the yelling was coming from. For a second Ari had him in his sight. He fired.

The bullet found its mark. Ripped through ids left arm, id fell to the ground. Ari ran closer to where the water made gentle, small waves as it touched the sand on the shore, the rifle scope still pressed against his left eye.

I swam as if a shark was lurking beneath, aligning itself to strike. With every arm stroke my heart beat faster.

I had to be in time.

The movement stopped and dissapeared into the dark as I closed in, and I dove into the darkness.

***

"Hold on, baby. Breathe baby, please breathe. Baby please don't go." I begged the girl with her wet, white hair pulling her back onto the shore where Ari stood offering us cover. Away from the monster.

"Breathe baby, please don't do this. Please." Every cell in my body screamed as I performed CPR.

"God, please let her live. Please." I pressed on her chest, blew air into her mouth. *Please.*

She coughed and I turned her onto her side, careful not to hurt her.

I cradled her in my arms, trying to warm her. "You're safe. I've got you. You're safe."

Ari phoned the police, and they arrived within thirty-five minutes. By the time they reached us we had taken her back to the SUV and found a blanket to warm her. I kept on talking to her and rocking her and after what felt like an eternity she cried and threw her arms around my neck. She held on, as I had held on to the man who saved me. The man who carried me out of that bunker, taking me away from monsters.

Uncle Tom ran towards us. The wailing of sirens replaced the gentle symphony of frogs and crickets as police cars pulled up. Tears still streamed down my face. Her face pressed into my shoulder, her cries so soft it stabbed at my heart. *She survived.*

"Finley, are you okay? Is she okay? What happened?" He hugged both of us, kissing both our wet heads.

"You're safe. You're safe. I've got you." I wasn't sure who he spoke to. Perhaps both of us. He looked towards where Ari stood talking to Captain Taylor. His eyes stayed on them while the paramedics spoke to the little girl. She increased the pressure of her hold around my neck. I willed my legs to stand and carried her to the ambulance.

"I'm not going anywhere, baby. I will stay with you until your parents come." I put her down on the stretcher, allowed the paramedics to take care of her, and make sure she would be okay; to confirm I hadn't lied to her. Her trembling hand held mine. She was safe.

"Ley, I'll meet you at the hospital. We can talk to Anderson and Taylor there." Ari turned and walked towards his SUV. I watched him get in.

How did he know Uncle Tom and Captain Taylor? Why did this girl turn her head towards Ari the second he said 'Ley'? She had been oblivious to everyone and everything around her since I pulled her out of the water. I turned back to her and put both my hands around her tiny left hand. Deep grooves on her wrist left by whatever he had used to tie her up and keep her his prisoner.

"Honey, what's your name?" My words hung in the air until she finally turned to look at me. Tears streamed down her pale face rimmed with drying hair.

"Riley." Sobs poured out of her as if she had, for the first time since he took her, or whoever sold her to him took her, remembered she was an actual person.

A little girl dragged into the abyss. But I found her. I saved her. Id could no longer hurt her. Ari shot id.

Never before have I ever hoped for someone's death as much as I hoped for the Angel Taker's.

When we reached the hospital, the ambulance's clock read 03:45 a.m. Not once during the drive had I let go of Riley's hand. I held on as they wheeled her into the emergency room.

A female forensic specialist came and took photos. She first took photos of me to show Riley what she was doing and that it wouldn't hurt.

I wondered how many times she had done this before; her gentle manner told me too many. A nurse came to do her assessment. She, too, was gentle. The nurse took the time to explain to Riley what was in the bags dripping into the tube that ran into Riley's hand. She even showed Riley how to put on the overhead television and adjust the position of her bed. Maybe she was trying to help Riley take control of her immediate surroundings, the only things she could control. The nurse reminded me of my grandmother.

A rape kit was useless as Riley was in the water when I found her. For how long, we had no way to determine. I didn't push the subject. What I had planned for the Angel Taker didn't involve evidence and I didn't want Riley to have to go through it. For a victim of rape, it's both invasive and demeaning. Vivid memories haunted me as I sat next to Riley. For what it was worth, I told Riley I had been through the same tests. Bad people had taken me, too, until one day someone had come and saved me. Just like I found her.

"It might feel strange when they look at you, but they won't hurt you. We need to do this. This is so we can find the very bad man who took you and hurt you. We will make sure he'll never hurt anyone else again. If you want them to stop, just say stop. They will listen to you, they're good people. I'll be right here holding your hand, I promise." Riley held on tighter to my hand, but a smile appeared on her haunted face. No longer the innocent smile of a once innocent little girl.

Riley's eyes focused on the Glock 19 strapped to my side; Ari had given me one of his. "Don't shoot them. They need to find him so that you can kill him. Please. Are the others safe?" Riley murmured. "He took them, and they never came back. Are they angels now?"

Riley sat motionless through the rest of the examination. Before the nurse left, she hugged both of us. Riley showed strength beyond her years and I stayed with her until she fell asleep. I pulled the blanket up to cover her, still trying to protect her, and walked to the voices outside her door.

Uncle Tom, Captain Taylor, and Ari's stark faces greeted me as I closed the door behind me. I turned to the two police officers stationed outside the door.

"I don't care who says what, no one, except the four of us, is to enter that room. No other police officer – I don't care if this is his case – goes in without us. Not a nurse. Not a doctor. No one. Not even her parents. Are we clear?"

"Yes," they said in unison.

I turned around and walked into Ari's arms. He kissed

the top of my head and held me. His warmth tugged at my composure.

We stood in silence and I inhaled his strength. I forced myself out of his embrace and looked at Uncle Tom.

"It was him. Is he dead?"

"The guys from forensics found a lot of blood. Ari got him good, but no sign of a body. They estimate from the blood spatter on the trees that he was shot in the arm." Uncle Tom rubbed his red eyes.

"I'm sorry, Finley. I had him and I didn't kill him. I don't know how I missed. I aimed for the kill shot."

My hands raised to Ari's face. "It's not your fault. I dropped the rifle, it affected the scope. It's my fault. I should've taken the millisecond to hand it to you."

"Ley." His hands on mine. "If you did that, that little girl wouldn't have made it. She's safe, and that's what's important. You did good. Real good."

"Riley. Her name is Riley." Tears stung my tired, burning eyes.

"You need to go home. It's seven a.m. and there is nothing more you can do here."

"Thank you, Uncle Tom, I promised to stay until her parents get here."

My words were barely spoken when Riley's hysterical parents ran into the ER. Captain Taylor went over to them and spoke to them. From where I stood, I could hear her mother's shaky voice.

"Thank you. Thank you." She fell into Captain Taylor's arms. "Can we see her?" Riley's father's cries echoed through the passages. He also fell into Captain Taylor's arms. His wife kissed him as he placed his arms around her. I fought back another wave of tears at the sight.

I didn't realise Ari had walked up behind me. He took me into his arms and turned me so that I could bury my face in his chest.

Before Riley's parents rushed in, I told Captain Taylor I was sure the Angel Taker was a police officer. Something about him reminded me of someone I had seen at both of the scenes where the other little girls had washed ashore. Whoever didn't show up for work that day, is the Angel Taker. The blood at the scene could be used for comparison against the exemplaries kept for all personnel who worked for the police, forensics units, and emergency medical teams.

Captain Taylor walked past us, escorting Riley's parents to her room. Ari and I stood next to the door. I was still guarding her even though there were two armed police officers. It was not my place to give them instructions, but it was. I had pulled her out of the water. He tried to kill her on my property. They stopped and looked at me. Riley's mother pulled me into her trembling arms.

"Thank you. Thank you for saving our little girl. Our angel."

"It was an honour. Riley is brave, she will get through this. Give her enough time, and never say the word angel around her. Ever." Her eyes widened, but she understood.

Riley told me he had called them 'my precious angel, mine' before he would hurt them. I didn't share the details with her parents. They didn't need to hear how he had violated that which was most precious to them. One day when she was ready, she might tell them, or otherwise carry it with her as most survivors do. A burden to be carried, not shared.

As Captain Taylor led them in to see their daughter, Uncle Tom cleared his throat next to me. "I see you know Ari." Straight to the point, I always liked that about him.

Thomas Anderson had the tact of a bulldozer when it came to me and Lizzie when boys were involved. I wasn't a teenager anymore and Ari wasn't a boy. The question as to how they knew each other remained.

"Yes." There was nothing else I could say. We had both given our statements. I explained I installed the motion detection cameras for security and told him and Captain Taylor about the farm I had purchased for the guests of Tabula Rasa.

It was to make them feel safe, which was not a lie.

"It seems you do, too." I waited for him to answer.

"Remember when I told you we have a contact in the Cybercrimes unit involved? I was referring to Ari's partner, Eli. He has been doing this for years. They are both part of a black-ops group. We really can't discuss this here. For their safety, and most importantly, for yours."

"You know I'm perfectly capable of taking care of myself." I hated when Uncle Tom forgot I used to be in active combat. He preferred to still see me as the tom-boy who grew up in front of him, loving me like his own daughter.

I looked up at him, saw the fear in his eyes and hugged him.

"I'm fine, Uncle Tom. You don't have to worry about me." He hugged me, crushing me against him.

He pulled me into a utility closet and whispered, "Ari is a good guy and one of the best in the world at what he does. It's up to him to one day explain to you exactly what that is. If I'm honest, I'm a little worried about the fact that your paths crossed. Any fool can see there is something going on between the two of you. Be careful Fin, don't get your heart broken. In his line of work, he can receive an order at any time to pack up and disappear, and he might never return. It is what he does best."

"How do you know so much about him?" It was not unlike Uncle Tom to do background checks on the guys I dated, not that he could've known about my involvement with Ari. But he suspected it. *Ignorant, almost old, hag.* Of course he knew. The way Ari held me and kissed my head screamed intimacy.

Never have two soldiers done that after coming out of battle unless they were related or sleeping together.

Uncle Tom got into his habit of doing background checks, starting with my first high school crush. It was his way of proving he had my back and that no guy would ever be good enough for me. I suspected he kept on doing this because every time I spoke about the crush of the month, he would pull information out of me. The very ignorant witness or suspect, I wasn't sure which role I took in his mind, as he subtly interrogated me. I'm forever grateful he never resorted to the tactics I planned to use on the id still in my wine cellar. Maybe I should've rather referred to it as my cave or something else. Wine is such a good thing.

What I was doing was a good thing. To id and the many ids to follow, who were not in any way good things.

"We haven't spoken in detail about what he does for a living. We met when I contacted him to train me. I told you I wanted to take up Krav Maga. Well, Ari is my instructor. I guess that's only his cover to do whatever it is he's really doing."

I wondered if I also formed part of this cover. It was always dangerous to get involved with someone while being undercover, but perhaps I had given him the perfect cover. People who saw us together would know who I am. Having a socialite for a girlfriend is a great cover. Socialite? I left that life behind me when I joined the army, never truly forming part of it in the first place. Finley is not pretentious. Well, maybe now I was pretending to lead a normal life. Ari didn't have to worry about me in any dangerous situation. I was capable of taking care of myself. He had someone watching his back. Even in bed.

There was a knock on the door, and Uncle Tom opened. Ari held a cup of coffee for each of us and I'm sure I looked as guilty as I felt. Ari raised one eyebrow and gave me a hint of his intoxicating smile. He turned his attention to Uncle Tom.

"I won't hurt her Anderson. I will keep her safe as much as she will allow me to."

"I am more worried about what she might learn from you, even if you don't realise it. And more importantly, what she will do with that knowledge. Finley is a born warrior and has never been afraid to go off the book. Her parents should have named her Rogue."

They were talking about me as if I wasn't even there, hiding in a utility closet with my non-related uncle.

Uncle Tom stepped out and turned to face me; his face

appeared older. "Finley, you need to watch your back. I have a strange feeling that he will come for you. It won't be to thank you for saving his angel's life. Because of you, he no longer has his cover in the police and Ari probably maimed him, if he doesn't succumb to the gunshot wound." I hoped with my whole being he would. "We are checking all hospitals and have sent a team to his house. You were right, Fin. He is a homicide detective and asked to be assigned to this case. His name is Tony Andretti. He is the grandson of the previous owner of Williams Manor."

"The sonofabitch probably thought it was his birthright to dump his victims where grandpa probably dumped his own. Oh, you sly little shark. Come on sharky, let's play." Hatred poured out of my words, every part of my being. I didn't even notice the shock that came over Uncle Tom's and Ari's faces.

"What?" My tone nothing short of a snap.

"You're doing it again." Ari looked at me concerned. "He isn't like the others, Ley. He's out for blood, your blood, and he won't stop until he has killed you."

"Not if I kill him first." Which I fully intended to do.

"What do you mean *others*?" Uncle Tom asked.

"What I meant with others is enemies in combat. This isn't war."

"Ari, I respect you more than I do most men. Don't insult me by lying to me. When both of you are ready to come clean, I will be waiting to hear the truth. For now, Finley, no going rogue. Are we clear?"

"Yes, sir." My attempt at humour didn't cover the truth. I lied. I knew he knew, which made it worse.

"I will stay with her and make sure she's safe." Ari turned to face me. His warm hands cupped my face. He forced my eyes to meet his. "No going rogue. Promise me."

"Yes, sir." I lied. I knew he knew, which made it worse.

As Uncle Tom turned to leave and get some much-needed rest, I hugged his worn body.

"I can find him." I said next to his ear. "I will tell you. If you promise not to ask any questions. Not now. Not ever."

"What have you done, Finley Williams? What have you done?" For a second I thought Uncle Tom would cry. Either from exhaustion or knowing I was doing something that not even he, nor Ari, could stop. Having a real-life, walking, talking, breathing lie detector for a godfather is no fun. Not when you're a teenager. Not when you're an apex predator.

"I can show you, but we need to get to Lizzie's. I left my laptop there. She's not going to be happy to be woken up so early. I'm not sure she's alone, either."

"I don't care who your sister has with her. And I don't want to know what you have gotten yourself involved in. Not if it means we can get Tony Andretti. I will deal with the two of you during lunch tomorrow." Uncle Tom, our new father. He was taking the role of being a daddy to his two grown-up Williams daughters very serious. I would have as well, if I had been in his shoes. He carried the memories of all the trouble we got into as teenagers and at university.

Now he would see how I had been spending my nights.

Seventeen

Ari and I drove in silence to Lizzie's house. My favourite song played on the radio as I watched as an aeroplane took off. I was too tired to enjoy the song or the thrusting sound of the aeroplane's engines. Ari loved Metallica, too; of course he did. He was in love with me. He pulled my hand from my neck and pressed it against his lips. The warmness of his mouth roused me – well, parts of me. My eyes refused to respond. Riley was safe. Uncle Tom seemed to think I wasn't. He followed us in his sedan, and I hoped he had better luck at keeping his eyes open. I couldn't lose someone else I love; I wouldn't survive it.

As we drove into Lizzie's street, I saw her driveway was empty except for my SUV. Its rugged exterior, standing forcefully, waiting for its master to come home. A comforting sight. It reminded me of my guardian, Texas.

As Ari turned the key in the ignition, I reached for his face and pulled his face so close to mine I could feel his breath on my skin.

"Thank you for being there with me last night," I said as Ari took possession of my mouth with his.

Our kiss was disturbed by Uncle Tom's tap on the window next to the driver. The raw, beautiful moment broken.

Ari reached for the door handle, but his eyes remained on mine. "Seeing you in action this morning and how you took care of Riley; you keep surprising me. I keep falling more in love with you. We need to talk about that dress." We kissed again, his hand no longer on the door handle.

By the time we forced ourselves to Lizzie's front door, she stood next to Uncle Tom, watching us. For a moment I felt like a naughty schoolgirl caught by her parents kissing a boy. The moment had been brief because my body ached for sleep.

Lizzie hugged me as I walked past her. The cloud of alcohol surrounding her made me hold my breath.

"What happened, Fin? Are you okay, what the hell happened?" She would never understand, and I lacked the energy to lie to her.

"I will tell you later. We need to do something very important and it's just as important that you have no part in it. Go shower."

"But," she hesitated. Her eyes pleaded for answers first from Uncle Tom and then Ari. They both answered her with silence.

"I will make us coffee. Fin, you get started. Liz, I beg you, please go shower and don't ask what we're doing. Ever. Trust me."

Liz and I had our orders. We obeyed without hesitation. I wrapped my arm around her waist as we made our way upstairs.

"Don't come downstairs until we call for you. Please, Liz. You don't want to get involved and never ask any questions." My sister nodded. She knew I wouldn't ask if it wasn't important.

Ari stood in the living room, observing my world. The one he hadn't seen before, but now found himself in, whether he wanted to be or not.

Before going downstairs, I sent a text message from the burner phone hidden in my overnight bag.

I made my way to the study carrying my laptop and face. How would I explain it? I didn't know. I hoped all earlier requests for 'no questions' covered this.

The curtains in Lizzie's study were made from heavy, royal blue material; as proposed by her interior decorator. I was grateful she took his advice. It set the scene for the darkness I was to bring into my loved ones' world. The laptop screen blinked at me. Dread settled as I entered my password, opening this world to Ari and Uncle Tom.

Uncle Tom walked in and placed our coffee on Lizzie's oversized, custom-made desk. He took a seat next to Ari, both out of view from the webcam. Silence.

My stomach turned on itself.

Time to let them see me.

"Whatever happens, whatever is said in the following minutes or hours, depending on how long it takes to find him, neither of you may ever ask questions and we will never talk of this again. Are we clear?"

They agreed without words. I cued my usual playlist; to cover real world noise.

My lungs filled with air. I held it, desperate to stall what was to follow. I exhaled and put on my face. My eyes focused on the screen in front of me, avoiding the eyes of the men seated across from me.

I only opened the webcam after I entered the first chat room. I stalked from one to the other, knowing where I was most likely to find him, avoiding it. No movement from either of the men on the other side of the desk.

"I know him." I slammed the screen of the laptop shut. My hands trembled as I removed my *face* from my own. Tony Andretti, aka Angel Taker, was not only the grandson of the infamous Tony Andretti.

"What are you talking about, Fin?" Uncle Tom edged closer in his seat.

"He was in my Ancient Cultures class at UM. We never told you, but one night at a party a guy tried to rape Ashley. I got him off her and pulverised him. If others hadn't shown up and pulled me off him, I would've killed him with my bare hands. I should've killed him that night. Not only for what he tried to do to Ashley, but then these little girls wouldn't be dead."

"Why didn't you tell me?" Rage simmered in his eyes.

"We didn't want you to pull her out of university. He didn't hurt her, I walked in before he had the chance."

"You shouldn't have kept it from me."

"I'm sorry. We were young and stupid. It didn't dawn on us what he was. I have no idea how both of us missed it. We didn't recognise the signs. When you study Criminology and

Psychology you start diagnosing everyone around you. But we were blind to the facts, ignorant. The sexual comments he made to all the girls, the way he stared. He always had this look. We just thought he was a loser. A pervert of sorts, maybe a peeping Tom or worst case, an exhibitionist. None of the girls paid him any attention. He didn't seem capable of doing any real harm."

"Not even after he tried to rape my Ashley?"

"You would've been proud of me. I broke his jaw." My eyes beamed with pride at the memory, forgetting the jaw-breaking kick ruined a perfect pair of pumps, and broke two of my toes.

He shook his head. "Let's focus on finding him. Make him pay for what he did to Ashley, and all the girls."

Uncle Tom was right. The only way to stop him was to find him. With my face back in place, I opened the screen and entered the corner of the abyss where I knew he would be.

This specific corner was only known to those invited to join the cult. This is how I referred to the group every time I entered. This specific group consisted of the worst of the worst predators ever known to mankind. Unknown at the time, except to other members. Here they came to gloat and share grotesque proof of their worthiness. A place for monsters to upstage each other. A place to master their craft. As far as they knew, I was one of them. Here, I was not Cerberus.

I became LordDante. The master of the nine circles of this hell. I stalked and learned as much as I could about the forty-nine members. Everything except their real names and where they hunted. Yes, there are many similar sites in the dark; this was, however, the darkest level.

I only granted membership to those I deemed the most dangerous and who brought an offering I deemed worthy. I saw the destruction they caused. Nausea overwhelmed me. I reached for Lizzie's wastebasket, my stomach cleared itself of the morning's coffee and the last of the Margarita still making its way through my digestive system. Ari and Uncle Tom sat unmoving.

I straightened myself out and resumed my position.

Baalares left me another offering. My stomach offered bile in return. Horrified eyes stared at me – Riley's eyes.

LordDante: *I find your offering unsatisfactory, Baalares. You have failed me. Your angel lives.*

I typed for all the members to read and waited for his response.

After five minutes, he was typing. With every flicker of the word 'typing' my rage grew into an uncontrollable beast. A beast I ached to unleash on him. Rip him to pieces. Remove his liver with my teeth. Leave the rest of him to rot.

Typing...

Uncle Tom changed his position, not making a sound and rubbed his eyes again. He paid no attention to the mobile phone that kept vibrating in his pocket. Ari kept his eyes on me. Rather, the face anyone who dared to hack my webcam would see.

Baalares: *Please forgive me my lord. Don't turn your back on me. I will do better. I will give you an offering better than any you have ever received.*

LordDante: *Don't be foolish, little sharky. You found out the hard way you're not the ferocious predator you thought. I'm done wasting my time on you. Does it hurt?*

Baalares: *Does what hurt, my lord?*

LordDante: *The stump. Where your arm used to be.*

Typing...

I suspect he started typing and then realised the implication of what I said. LordDante knew he was shot. Impossible. Unless LordDante was working for the police, forensics, or one of the people at the lake. Five minutes later he pressed enter. I suspect it was more a case of hitting enter. But then again, I didn't know the extent of his blood loss.

Baalares: *How do you know?*

It didn't take five minutes to type four words.

The little sharky was squirming. I relished in my small victory. Little sharky was what I called all forty-nine of them.

My predatory nickname for the pieces of trash I had to talk to hoping they would let their guard down. Just enough in their attempt to be seen as worthy by their master. It was more a matter of them trying to outwit each other. LordDante created the perfect place for psychopaths to play and be crowned King of the hill, or Queen. A place to stake your claim. Prove you are the worst killer to ever walk this earth. I often smiled at their comments behind my other face. No matter how they tried to proclaim themselves as master of darkness, I was always twenty steps ahead.

I hunted hunters, on the verge of seeing their faces.

While I baited Baalares, Eli was hacking into their laptops. A tiny little Trojan horse which clung to their IP addresses the second they were given membership. There are others like myself who use their skills for good. I considered the hacker who created the Trojan horse one of the good guys. In a matter of seconds, we would have their addresses and pictures of their faces if they were too stupid to cover their webcams.

Narcissistic psychopaths tend to be too self-involved to consider consequences. No more hiding little sharkies. My phone vibrated in the zipped pocket next to my right knee. It was done.

LordDante: *Wet, white hair sinking into the dark. A small little sharky circles it. Desperate to rip the luminous wings off and devour it. Bang! You have much to learn, little sharky. The others have been found. The only offering I want is your life. Take it by your own hand! I will find you, and I will show you no mercy! Not the mercy you gave your angels! Take it. Take your own life you fledgling. You don't deserve to hunt in this world. You're a failure and we laugh at your inadequacy. Take it. Take your own life, Tony Andretti.*

I logged off. Closed my laptop. Removed my face. Unaware of the smile and rage that contorted my Finley face. Uncle Tom and Ari didn't move as they stared at me seeing the face of an apex predator. I had called Tony Andretti out to play. None of what I had planned for him would be merciful. If there was righteousness in this horrible world, it would be for him to die a slow and violent death at my hand. The same hand which had saved Riley.

The silence became deafening. I realised I was smiling and looked away. They had seen what I wanted no one to ever see. A face reserved for the predators of this world. The last they would see as they took their last breath.

"What have you done, Finley?" Uncle Tom wiped his eyes. Tears, not exhaustion.

"What I had to do." I stood and opened the curtains, hoping sunlight would erase their memories. Never to remember the face they had just seen.

His phone vibrated again, and this time he took the call. "Anderson." He shook his head, still staring at me. "Thank you. I am on my way." He drank the last of the cold coffee from his mug and cleared his throat. "They found the others Riley told you about. Two others in the garage of Tony Andretti's house. Alive." He left without saying more. I wondered whether we would ever be able to go back to how things were before.

My body yearned for sleep as much it yearned to hunt Tony Andretti and make him pay for what he had done. Ari's phone rang and he looked at me for the first time since he had seen my predator face.

"Eli?" He listened as Eli told him everything. Without me telling him first. I regretted it, but there wasn't enough time. He put his phone on the desk in front of him, his eyes remaining on mine. I waited for him to shout, to do something, anything. He didn't.

"Let's go to bed. Do you think Lizzie will mind if I sleep here? I'm too tired to drive. You're struggling to stay awake." He got to his feet, took my hand and gave it a squeeze as he led me out of the study towards the stairs, only asking where we were going once we got to the top of the staircase. Lizzie came out of her room as we reached the guest bedroom door. Ari walked in, leaving me alone to face my sister. One person who didn't see my other face.

"Fin, are you okay?" she whispered. I wondered if she

didn't want Ari to hear or if she was, after all, hungover.

"I'll tell you later Liz, I promise. Everything I can. For now, I need to get some sleep." When I switched my laptop off, the monitor showed 11:00 a.m. I was tired in a way I hadn't been in a very long time. In an effort to control the walls that held my emotions in, I refused to allow my mind to remember the last time I was that tired. Soldiers don't cry, yet I had holding Riley. I hoped hers would be a story like Ashley's. A story of triumphing over evil.

"Forget lunch. We can stay in tonight, I will cook. Ari is welcome to join us if he wants. I will ask Eli to come over."

I willed my eyes to focus on her. How could I forget? "Happy birthday Fizzie-Lizzie. I love you." I sank into her arms and cried. The walls crumbled. "I'm sorry for ruining your birthday. It's just, we found her. She's alive. They found the others. We know who he is."

"Who are you talking about?" she asked afraid of the answer she already knew.

"The Angel Taker. We found him. We were in time to save Riley. Uncle Tom said the police found two more girls still alive at his house. They're alive, Lizzie. They're safe now." I struggled to say the words in between sobs. Lizzie held me tight in her warm arms.

"I'm proud of you. Always. Those girls being rescued is more important than a silly birthday. Now go to bed and let Ari hold you. You're safe, Fin."

She stood and helped me to my feet. I kissed her cheek and walked into the room to face Ari. The room was empty.

I fell on the bed and cried until I was empty of all emotion. The door to the adjoining bathroom opened.

Ari walked out wearing only a towel. He pulled me into his arms and held me.

"Let's shower and sleep. I need to hold you. We can discuss the dress later." He lifted my tear-soaked face towards his and kissed my forehead. I let him lead me into the bathroom and we showered together, got into bed, and slept. Ari's strong arms around me. He was there. He hadn't left at the sight of my other face.

Mid-afternoon I woke up. Ari was still asleep next to me. I couldn't help but snuggle into the hollow of his shoulder and rest my head. With the rhythm of his heart, the gentle rocking of his chest, I fell asleep. Late afternoon, I awoke to him stroking my hair.

"Do you really want to be here?" I found the courage to ask. I needed to know.

"Ley, I will always want you. Nothing will ever change how I feel about you. I've seen the worst sides of you and I'm still here."

"Why does it not scare you?"

"Because I know that face. It has stared back at me from the mirror. Too many times to remember. This is what I wanted to protect you from. To be in their world, like this, it changes you forever. You mean too much to me. I don't want you to turn into one of them. Let Tony Andretti go, the police will find him."

"Not before he finds me." I pushed myself up on my elbow to face him. Black, bristle stubble framed his strong face. I wanted to forget Tony Andretti. Lose myself in the moment.

"What have you done, Ley?"

"I called him out. In time he will figure out it was me. I hope he doesn't think you are LordDante. I haven't even considered that possibility before today. Ari, I put a big target on your back. What have I done?"

"He knows it's not me."

"How can you be sure?"

"He heard your voice – a woman's voice. You gave the order to shoot, to kill him. You were in control. Finley, he's going to come after you. Just the way you want him to. I don't know if you're fearless or stupid. What did you say to him? What put that look in your eyes?"

I told him everything. How I created the group, how

I found out Eli was working with Uncle Tom and Captain Taylor. Stealing Uncle Tom's phone at the hospital to get Eli's number and how I sent him a message before I logged into bait Baalares. I even told him we now had photos of the other forty-nine. After I logged off, Eli sent it to various agencies across the world. Through facial recognition software and the beautiful tiny Trojan horse, the hunt would begin. Technology has its positive sides.

"You keep surprising me." He cupped my face and pulled me on top of him.

I had to ensure Tony Andretti never considered, even for a second, Ari of being LordDante. He had to come after me.

Months later, he did.

Eighteen

"Promise to never wear that dress again. Unless it's for me and we're alone." Ari watched me as I dressed for dinner. I felt terrible that this had affected Liz's life, but she was right. The safety of the girls was more important. I would make it up to her when the time was right. When Tony Andretti was dead. Swimming with the fishes.

"So, should I only wear the underwear and high heels then?" I teased.

"Yes! Do you have it here? We can order room service and just stay here. Forever." I knew a part of him felt the same understanding and intimacy I did. It had occurred to me during the drive to Lizzie's that I should perhaps take the risk and let Ari in and give in to what I felt for him. Maybe I didn't have to hunt alone. Maybe I didn't have to be alone.

"As long as you promise to rip it off." He was about to lose all control. His eyes had the same fire they did the previous night at Rip Tide, and when I had walked into the penthouse.

"Stop it, Ley. We need to have dinner with your sister. It's the first time I will properly meet her and get to know her. I can't be thinking about you the whole time. Not like that."

"I know." I wore my most innocent face, sashayed towards him and sat across his lap facing him.

I bit my bottom lip and gave him my best bedroom eyes. "I'm sorry." The kiss that followed was anything but innocent. I pulled away from his hungry mouth and kissed his eyes and down to his neck. I jumped off him and headed for the door.

"Let's have dinner, I know my sister is dying to get to know you."

"I will make you regret that." He readjusted as he stood.

"I would hope so." I smacked his rock-hard ass and headed

for the kitchen towards the voices.

Lizzie's laughter guided me to her. "I didn't. How dare you say that?" Her face lifted towards the ceiling, she looked radiant.

"Yes, you did. Do you want me to take out my phone and show you?" Eli had accepted her dinner invitation.

"You didn't?" Lizzie couldn't stop laughing, even if I had told her Williams Pharmaceuticals was on fire.

"No, I didn't. But I'm telling you, you threw yourself at me." Eli joined her in laughter.

I wondered how long it would take for them to realise they were no longer alone. Ari filling the door behind me did the trick.

"So, what happened last night?" I ventured into the conversation.

Eli walked over and gave Ari a bro-hug. The kind of hug men give each other but it's not a hug. It's more a – my chest is bigger than yours, see when I press it against yours, let me pat your back twice while you are this close, we are such manly men – kind of thing.

"Thank you for helping, Finley."

"An absolute pleasure. I should thank you."

"This is the first time, in a long time, we got so many of them at the same time. I got feedback from my contacts. They're actively tracking suspects. They've already found names and addresses for some. Finley, you did a good thing."

Eli walked over and gave me a hug. I would assume this is how brothers hug their sisters. He picked me up and squeezed me so tight I thought he intended to break my back. "Do you realise how many lives you saved today? I can't thank you enough, on behalf of all the agencies involved."

Lizzie finished stirring the sauce and put a tray in the oven. She didn't ask any questions. A fragrant aroma filled the kitchen, and she poured herself another glass of wine. She poured me a whiskey, and asked Ari and Eli what they would like to drink. Being the manly men they are, they both asked for beer, which she diligently removed from the fridge. I realised she was not wearing high heels for the first time since I had come back. She looked beautiful in a pair of jeans, a white button-down shirt, one button too low in true Lizzie style, and comfortable flat shoes. Her hair looked more like her own tonight, not Favio's creation. She was comfortable having us in her house. Three people dressed in all black; guns unconcealed. I hugged her. A normal sisterly hug with no need to measure chest sizes; we had the same surgeon.

"Thank you, Liz. For dinner, for everything." She held me tighter.

I turned my focus to Eli, still holding Liz. "So, what did – or didn't – happen last night?"

Eli smiled and looked at Liz. "Well the thing is – and I swear this is the truth – as you remember, I was the sober one last night. My recollection of past events are much more plausible than that of a certain young lady who had a few too many." He still looked only at Liz.

"Liz hit on me. Actually, she threw herself at me, but me being the gentleman I am, ensured she got home safely. I walked her to her front door and left. Of course, I could only leave after I had pulled her off me. I had to maneuver myself out of the death grip she had on my shirt as she tried to kiss me." He saw nothing but Lizzie.

"Did not. I simply grabbed at your shirt to steady myself. I tried to kiss you, on your cheek. To thank you for being a gentleman."

"Told you he's a gentleman, and she's safe." Ari raised an eyebrow and the thing of intoxication became visible, my heart went wild. I walked over to him and kissed him in full view, for everyone to see.

"Get a room." Eli sounded like a frat-boy. Maybe he and Lizzie were a match. Well, maybe him and drunk adolescent Lizzie.

"Please don't. Not again." Lizzie shook her head.

"What?" My cheeks caught fire.

"Yes, sister, I heard. By the way, good job, Ari." Adolescent Lizzie joined us.

"I'm going outside." I took my Walker and left. The patio was a good place to hide my humiliation. The fairy lights made everything look magical. Ari on my six.

It was another cool night, the wind quiet, and I was grateful to hear only crickets and traffic in the distance. People on their way to enjoy a night on the town. Simple sheep having fun, enjoying their lives until a wolf came along and tore it to pieces. I was in no mood to think about sharks.

"That was uncomfortable." Ari pulled me into his arms before I could sit, pulling me onto the patio chair with him. I snuggled into his warmth and took a sip of my whiskey.

"I blame you."

"How is it my fault your sister has supersonic hearing?"

"No one needs supersonic hearing when it's you. You're that good. Too good."

"I'm sorry. I won't do that to you again in future."

"Don't you dare. It's the only reason I let you hang around."

A future. Did we have a future? Did I have a future? Would there ever be a time when this was our life, just normal banter between lovers, between friends and family? I hoped so. But is life ever that simple? Mine surely hasn't been.

I thought of id in the room. With everything that had happened in the preceding almost twenty-four hours, I didn't have time to check up on id. Would I get up and sneak off to do that or remain in the arms of this man?

I took in the sound of my sister and Eli joking and laughing as he helped her with dinner, shocked as I realised Liz allowed him to help. She ruled her kitchen like a small dictator. A few dictators came to mind but predators like that do not deserve to be named.

"You need to check up on him." Ari opened his beer with one hand, putting the screw cap on the table next to him.

"Him?" I didn't realise who he was referring to.

"The monster you're holding."

"I don't want to. I don't want to leave this world even for a second." I snuggled into him, putting my legs over his right leg.

"You don't have different worlds anymore, Ley."

"I can keep it separate." I tried to convince myself.

"It's too late. Until you stop, they will remain merged. It's going to get harder for you to differentiate between the two."

"I know." I didn't want to. "But right now, let's be here. Celebrate the fact that fifty of the vilest of them are no longer able to hunt in the open. Or in the abyss, for that matter. Three little girls are safe."

Police forces and other agencies whose names I didn't care for as long as they kept on doing what I was doing, kept on fighting until this war was over, and were hunting them down as we sat in a moment of peace I prayed would never end. It did. My life was about to change in ways I never thought possible. Powerless to stop it. Sometimes I wonder, in moments like these, if I would have. Had I known.

"Life doesn't work that way. Once you have set a course there is no turning back and you need to live with whatever lies ahead," he said, as if he had read my mind. Ari took my face in his hands and brought my mouth to his.

"Seriously you two. Enough with this 'being in love all over the place' thing." A hint of jealousy in Liz's voice as she and Eli walked out to join us. The moment forever gone. A memory made.

The rest of the evening we spent as friends do. We laughed and got to know each other better. Eli looked forward to training with me. Ari explained he couldn't hit me anymore as he was already 'hitting it'. It made sense, I believed him. From what I gathered during the evening, Eli was every bit as formidable as Ari. They had been partners and friends for fifteen years. They had shared more than most people do in a lifetime. More like brothers than friends and I felt safe with them.

So did Lizzie. The electricity between her and Eli was

visible from space. I picked up on reluctance from both of them.

I wondered why Lizzie wouldn't pursue a man like Eli. He was perfect for her and I trusted him with her. Lizzie adored Ari. She told me as much when we cleared the table. The dinner itself was one of her masterpieces. It can't be described in words. Lizzie had made the pasta for which she had given me the recipe the night Ari and I were at the lake house. A lifetime had passed between the two nights.

"So, what's going on with you and Eli?" Normal birthday dinner conversation.

"He is amazing." She almost giggled. "But it's also complicated. With you and Ari being whatever you are and Eli now being your new trainer. What is it you're training for exactly?"

"Don't change the subject." I changed the subject.

"I don't know, Fin. I think a part of me is scared that this could be something real. A guy like that, you don't have only one night with him. One night isn't enough. I could want it all with him and that scares me. I haven't allowed myself to even consider letting someone into my life on a relationship level again. Not since Robert."

Robert. Six years later and I still wanted to strangle him for the way he had left my sister. And of course, he had to leave my sister for her best friend. On their wedding day. He couldn't turn his back on Margaret, not when she was pregnant with his child. *Robert.* The mere thought of him still made my fists clench. I considered giving him a position in the room. I couldn't do any of the things I had planned for the many of ids who would still take up residency. You can't do that to a person for being a womaniser. He stayed with his baby-mama. Married her exactly five years before, on Lizzie's birthday. Such a valiant man.

"You deserve to be happy, Liz. No one deserves it more than you and you will be safe with Eli."

"Why is being safe with a man so important to you, you

never used to...oh, I'm sorry. I get it now."

"Get what?" I didn't like her tone. She scratched at something I didn't want scratched.

"What happened to you, it must be important to feel safe with a man. To know he won't hurt you like that."

"No, Lizzie. I'm not talking about rape." My words came out harsher than I intended, but I didn't want to talk about it. "There are horrible things happening all around us and with me spending so much time at the lake house, I need you to have someone close by should you ever be in danger."

"I'm sorry, Fin. I just assumed—"

I didn't let her finish. "Assume only makes an ass out of you and me."

"Well, your ass does look better than mine. This Krav Maga thing is good for you. And I'm not referring only to the instructor." On to a better topic. My ass did look good. I was glad people noticed.

"Why don't you go for private lessons? It's amazing training and I would be much more at ease knowing you can protect yourself. I really hope you never have to."

Lizzie looked at me and mischief played on her face. She spun around calling out to Eli, who sat on the patio with Ari. They were speaking in Hebrew, about us. The topic never came up, but I can follow a conversation. Remnants of the war.

She hurried towards them, red waves in the glass in her hand. "Eli, you're going to teach me Krav Maga. I want an ass like Fin's."

Eli spat out the sip of beer he had just taken and laughed. Ari did the same. "What?" Eli still laughed.

"Yes, you are. Let me know which days and times, and I will be there. I'm sure I can throw a punch if I have to." Lizzie couldn't throw an apple never mind punch someone hard enough to not make them laugh at her. I would know.

Teenage girls, especially sisters, can get violent. I always punched her where the shoulder meets the clavicle and she would run crying to our parents. Each time she tried to physically attack me, I punched harder. She never learned. Maybe this would be a good thing. Beautiful and naïve. She is by far one of the most intelligent people I have ever known. A woman like her; easy prey for a ruthless predator. She was trusting and trying to fill a void created by Robert's betrayal, and my parents' deaths.

Who knows, perhaps if she and Eli spent more time together, she would realise she could have something better. Something honest and real, maybe with him. I liked him, not just because he had my back, but because I saw how he looked at her. The way he looked at her in that moment, he no longer laughed.

"Okay, sure." He forced his mouth to not smile, but I saw it. "Come with Fin on Monday morning and we will get you started. But Liz, I'm not going to go easy on you. If you're in this, you're in, and I'm going to push you hard. I don't train people for self-defence. I make weapons out of people."

"Promises, promises." She skipped over to him and gave him a kiss on his cheek. Even in the dim light, I saw his face turn cherry-red. Lizzie saw it, too.

"Thank you, Eli. You won't regret it." She gave him another peck on the cheek.

We spent the rest of the evening talking. Neither Ari nor I were tired after sleeping late into the afternoon. Lizzie and Eli got to know each other and flirted like teenagers. Perfect for each other.

Ari held me close and every so often would kiss me, a long tender kiss, on the top of my head. An intimate kiss reserved for those who are in love.

Ari excused us and pulled me to my feet. "Time for bed," he said. I think he wanted to give them privacy. I was about to do the same just as he stood.

Eli ended up spending the night, in the other guest bedroom. *Eli the gentleman.*

Ari and I spent the rest of the evening talking about our

lives. Lives lived before war and how it had shaped us into who we were now.

I wondered whether what he told me formed part of his cover or if he showed me the real Ari.

Nineteen

Uncle Tom came over for lunch that Sunday afternoon. Lizzie allowed me to cook, under her strict guidance. Guidance in her world means orders. I enjoyed having Ari in this part of my world. No matter what he said, I could keep it separate. I checked in on id earlier and it was time to leave id in complete silence. Time in silence to reflect on what id had done, the reason id came to be in that room. In quiet contemplation, id would realise what awaited. The following day, id and I would have a chat. Followed by making him my first official, not legal, first. The next transfers were arranged for Tuesday, Wednesday, and Thursday nights. A busy week lay ahead of me.

"Uncle Tom, would you like a whiskey?" I tried my utmost to make him forget seeing my face.

"Only if you pour one for yourself and one for Ari."

"I would prefer a beer, or a brandy, if you have any." *Not the perfect man. How could Ari or anyone not like whiskey?*

"What's happening with the sniper case?" I needed to push the idea of Ari not being perfect out of my head.

"Finley, on a Sunday? Why don't you finish your doctorates and become the profiler you were destined to be? Surround yourself with serial killers." Lizzie sat across from me on the patio. It was a standard Sunday afternoon, inappropriate conversation, good food, each enjoying their alcohol of choice. She had no idea I was surrounded by serial offenders, and meeting more every day. Not as potential new friends.

"You wanted to be a profiler?" My once biggest desire Ari questioned, but my other face he took in his stride.

"Our Fin would have been one of the greats. It's uncanny how well she understands them. In all my years I have never seen someone grasp their motives as much as she can. I can't tell you how many times she cracked a case even when she was still a student." Uncle Tom beamed with pride. His words gave me hope we could restore our relationship.

"Yes, that was the dream. But I joined the army, and the rest is history. So, what has our boy been up to? I've heard nothing new on the news."

"Because we are banning the media from reporting on him. If he's doing it for the attention, we don't want to boost his ego anymore."

I drank the rest of my whiskey staring out towards where the ocean glistened under a cooler autumn sun.

"You're not doing it for the attention, are you? No, you're on a mission. Show me what that mission is. I want to understand. I know it hurts you, makes you angry, and these people you see on the other side of your scope remind you. What is it about them? Do you work shifts? Is that why there is no discernible pattern? You don't want to be violent. You're not using your hands, not torturing them. But something is torturing you. I want to help you. Show me." I kept my eyes on the golden ripples on the ocean. A small portion of something large became visible, maybe a ship or something in my mind's eye.

"Finley, stop doing that. I hate it when you do that." Lizzie rubbed her arms. It was nothing new for me to give her the creeps, I've been doing it since we were children. She could never know, she wouldn't understand.

"That, right there, is why you scare me. It's time you finish your studies and do this the right way." I prayed Lizzie wouldn't pick up on Uncle Tom's words, *the right way*.

"Is he telling you anything?" Ari's dark eyes fixed on me. Did I give him the creeps as well? Before I answered, his phone rang, and he excused himself to take the call.

Ari didn't return for quite some time. Uncle Tom and I discussed the sniper, without discussing anything new. Calculated, cunning, and above average in intelligence. *A ghost*.

"He's definitely in a line of work where he works shifts.

Somehow, he's coming in to contact with the victims. It's not random. You need to have the task force look into that. As I told you before, I still think he has some form of official training."

"I agree. His last kill was at a distance of 800 metres, in a very dense area."

"He has more than one rifle. Each suiting his mission."

Ari joined us, but something was different about him. I sensed the weight of the world weighed on him and I didn't like the vein on his forehead.

The moment his eyes met mine, I knew.

Twenty

Late afternoon, Ari asked me to pack my things. He wanted to spend the night alone with me at the penthouse. I knew. When he walked Uncle Tom out to his car, he and Ari spoke for a long time. I watched them from the safety of the porch. I didn't hear Lizzie as she came and stood beside me. She wrapped her arms around me. She knew too. *Everything is going to change.*

Ari gave Uncle Tom a bro-hug and my heart fell into the abyss. The notion sank to its knees. I think it prayed.

Ari followed me in his vehicle as I drove home. I didn't want to reach my destination. I wanted to drive around forever, with him behind me. But fuel is expensive and the hole in the ozone is getting bigger.

We shared the elevator ride in silence, his reflection solemn. I unlocked the door and walked into the emptiness of what lay ahead of me. Again.

"When are you leaving?" It was pointless to delay the inevitable. Tears dripped on my chest as I put the Remington back in the safe. My back to him. Ari put our bags down and walked up behind me. His warmth, his smell, I couldn't let him go. I didn't want to be on this road alone, not when I had just decided to open myself up to him. Ari held my aching body, kissing the back of my head.

"Tomorrow night." Silence, the only sound; my life slipping into the abyss.

Ari was the only reason I had held on to the last bit of light. I kept fighting the darkness which tried to consume me. He took my hand and led me to the couch, my favourite place to sit and contemplate a life without war.

"Ley, I love you. I don't want to go, but I've spent the past two years trying to infiltrate this organisation. As life would have it, I'm in. Now. The things these people are doing, I can't turn my back on it. Please understand, as much as you won't give up what you're doing, I can't either."

I breathed into my hands, desperate to hide my tears. I understood. "Who are they?"

"I can't tell you their name, but they have an extensive international network. Arms, drugs, the usual. The worst is what they're doing to the people. They traffic children and adults across the world for whatever reason. They are ruthless. We estimate eighty percent of their victims don't make it to where they're being sent. They are worse than anything we have ever seen. They make drug cartels look like Care Bears. Please understand I need to do whatever I can to stop them."

"Is Eli going with you?" A part of me hoped. I didn't need a reminder of Ari.

"No. He's staying here. To keep our cover infiltrating the local branch. Promise me you will never go to Rip Tide again. Promise me, Finley."

"That's why you were there on Friday night. Why you told me to watch our drinks."

"Yes. Leave it, don't go after them. You going rogue will only jeopardise what we have spent years doing. It could get me killed. Please promise me you will let this one go. Let me handle it."

"I don't want to let you go. Not when we just got started." The notion still on its knees.

"You have to, babe." I preferred when he called me Ley; babe is a pig's name.

The emptiness inside me grew, soon darkness would fill the void.

"Ari, I know how this works. You leave tomorrow and I'll never see you again. Not because you won't survive, but for your safety, mine, Eli's and countless others. Even if you cut off the head, more will grow in its place; it's an unstoppable cycle. We can't stop monsters like this, and you know it."

"I do, but I can't stand by and let them continue doing this.

This kind of monster can't be stopped, but I can wound it. I will. How can I turn away from saving the lives of countless people? Isn't that what we are both destined to do?" He wrapped me in his arms.

"When you're done, come find me. I will disappear with you."

"Ley." He cupped my face in his palms and forced me to look at him. "I love you. I always will, but you need to move on. Don't wait for me like one of those girls we used to pity when we shipped out. You deserve a full life; to love and be loved. To put this crusade of yours behind you. I want nothing more than to tell you, just give me a year and then I'll be back. We will pick up as if nothing has happened, nothing has changed. But Ley, it doesn't work that way. It can take me a year, ten years, the rest of my life. We can't put our happiness above the lives of those people who have lost hope, dignity, and their own identities."

This was the moment in which I knew I was falling in love with him, but I couldn't bring myself to say it. I hated the truth Ari spoke. I hated the monsters of this world who destroy so many lives, not only of those they keep captive.

No, the lives of the men and women who sacrifice their own lives to hunt them down and put an end to their reign. The men and women who sit through hours, days, weeks, and years looking at the images. Seeing what these monsters do. They keep their sights on saving as many as possible, never giving up hope of finding the ones whose cases steal their sleep, never stop searching for them, not even when they go to the grocery store.

God bless them.

They are the true warriors of our age.

"No matter what happens, come find me when you're done." I kissed him, consumed by my desire to cling onto the last bit of light in my life. The last bit of what other people have so easy. I made love to him countless times that night. Each time as if it would be the last.

A desperate attempt at intimate human contact as I knew the darkness of the abyss awaited me.

The following morning, Ari left. Darkness swaddled me. I felt as lonely as the island on the horizon. The crisp, clear day didn't change my mood. I prayed he would be safe, finish his mission, and win his war.

I opened the door; rage and hatred stormed in. Hatred for the monsters who caused all these wars. For making Ari, myself, and countless others put our lives in danger to stop their depravity. I would make them suffer, starting with the one in my room.

I phoned Eli and cancelled our training session. He claimed to understand. Eli couldn't understand the depths of the darkness I had embraced.

My soul in stark contrast to the beauty of that day.

"Clive Baker. I see you're still here," I spat id's name out. The vile creature clinging on to the last bit of life id had. Not for long.

"Please. Please let me go."

"No, Clive. Pay attention, this is how this game works." I pressed the record button on the voice recorder. My voice hidden behind the altering device. "You tell me the truth and I won't hurt you. If you lie to me, well then, Clive Baker, you will think you spent the past three days in a five-star luxury beach resort."

"Please." The wretched thing had to muster all id's strength, dehydrated and in excruciating pain. Vivid memories from a time when I was on the receiving end, not for any fault of my own.

"Did you show them mercy, Clive?" I collected the hammer and nails from the shelf.

"Who? What are you talking about? I didn't do anything!"

I forced laughter down, deep down.

"Are you thirsty?" I held up a bottle of water. Opened the

bottle and poured its contents onto the concrete floor. Close enough for id to see, out of id's reach. Only my thirst would be quenched.

"Please!"

"Clive, Clive, Clive." I failed to suppress the smile. "Begging won't help. What will help is if you answer my questions." I gave id a sip of the LSD laced water. Followed by another. Many experiments have been done in the past on the effects of hallucinogens in interrogation. *Shoot me for having a scientific curiosity.*

I gave id just enough for this to be short of an overdose. Would id experience a bad trip? I was desperate to find out. Id did.

Poor little sharky saw horrible things, screaming at it to go away, trying desperately to get away but it only left him looking like a marionette. I hope id saw the faces of the young boys id had devoured, coming for revenge. I left id alone for a few hours. Once the effects wore off, I hoped id would be a little more forthcoming with answers.

I closed the door to the room and stepped back into my other world. *Tony Andretti.* How long before he found me? What was he fantasising about doing to me? I wasn't a helpless little girl, I still had the use of both my arms. If only I hadn't dropped the rifle, Ari would have killed him.

For the first time, a Walker didn't help. Neither did three, so I drank the last with a painkiller. My face had started hurting again the morning Ari left. I drank alone, the lake and house my only company.

Winter was coming fast. Fewer people would be around the lake, only finding their way back for Christmas and the odd long weekend. They would spend time with their loved ones, celebrate the past year and look forward to the new one. Make memories. Love and be loved.

The rage consumed me. I didn't fight it anymore; I embraced the grip of its cold, dark hands.

I allowed it to change me. The darkness covered memories

of war, of Ari who left, and knowing what lay ahead of me. I loved being in the dark.

"Clive? Are you ready to talk now?" Recording what I hoped would this time be a confession. Id's begging had become tiresome. It was time for id to go, I needed space for the other three which would soon arrive. Id didn't want to look at me so I removed the heretic's fork as a sign of good will.

"Thank you," id uttered.

"How many, Clive? You being a commercial pilot, I'm sure you must have at least one in each city. How many?" The disbelief in id's eyes was laughable. "You're a pilot Clive. You get around. How many?" Id's head bobbed as electricity rushed through id. I don't believe in shock collars for dogs, but I do for sharks. Not the aquatic kind, though.

"How do you know?" The effects of the LSD were wearing off. Whether the experiment was successful, I couldn't say. I upped the dosage for the next one. What was the worst that could happen?

"Your stupidity is boundless. How did you ever qualify for your pilot's license? Let me explain it to you, it's simple. You think because your real life is spent on the dark web the life you spend on the normal web is untraceable. But a predator such as yourself is a special kind of dumb. Such poor security settings on your social media accounts. I guess it never occurred to you that there was something – someone – bigger and far worse than you in this world. You had a beautiful wife. Did she figure out what you are? Is that why she left you?"

"Who are you?" *Poor, little dumb sharky.*

"I'm bored, Clive. To be frank, I need to make room for three more. As you can see, I never made preparations for more than three of you at the same time. So, guess who needs to leave now? How many, Clive?" Id's body convulsed as electricity rippled, making a wonderful sound which reminded me of bees.

I picked up the hammer and nails. Had myself some fun.

Blood streamed from id's fingertips, the very fingertips that touched what wasn't supposed to be touched. Id's pathetic cries for mercy pushed me further into the darkness. The hammer did what it was made for, nails rammed into the soft flesh under id's nails. You have to love the irony.

I removed the chains around id's ankles and id tried to stand. Frivolous attempts making for much needed comical relief.

"You need all your bones in your feet uncrushed, idiot." A horrendous laugh came out of me, one I had never heard before. The look in id's eyes made it worth scaring myself, not that id saw my fear. "How many?" *Hammer, push, hammer, deeper.*

"Fourteen! Fourteen."

"Where did you dispose of their bodies?" Silence. I fetched the cat-o'-nine-tails. I needed to get a workout in after cancelling my session with Eli that morning.

Id listed each city with exhausted screams. The cat did the trick. More details offered each time flesh tore and ripped from id's body. It was a great workout, but I regretted needing to clean up after I was done.

"Anything else you want to share?" I wiped wetness from my face with the back of my hand. Forced compassion into my voice, even tilted my head for effect.

"No, please. I told you everything. I promise. Please let me go." Id remained oblivious to the fact id was not leaving.

Not alive, anyway.

"Thank you for sharing, Clive. Don't you feel better now? No longer carrying the truth all to yourself? Now the world will know who you are, what you've done." I dragged id to the chair. Id didn't fight. I made id sit for the last time. Three options lay ahead of id; presented on the cold steel table. In the right light you could see your reflection in it, I didn't want to see mine. A lot of thought went into the three options. I had considered quite a few others, but these three spoke to me. *What would they choose?* All chose darkness before. *Would they all choose the same way to enter it for the last time?*

"You have an enormous choice ahead of you, Clive. Just as you chose to sodomise and strangle fourteen innocent boys. Your decision. You destroyed them and everyone who loves them. Make your choice or I will get more of the toys from that shelf and help you decide. If you are unclear as to what your options are, let me explain them to you. First, to your left, you have water. I know you're thirsty, but wait, that's not all! One chosen just for you – that's how special you are, Clive – much need water with just enough ant poison to end a colony – and you. Your second option is this stunning syringe. The bonus of this option is you get to take the purest heroin. Only the best for you, Clive. Your third and final option is behind door number three. This delicious bowl of pasta. With a secret ingredient which is sure to surprise you, make you all warm inside. A dash of broken razor blades and a splash of arsenic. For added texture and taste. Wow, now isn't that something? You might be the first person ever to eat this very dish. What will it be, Clive? Don't let the audience in your head influence your decision, your choice brought you to this point. Choose carefully Clive, and do hurry up, I don't have all day."

I waited. Contemplated whether I should give myself a manicure while I waited for id to die. It seemed like a waste of time to sit and stare. 'Don't stare, it's impolite,' as our parents teach us.

Id chose the heroine. Id must have thought death would be euphoric. Not knowing what happens when it's this pure and uncut. *You get what you pay for.* Id didn't think of how id's brain would forget how to signal id's lungs to breathe, id's heart would malfunction, forcing organs to shut down. Death would not come swiftly. I watched as id injected the liquid into the fold of id's arm. Dehydration and the earlier dose of LSD might speed things up, I had a lot to do. I waited for id to make id's final attempt for breath. Id's blood is not on my hands.

Id took id's own life, I didn't.

Id died in a delightful, yet undignified, manner. Id deserved far worse but that would mean I would have to get involved. I wished id could kill id-self again for leaving me to clean the mess id had left. Vomit and all kinds of other nasty bodily secretions and excretions.

It was time to bring answers and closure to fourteen families, and to honour fourteen young boys. I rolled id up in a black plastic sheet. I pushed the memory of Ari far away from what I was doing. No part of him, not even the memory of him, should be in that place. There was no point in entertaining the memory; Ari had left, doing what he had to, and so was I.

I dragged id's lifeless carcass to the illegally purchased Ford Ranger. My mobile phone I left in the kitchen, in case my whereabouts needed to be verified on these nights. I set up an automatic function to send text messages to Lizzie or Ashley or some other acquaintance. They didn't know I had made them my alibis; I hated doing it, dragging them unknowingly into this. But it was for the greater good, I told myself. My Walker had to wait until I got back, I couldn't risk being pulled over for drunk driving.

With id loaded in the back, I headed into the city, the music loud. Background music for focus, a soundtrack to this episode. The pilot. Pun not intended. Happy accident. I didn't listen to Metallica, it reminded me of hunting with Ari. I missed him. The longing for normality I would harness to fuel my growing rage. The notion paced, moving closer to the pit with each step. It might have considered hiding had it known how busy we would soon be.

Twenty-one

There were few cars on the road as I headed towards the building. I had chosen it days before; there was no security. Not as many prostitutes and johns in the area; weekends tended to be busier. The perfect part of the city to get rid of something or someone. Here people kept their eyes to themselves. A derelict old building doesn't draw unwanted attention, a parking structure in its former life. A long time ago this area housed the headquarters of several global enterprises, and Williams Pharmaceuticals used to be only a few blocks east. I drove to the fourth floor and parked close to the side of the building, taillights facing the street below. I pulled id out and every part of me was exhausted.

The night before had not been spent sleeping. The thought of never seeing Ari's rugged, handsome face again kept me awake. He didn't sleep either. We lay in the darkness holding hands, each other, as the moonlight kept complete darkness at bay. We made love as many times as our bodies allowed. More times than either of us expected. Neither of us said anything meaningful after our conversation on the couch, there was nothing left to say.

I opened the sheet and placed the rope around id's neck. A perfect hangman's noose if I do say so myself. Well, I had to, there was no one around to admire the work of my hands. I doubt my father would be proud of what he had taught me, not for what I used it.

As I tied the other piece of rope around a pillar, there was a different sound in the distance. Distant, but in the building. *A door opening or a footstep?* My heart didn't race, adrenaline didn't pump through my veins. I felt no fear.

Have I become a predator like the ones I hunt? Unfeeling, unremorseful, no sense of fear of being caught. One can't become a psychopath. The sound again. A faint sound which became louder, closer. Instinct forced me into a crouching position. Without a sound, I removed my SIG from its part on my body, snug against my right hip.

I waited.

Nothing. Only cars stopping and pulling away down below. A few prostitutes making a living. Family men paying for minutes of pleasure, taking lifelong diseases with them as keepsakes to their unsuspecting wives.

Again, the sound. Closer.

I had parked a few parking bays from the door which led to the staircase. Whoever came through the door would see the carcass. Displayed on a plastic sheet, too dark for anyone to notice the rope around id's neck. The end wrapped around the pillar was visible. The door handle moved. My heart started beating erratically, fighting against psychopathic traits. Adrenaline and a faint trickle of sweat running down my spine joined the fight. *Not a psychopath!*

Hair stirred all over my body as the door opened. *Him.*

He saw my vehicle, not a sound, not as much as a flinch. How could he not flinch? The building should've been empty. The only plausible explanation being that he had come looking. He must have known someone entered his world. His own curiosity compelled him to risk being seen, perhaps getting caught. Or he didn't want to share his territory. I chose his nest for my first. He saw me.

Expression obscured by a mask, the same as mine. Without considering all possible outcomes, my trembling body shot upright. No longer hidden behind the SUV's front tyre. I gave up my protection. He took a step back. Our eyes met.

He took another step back. My arms on the bonnet, gun barrel pointed at a ghost.

Two figures in the darkness, mirror images of each other. Hoodies over our heads, drawn low to cover our eyes. Eyes fixed on each other. I don't know why I didn't shoot him. He didn't shoot either. Ripples ignited between us.

The notion stirred.

I often spoke to him; now he stood right in front of me. My finger on the trigger. *Why are you not squeezing?*

"Why?" Stupid Finley and her stupid words. Words that didn't know when to cling to the railing of the sinking ship of my mind.

"Why?" I asked again.

His head tilted to the right, his right. *Is he considering my question or my idiocy?*

"Why are you doing this? What are you trying to undo or change? Please, tell me, I want to understand."

His neck twisted and he saw my reason for being there. Even in the relative darkness it was visible. He heard my female voice. I didn't think to wear the voice altering device. Not for one second did I consider I was entering his world, his hunting ground. I stepped onto his turf, where he was the killer king, never considered how a possible encounter might end.

Ghost face resumed staring at me.

I sensed a man carrying an unfathomable amount of grief. A gut-wrenching pain which has forever changed him and made him a killer. I didn't need to hear his voice, he told me without saying a word. For some inexplicable reason a part of me wanted to walk over to him and hug him. I wanted to tell him everything would work out. He would get through whatever it is and survive.

I didn't get a chance to act on my foolish idea, he disappeared into the stairwell. I let him leave just as I had let Ari leave. I watched, powerless or unwilling to stop them.

He made no sounds as he left, and as I listened I realised he made no sound coming towards me either. *How did I hear him without hearing him?*

Whenever I encounter a monster, I can sense his or her depravity. I sense the evil masquerading as human. It's an ability I have had for as long as I can remember. My palms itch. It did at both scenes where little blonde girls with wet, white hair were returned by the ocean. Where Tony Andretti stood, close enough for me to have killed him. Evil. The man in that derelict building was not. My palms told me so. He is a killer but not evil. *Is that even possible?* I had entered his world, walked – drove, to be precise – straight into his nest. The perfect sniper's nest.

I sat on the cold surface of the dilapidated parking structure, inner turmoil surrounding me like a violent storm. Confusion held me in place. What drew me to him? How was it possible I didn't sense evil under that mask? Why did every part of me ache to hold him? *Is he me?* We wore the same face after all. I shook it off, blamed my dance with the abyss.

Time to leave, this was no place for self-therapy. I ensured the rope was tight around id's neck, rallied all my emotions for strength and pushed id's carcass over the ledge. Id would hang there for the world to see. As a warning to others.

The following day, Captain Taylor received id's wallet, together with the confession I had taped. An unlucky person will lift his or her head and find id's body, hanging. Like all murderers, rapists and paedophiles should be.

Soon more of them would take their place across this city.

He drove with me all the way to the lake house, not once leaving my mind. The way he watched me fascinated me. I tried to understand what stirred in me as we stood facing each other. I had to know this man. This man who carried so much pain and grief. He was a killer. I wasn't delusional about that fact; but not violent to the extent of killers who strangle, stab and bludgeon. He didn't rape, he didn't mutilate; his acts were precise. He stood so close I could've shot him with my eyes closed. *Why didn't I?*

I never once gave killing a second thought, not even the first time I had killed, when only a teenager. Chased him down, slit his throat without hesitation.

I cleaned up the mess id had left as soon as I got back.

The following night, the next one would take id's place. Another would join the night after that.

He stayed in my mind, no matter how many times I tried to evict him. What drew me to the sniper? This man who killed seemingly innocent people.

Why did I feel compassion for *this* murderer?

In the months that followed, I lost myself in what I was doing. I ran into the abyss with open arms and embraced the darkness. It consumed me, more and more with each passing month.

There were never fewer than three in my room, running at full capacity, no long-term vacancies. My plan was simple, yet perfect.

They drove to a certain point outside the city, left their mobile phones and took the burner phone I left, watching them as they did so. I had strategically placed all the motion detection cameras, ensuring I saw in advance who I would meet, who was making their merry way to meet their end. Depending on which chat room we had met in, the voice of a helpless girl, boy, woman or man's murmured screams sounded from under the tarp as they stepped closer. Their eyes always held that excited spark, igniting bloodlust in me. I shot them with a tranquilizer dart, the feather of the dart always pink. There was a speck of a girl still left in me, or at least my desperate attempt to cling to it through a whimsical act.

My sedative of choice, a mixture of Azaperone and etorphine carfentanil, depending on what my supplier could get a hold of that month. Azaperone is commonly used to sedate pigs, fitting considering the monsters I sedated.

I winched them up and into the emptiness under the tarp and drove them to the room to keep the others company, although they never conversed. I considered removing their tongues, but it was pointless until they confessed. I resorted to using good old duct tape. And sometimes when I was bored I removed the duct tape but kept them quiet through the mere push of a button. Shock collars for sharks – brilliant idea.

I played them a wonderful mix of death metal music and kept an eye on them from the luxury of wherever I found myself. A few quick dabs with my finger and I watched my own reality show, I wasn't the star, but the creator. If I deemed it time, I switched the music for the flashing red light and started taping their eyelids open. It was such a waste that I spent so much time getting everything ready only for them to close their eyes or look away. *How dare they?*

When the light finished playing its part in my well-rehearsed production, I switched their sensory experience. Water dripped on their foreheads, the heretic's fork ensured they kept their heads in place. When the time came, I ensured they gave their confessions, by whichever means necessary, always giving the paedophiles and child murderers just that little bit of extra attention, even after they had confessed.

The extra attention being a choke pear, also known as the pear of anguish. Inserted in their mouths, I didn't have the stomach to put it in their anuses. I found that out the hard way. The mechanisms are quite simple; you insert the device into an orifice, turn the screw and with each turn the metal leaves open.

I made their final decision for them. You need an intact and functioning jaw to swallow water or chew food. I hoped the others didn't feel left out, not that they were able to see what I was doing, but they heard. I made sure they heard everything, except the confessions. The victims didn't deserve to be raped and murdered again in their minds.

The confessions were for the ears of Captain Taylor, Uncle Tom and everyone else working on these cases, many victims they had no prior knowledge of.

Without fail, I sent a text message from the burner phone used only for contacting a specific person. A young man came and took their vehicles. I didn't care what he used it for as long as it disappeared and was never traced back to me. Vehicle tracks were no longer a problem; I paid to have the road leading up to the farm and even further covered in gravel. It made it easier for Tabula Rasa's bus to drive out over weekends, bringing with it the excited guests to enjoy their weekend in the fresh air of the countryside.

Ashley and I decided to put in a swimming pool, hot tub, tennis court, and vegetable garden. The refurbishments of the farm and the new building in the city I personally oversaw, giving Ashley enough time to focus on her wedding and her daughter. Hope had started crawling; she grew up too fast and was deeply loved by all.

Disposing of the carcasses remained the same as the first, only displayed in different locations. A part of me always hoped to see the sniper again.

He remained elusive.

A vivid memory.

A fire in my core.

I sat overlooking the lake enveloped by a snug grey blanket. Whiskey in my favourite crystal tumbler in hand, its contents warmed me from inside. Mindless, my thumbs traced the abstract, engraved design. Spring had settled in as new leaves sprouted from branches on deciduous trees.

In these moments where I sat in complete silence, only my Walker to keep me company, I realised it was time for me to re-enter the normal world. I grew tired of the hunt and the darkness which had hung over me the preceding months.

The last time I counted I was up to forty-three, each time tallying the total as I pushed a carcass over the ledge or barrier.

Not once did Uncle Tom discuss this killer with me, the one the media called The Hangman. If only they knew it was Hangwoman; journalists and the general populace can be so sexist. Uncle Tom never asked for my insights and I wondered if it was because he suspected or if he knew.

I often wondered in those quiet moments sitting on the deck whether he appreciated my service. Did he have gratitude for what I was doing, ridding the world of monsters?

Man-made laws didn't bind my hands, only my own laws.

I never took a life, they died by their own hand. My hands were clean.

Twenty-two

My phone rang for the first time the following afternoon. I considered not answering, but the caller is known to be relentless.

"I miss you. How about I come over tonight and spend the weekend with you?" Lizzie spent the preceding months trying to help me mend my broken heart. Broken heart; in her mind I needed to get over Ari. There was nothing she nor anyone else could do for me, I needed to rescue myself from the person I had turned into. *Person?*

She was still training with Eli and a deep friendship formed between them. I kept hoping it would blossom into something more. Eli also became a dear friend to me. Not once did he ask me to stop when my punches and kicks were so ruthless it left bruises. He held me as I cried, missing Ari, he thought. What I did left me a shell of my former self and I couldn't carry the crushing weight of it anymore.

It was time to be me again, have a life and enjoy it.

I had to find my way back to myself.

"Please come, Lizzie. I miss you and to be honest, it's time. You're right, I can't go on like this. It's not what Ari wanted for me when he left." I meant most of it.

Lizzie cooked, and I took in the sight of her. That day I made my choice. I would no longer let the hunt consume me. In all honesty, the fact that there was a lot of pressure on the police to find this vigilante and bring him to justice, helped push me to make my choice. How ironic, they had also never considered a woman to be responsible. Many of the city's more prominent people were found hanging around, too many.

Preachers, teachers, pilots and cleaners, the list varied.

Men, women, all races and various nationalities. I didn't discriminate, I showed no mercy.

Having three down in the room always made me laugh. I cherished my dark sense of humour during that time. It made for the beginning of a distasteful joke. A paedophile, a serial killer and a rapist walk in to a room...I never had a necrophiliac in that room. I didn't come across one in the chat rooms where Cerberus became a household name.

I switched roles between seller and buyer, saving the captives and taking them to Tabula Rasa. They never knew my name, and they never said a word to the police. Deep down, they knew the person with the ghost face protected them, saved them.

Days after they became a guest, I put their captor on display, a visual reminder they were free. The monster vanquished. It was time for me to lay low, let the police think the person they secretly admired had moved, packed up shop and took his trade somewhere else. *His? Ha!*

"How are you, Lizzie?" The Walker gave me sanity and enough liquid courage to attempt small talk.

"Been worried sick about you, to be honest. I knew you would take it hard. Uncle Tom said to give you time, you're mourning more than just Ari's departure." So much for small talk. Uncle Tom knew me too well.

"I've been worried too, Lizzie. I didn't think I would get through it all. Looking back, I should've started seeing someone months ago." She didn't let me finish my attempt at hiding the truth, yet remain conversational.

"You should've started dating months ago, Finley. Do you want an introduction at Alias? That way you're in control. You can have meaningless sex until you're ready for something more. Get some to get rid of the strain on you."

"That's not what I meant. If you will let me finish, I meant to say a psychiatrist."

"Oh. But you really should consider it. I'm still having loads of fun. Sure, I don't go as often as I used to. But at least the option is there when I want to." She placed a casserole dish in the oven.

What is it about the Williams sisters and our self-sabotaging ways? Eli was smitten with Liz but she refused to be with him, although I could see she wanted to.

"I'll think about it. Promise." I lied, but we were having fun that evening, being sisters and best friends, like we used to before. The rest of the evening was spent laughing, reminiscing and making plans to go away together. Perhaps a cruise would do us both good.

After Lizzie had gone to bed, I remembered the cruise we had fantasised about earlier and put my laptop on. I absentmindedly logged into one of the chat rooms I frequented.

A private message waited for me. I didn't want to open it, but curiosity got the better of me. I steadied my hands and clicked on the link in the message. The video played, and I saw what he did to her.

Someone was raping her.

Lizzie looked dead, yet she was very much alive in the room right next to mine. Who sent this? The sender's name was Pandoras_trunk. *Pandoras_trunk?*

The sender included a message:

Look.

Your darkness should answer.

Every day.

He knew me. My darkness would answer.

Ari. I referred to the compartment in the back of his SUV as Pandora's box. Using it as a pseudonym was his way of letting me know it was him. Alive. I hoped it also meant safe.

I would hunt this shark and rip him to pieces for what he did to my sister.

I fought back tears, allowed the dark rage to fill me once again. Someone raped my sister, my Lizzie, and posted it for the world of predators to see. In the video she lay motionless, a small trickle of blood ran from her mouth. He strangled her with what looked like a scarf. I forced myself to watch, watching for something to show me who this shark is. Right at the end of the video, in the last seconds, id showed id's face. I clicked pause and took a photo of the screen with my phone. I wanted to keep it on me, to be sure it was id when I found id.

I replied:

Kindred spirits you and I. Forever bound in our quest.

I wanted to reply:

I'm done. I want a normal life.

Sleep didn't come that night. I paced outside on the deck so as not to wake Liz. Where did he find her? She didn't go to bars and never went home with strangers, she told me as much during dinner. *Alias.* That must be where he found her and the others. For reasons I can't explain I couldn't bring myself to click on any of the other links. I didn't have to see id rape them. I had seen id's face. Id would pay for what id did. One last time and then I would be done.

Over breakfast the following morning I told Liz I gave our discussion from the previous night serious consideration. Perhaps becoming a member at Alias would be good for me. She sent a text to her friend, Sam, even before we finished our conversation. Sam invited me for an interview later that same day. I was eager to get started; the sooner id was dead the sooner I could put all of this behind her. En route to Alias, I dropped Lizzie at her home.

Sam met me at Alias. I don't know what I expected, a place that looked similar to a BDSM dungeon or a strip club, but it was tastefully decorated. It had a flair of sophistication to it with its ebony bar and dark leather couches. Alias' interior reminded me of a cigar lounge or a gentleman's club, but there was one or more men who were not gentlemen.

I completed the form and gave a copy of my driver's license for her PI to do a background check. Because she had known me and Liz for years, I was welcome to attend from that night. I wanted to, telling her I had recently gone through a terrible break-up and I needed a distraction. The divorcee in her

consoled me and agreed that I needed a palate cleanser.
Alias' rules were simple:

1. Never talk about Alias to anyone not a member of Alias.
2. Never use your real name or share your contact details.
3. Never have sex with the same person on more than one night.
4. If you start to get emotionally attached or have any interest in a person past the one night spent together, you are to leave Alias at once.
5. Always use protection.
6. In the unlikely event you wish to cancel your membership, an exit interview will be held at Alias on the first Friday after you have given written notice. Interviews will be held at 20:00.

As I walked out of Alias, I phoned Lizzie and put my sunglasses on. I didn't want to be recognised and the sun seemed brighter than usual coming out of that dark place. Not due to bad lighting. It was time to go shopping. I needed a dress, shoes and whatever else Lizzie deemed necessary to make me appear acceptable.

I contacted a dark web acquaintance, and he or she supplied me with whatever I needed to make this hunt successful. The thing that raped Lizzie spiked her drink. I had to make sure that whatever id used to spike my drink would have no effect on me. To id, I would appear eager. If I ever won an Oscar, it would be for this performance. As I'm such a thoughtful person, I purchased something special for id from my acquaintance.

"Finley, I'm so excited. Do you want me to call Favio?"

"Please Liz, no Favio. I think between the two of us we can get me dressed. Make me look more feminine. The way you keep reminding me I need to dress. I still need a dress and shoes. I'll pick you up in half an hour and then we can go to the boutique you're always talking about."

"Versace is not a boutique, it's an experience." She was giddy and her happiness made me angrier.

How could someone do this to my beautiful sister?

We found the perfect dress, shoes and everything else to make me blend in. *Camouflage.* The only things I needed were my bare fists and my hunting knife. Maybe a knuckle duster to use when I got tired, but I wouldn't.

Dressing up and getting ready was fun, it brought back more happy memories of us doing this very same thing at UM.

Id sat at Alias' bar with id's back facing the door. Id was laughing; the sound activated a timer. *Tick-tick-tick.*

Drawing id's attention from the gorgeous red-headed woman id was talking to wouldn't be easy I thought, as I made my way through the crowd towards the bar. Luck was on my side. She showed no interest and took off before the bartender gave her the cocktail she had ordered, or perhaps id was brazen and had ordered the drink for her.

"I'm Jen." My hand stroked id's back. An orca playing with its prey.

I slid on to the stool next to id not sure how to go about seducing a shark. *You learn something new every day.*

"Well, hello, Jen. I'm Damian." The mandatory small-talk people make to get into bed or a bathroom stall ensued. *How could my sister enjoy this life?*

We spent an hour talking about nothing before I had my chance to slip a little something into id's bourbon. I had crushed it before leaving Lizzie's; it dissolves quicker and is less visible. Until that point I had been cautious of my own drink, not yet trusting the vaccine I had purchased. Another forty-five minutes and id was ready to leave. Award-winning performance by Viagra, standing ovation. *Tick-tick-tick.*

I followed id home; the perfect stage for id's final show. Id's touch repulsed me, my hands drew into themselves, and my heart rate increased every time id's vile fingers found my skin.

I reined back the darkness. *Soon.* Seducing, teasing and waiting for the perfect moment to strike, I played my part with perfection. I was, after all, the apex amongst other predators.

Id poured us drinks, and I knew what was in mine, always twenty steps ahead, awaiting id's arrival in the main bedroom.

The hidden camera was easy to find, and I switched it off until it was time. Id found me, leaning against the doorframe, the little black dress' zipper pulled down to just below my navel. Id touched the roundness of my breasts and I gripped the reins, one doesn't merely go in for the kill when you can play with your prey. *Orca's are so playful with their food.*

Id was eager to play, not knowing the rules of my game. *Dumb little sharky.*

I moaned as id's hand slithered down my stomach and I pushed myself against the door frame, and told id to lie down on the bed. Id swam past me in excited obedience.

A quick sip of the drink id gave me to make my role appear natural. Should the vaccine not be effective I had roughly 30 minutes to bring this story to the climax. No one hurts my sister.

Tick-tick-tick.

Id followed my orders and lay down on the bed without asking questions. *Good little sharky.* Id's vulgar excitement visible.

I climbed on top of id and bent down, pulling away just as our lips were about to touch. With my breasts pressed into id's face I leaned forward and tied ids wrists to the bedpost. Id's excitement grew, id's body arched as id licked the parts of me id found. I clenched the reins.

I whispered next to id's ear, "You have no idea what I have been doing to you in my mind since the first time I saw you." Biting my bottom lip, passion exploded in my eyes, but not the kind id expected. Id didn't notice the difference. *Stupid little sharky.*

I slid down towards id's feet, my body warm and excited. Excited for a different reason. Id's breathing became louder as I tied id's ankles to the feet of the bed. I walked to the bag id thought was an overnight bag, and removed my toys. As my dress fell at my feet, id pulled against the restraints. I watched id thrash at the sight of my naked body. Laughter filled the room, my laughter, the same laughter I had heard the first time. This time the sound didn't scare me.

I got dressed in my hoodie top, tracksuit pants and put my other face on. Id's miserable attempts at screaming made me smile, duct tape is such a handy item. I switched the camera on and stared into the abyss. The abyss staring at the face of my darkness. My last dance for this season of 'Dancing with the Darkness'.

Tick-tick-tick.

The knife's blade cold; id twitched with muffled screams as I dragged the knife along id's body. Slicing clothes from id's body. Pushing and twisting with the precision of a hunter skinning his kill, the knife explained the rules of my game. An extension of myself, the knife kept doing what I commanded, until id's eyes were filled with the same angst as the defenceless faces I had to see.

The same angst which once filled me.

Tick-tick-tick.

Id thrashed again as I rested my full body weight on id's lower legs, running the side of the blade against the weapon id cherished.

The blade's penetration fuelled by memories and words. Words uttered by the id's who found their way into my room, into the chat rooms I stalked, my sister's body, and my own.

Stab. Kiss. Rip. Lick. Bite. Bludgeon. Penetrate. Torture. Laugh. Thrust.

Forty-three times I maintained control of the reins, not giving into the darkness, keeping my hands clean. I let go, allowed the darkness to do what I kept it from for so long. *Boom*.

What this id did to Lizzie and all the others. *Boom*.

Four months of having those words ingrained in my body. *Boom*.

Ari who had to leave to wage his own war against these beasts. *Boom*.

Tony Andretti who was yet to emerge from the dark. *Boom.*

The knife plunged for all of it. After the knife played its part I ripped everything from id with my gloved hands. *Clean hands.* When there was nothing left, I cut id's weapon off and thrust the repulsive thing down what remained of id's throat. My personal version of a Columbian necktie.

Turning towards the camera I stared at those who were seeing their own fate.

"You're next. Escape my wrath and take your own life. I will not grant you the mercy you have shown your victims. This here," I pointed to what remained in view, "merciful."

I left the camera on, found the glass I drank from earlier, ran a cloth along the surfaces I touched, and left with my knife.

In my wake, debris lay scattered by multiple explosions.

Not my mess to clean.

For the first time, it felt strange to wake up at the lake house. I thought of the first Tony Andretti and what he did in that house. He and I were alike. I could no longer continue on this path. Cut one head off, three more rise out of the abyss intent on destruction. I was done.

I must have drifted back into a nightmarish sleep as I lay there tortured by visions of what I had done. The ringtone of my mobile phone woke me. The clock displayed 15:00. It was Sunday. *Impossible.* I slept through Saturday and most of Sunday.

"Hello." My voice groggy.

"Finley! The police found one of the members of Alias, I recognised him from the photo in this morning's paper. You left with him on Friday night." Lizzie was hysterical.

"What?" Forced calmness. I had known it was only a matter of time before the debris would be found.

"The guy you left the bar with Fin, he's dead. Murdered. The paper said it's the most violent murder the city has ever seen. Where are you?"

"Calm down, Liz. I'm at the lake house. Drove here from

the bar. I didn't go home with him."

"Finley, I slept with him a few weeks ago. This is surreal."

"You slept with him?" Pacing between the bedroom door and window, nothing in the room but Lizzie's words.

"Yes, a few weeks ago."

It didn't make sense. Was this a sick, twisted fantasy of Liz's and I killed him for indulging her?

Confusion propelled words out of me as my hand struggled to keep the shaking phone next to my ear. "You wanted him to strangle you?"

"What? What do you mean, strangle me?"

"Liz, did you play some sex game with him where you appeared dead? Did he strangle you while you had sex? Are you a gasper?" In the midst of the chaos and rage, I remembered the term for people who enjoy partaking in erotic asphyxiation.

"A what? No! What are you talking about, Finley? What's going on?" Her frantic voice forced the strength from my legs.

"I'm on my way. We need to talk." I ended the call, dressed in a frenzy and raced to Lizzie's. I had to know. Had I killed an innocent person? Had I reached a point of no return?

Am I one of them?

"Fin, what's going on? You made no sense over the phone. You look terrible." I had driven to Lizzie's in half an hour and I don't think I breathed once the entire time.

I took my laptop out, and showed her what I never wanted her to see.

"What did he do to me?" Glass shattered as she threw everything within reach, a violent storm tore through her life. I didn't stop her.

"Did you have sex with him?" My voice much calmer than I felt.

"I didn't consent to that! Not that. How could he do that to me?" The storm raged until it had done what all storms do. It left carnage in its wake. Lizzie's world destroyed.

"Tell me what happened." I needed her to talk, to start

dealing with all of it as soon as possible. Not allow it to steal more from her than it already had. The following day I found her the best psychiatrist in the city.

"We met at Alias, at the bar. He was intriguing and attractive. A smooth talker. I went home with him willingly. We had sex and I guess I fell asleep. It was frenzied; crazy. He was really good and knew exactly what I wanted. But nothing like that. Not like that! Why did he do that?"

"Lizzie, did he offer you a drink when you got to his place?"

"I can't remember, I think so. Why?"

"He spiked your drink with GHB, or something similar. You would have been out cold fifteen to sixty minutes after drinking it, depending on how strong the dose was. Lizzie, I'm so sorry."

"Where did you get the video?"

"Someone sent it to me. I'm so sorry. He can never do this to anyone else, ever again." I refused to open the door to the dark and dangerous world she had no real acknowledge of. Lizzie's knowledge of the dark web was that of the general populous – it exists. I wasn't about to open doors, inviting her to look for herself. I wouldn't allow her to turn into – well, me.

"Why didn't you go home with him?" A crease appeared between her eyes. It was not the time to mention Botox.

"I don't know, something about him seemed a little off. Lizzie, you can never tell anyone about this video. It will make us both potential suspects."

"I know. But how do I go on after seeing that? How did you, how *do* you carry on?"

I really didn't have an answer for her. "You just have to. The only way to get through it, is to get through it. Tomorrow we will tell Sam what happened and you and I are both putting that place behind us. We will tell her you remembered, or I'll think of another reason."

I stayed with her that night, sleeping next to her, and first thing the following morning we phoned Sam. It outraged her, but she refused to shut Alias down. 'One bad olive didn't spoil the martini.' Sam was adamant we still come in the Friday night for our exit interviews, and I said I would do it for the both of us, Lizzie had been through enough.

The rest of the week went by in a blur. I stayed with Lizzie and made sure she got the help she needed to work through this in a healthy and hasty manner. It would take time, but I didn't want her to give herself time to slip into the pit that swallows victims of any violent crime. I tried myself to get out. I yearned for the light for a different life, to be done.

Driving to Alias the Friday evening I thought about the sniper for the first time that week. The previous Friday night I had left id's house and dropped the bag holding the blood-soaked clothes, gloves, mask and motocross goggles into the lagoon. No blood on my hands, no blood in my eyes either. You can contract HIV and many other nasty diseases from blood spatter in your eyes.

I planned it all out, down to the free weights I took from my home gym to weigh the bag down. The glass in which it had offered me a spiked drink I crushed in the towel and tossed it into the water. Water washed away traces of my DNA. The knife I wanted to keep; it was a gift from my father for one of our hunting trips. But I wiped it down and then watched as it fell into the water of the lake. I didn't want to just toss it into the lagoon; I'm sentimental.

I parked the vehicle I used for transfers in an alley two blocks from where the first one had been put on display.

As I got out of the vehicle, I pulled my clean hoodie over my head. I welcomed the smell of New Dawn, a fitting name chosen by the fabric softener manufacturer. I was ready for a new dawn. I opened the car's windows a quarter of the way, took the canisters from the boot and poured the contents out over the interior of the car and the exterior body.

The notion stirred, but I brushed it off as a result of the aftermath of what happened earlier.

I pushed a soaked rag in the petrol tank and stood back.

The notion tried to draw my attention, but I was too focused on my first act of arson.

I removed the Zippo from my pocket, its flame beckoned me, and I wondered how pyromaniacs differed from murderers.

Do murderers have impulse control disorder? My vote still out on that one, even after doing extensive research on the topic while at UM. I lit the soaked rag and tossed the Zippo into the car through an open window. The yellow-orange glow of the flames complemented the dark exterior of the car.

It was time to leave. *I forgot to pack marshmallows.*

The notion scampered as I turned and saw the reason for the uneasiness.

He stood across the street under a broken streetlight, watching me. Not wearing his mask, his hoodie blacking out his face. Our stares locked, the tingling sensation returned to my core but my palms remained itch-free. I held his gaze and waved, knowing for reasons I cannot comprehend that he wouldn't kill me.

I kept walking to where I had hidden the Ducati Monster, pulled the helmet over my head and looked back to where he stood.

He was gone.

Sirens echoed in the distance and I opened the motorcycle's throttle. Buildings and lights streamed past me. *Who is he?*

He saw my face.

Twenty-three

Sam texted to say she was running late as I drove to Alias that Friday night. A cunning ploy to give me time to meet someone while I waited for her. She knew damn well why we wanted out; she was wasting my time.

Music and laughter filled the night, people were having fun and enjoying their lives. I wondered how many of the others still frequented Alias, oblivious to what id had done to them. Perhaps it was better they didn't know, their psyches untouched by evil.

Time stood still as I opened the door, no voices, no music, no thoughts. Only him.

My eyes could've focused on anything and everything as I opened the door, he was seated to my left on a sofa, laughing. Perhaps it was the sound that drew me to him, but whatever it was, I was captivated. A word has not yet been created in any language to capture him in his entirety. His face could launch a million ships; Helen of Troy had nothing on him.

A light stubble framed his strong jaw, his hair a sun-kissed brown. He reminded me of a movie star, but I couldn't quite place him. Before I could tear my eyes away from him, he lifted his chin. Electric blue eyes ignited an unfathomable spark in me and deep inside me, something stirred. The notion was riddled with excitement.

I had to know him.

A hand tapped on my shoulder, I ignored it. It tapped again. "Finley?" Sam's voice didn't penetrate. "Finley?" I was back in a world I didn't want to be in; I wanted back into his gaze. To be his captive.

"Are you sure you want to give this up? You can have him.

Tonight is his first night, show him how much fun this can be." Sam tried to sell her product. "Are you sure? You haven't even given this life a chance. You can have a man like that every night of the week."

"One night? A lifetime might never be enough. Who is he?" I forced myself to focus on Sam but found myself glancing at him in the mirror behind the bar. His eyes teased at the strap of the asymmetrical satin top, teased around my derriere and I would thank Lizzie later for telling me to dress the part. My heart unwilling to slow down even as I took a sip of my beloved Walker, which Sam had ordered for me. Another sales gimmick. *Focus on Sam.*

"Sam, you know what happened to Lizzie. You need to close this place. It's a hunting ground for predators. You don't know how many other women that vile thing raped. I assure you it's not only Lizzie." I didn't tell her I knew for a fact it wasn't only Lizzie.

Sam gave her best pitch, but it wasn't good enough. My heart fought against my logic. I stood strong and pushed his face out of my mind, not searching for his reflection in the mirror behind the bar.

I signed the papers, making the termination final and signed on Lizzie's behalf. Taking one last sip for courage before I would turn around and leave, never to know this man. I felt his heat behind me and turned around, taking my time, desperate to still my throbbing heart. My legs failed me as I looked into his eyes, a boyish grin had replaced that smile as he reached out and took hold of me. His body was strong as he pulled me against him. *Steady legs, steady.* My hand found his chest; his heartbeat echoed the erratic rhythm of my own.

"If I asked you to leave with me, to go to a coffee shop and have a normal conversation with no strings attached, would you come with me?" Mischief ran wild in his eyes.

"Yes." It was out before he finished his question. His smile reached his eyes.

"Then let's go. This place gives me the creeps."

He took my hand and led me out of Alias, his touch an automatic switch to my senses. I saw only him, heard only his voice; his scent overpowered the salty ocean breeze and I was desperate to taste his mouth, his skin.

The coffee shop down the street closed just as we reached it. The annoyed waiter kept pointing at the closed sign still shifting against the glass door. We both laughed at the odds. There had to be somewhere else we could go. The restaurant at The Marcella Hotel was still open and served the best sushi in the city. I couldn't remember the last time I had sushi.

We spoke for hours until the manager came to ask us to leave and make our way to our room, adding room service was available twenty-four-seven. Conversation flowed like a raging river during dinner. It was exciting in ways I can't explain. I wondered how much of what he was telling me was true; we had met at Alias after all.

Each time I asked the waiter for a Walker, he looked at me and asked, "You do love a good Walker, don't you?"

"Yes, it's my poison." No point in lying about this fact. After the third time I found my nerve and asked him why he kept asking. He reached for my hands, stroking my palms with his fingers, teasing my fingertips with his touch as currents rippled through me.

"My surname is Walker." Coincidence? I never believed in such a thing.

We got to know each other more in those few hours than I had gotten to know anyone in a long time, including Ari. We didn't share our first names, I found this strange, it's how normal introductions are made. Nothing about him or that night was normal. When he finally did ask, I blurted out Victoria, my mother's name. His name: Aidan.

We stood in the hotel lobby and I didn't want to go home, not without him. Most of what I had told him was true, apart from my hunting, and I hoped most of what he had told me was as well.

"I have another crazy idea for you and I hope you will say

yes." Who could ever say no to his boyish grin? His dimples tried to crush my self-control.

"Depends. How crazy?" His fingers intertwined with mine and he pulled me closer, wrapping his arms around me. My hands found his chest, and I felt the hastened rhythm of his heart, squeezing the air from my lungs.

"Let's get a room. Hold on before you get scared off and run for the door. Not to have sex. Well, maybe something, if you behave. I'm dying to know more about you." That grin, those eyes, his smell subtle but pulling me in, his naughtiness tugging at a side of me I never knew existed. "I don't want this night to end, I have never met someone as compelling as you. I don't want to walk out of those doors and face the reality of this world, not knowing if I'll ever see you again. Does that scare you?" The warmth of his hands sent shivers through me.

"No." I couldn't fight the desire to know him, laugh with him as he kept pulling me into something I had never known before.

"Wait right here." He spun around and headed for the reception desk. Three steps later he turned around, his gaze grabbing hold of me.

He closed the distance between us without taking his eyes off mine, standing so close I felt his heartbeat. He ran his hand through my hair and held the back of my head, stroking my scalp with his fingers. That boyish grin again. He brushed his lips against mine; teasing, tantalising.

My hands found and pulled on his unbuttoned shirt collar. His lips tasted like honey as his tongue met mine. It might have been the Baklava we shared for dessert. My legs failed me; he held me tighter and pulled me close against him.

I lost myself in the tender, eagerness, of his kiss. It was one of those moments you see in the movies and laugh at how ridiculous it is. I opened my arms to ridiculous and held on for the ride.

He eased his hold, his mouth still against mine. "We have a serious problem."

"Why?" Sucking on his bottom lip as I pulled away from his perfect mouth.

"I can't stop kissing you."

"Then don't."

Mister Walker found us a room, the presidential suite, 'just in case we never wanted to leave'. I couldn't think of a single reason I would ever want to leave. *Captivating.*

The suite was exquisitely furnished in whites and creams. Large sliding doors opened onto a private deck, a pool, and loungers. The bedroom and adjoining bathroom were separated by a glass panel.

"I'm going to love watching you take a shower." That boyish grin of his made me want to take a shower. A cold one, if he didn't join me.

Aidan pulled me onto the oversized couch, our bodies finding comfort in the embrace. "Do you want to watch a movie?"

When last did I watch anything but the ids on my phone's screen? Perhaps occasionally the news to see if there were any new developments with the sniper or if Tony Andretti's carcass had been found. I constantly hoped for the latter.

"Yes. Do you want me to fetch us a drink from the mini fridge?"

"No." He kissed me until my chin was raw from his stubble and we laughed like teenagers at the redness.

No matter the sting it caused my chin, I couldn't get enough of his mouth, eager for what would follow.

He sensed my eagerness and pulled away from my ravenous mouth. "This might be the strangest thing I have said to you all night."

"I doubt it can be stranger than what you hinted at in the lobby." Seduction dripping from every word like honey.

"Don't look at me like that. You're making this even harder to get out."

"Do you need help to get it out?" Sounding like a porn star,

I wasn't proud. Maybe a little. I could play his game and not care who won.

He laughed, shocked that I could match his naughtiness. He told me later he laughs when he is nervous.

Win for Fin, I make him nervous.

"No, that's not what I meant. Hold on before you say anything and make me lose my nerve because this is hard."

"Yes, it is." I pushed my body against him, feeling what I referred to.

"Woman, you're going to be the end of me." He kissed me before I could say anything else, each kiss better than the last. We found each other's rhythm.

"I don't want to have sex with you."

"What?" Shocked at his abrupt statement mid-kiss.

"I want to. Desperately. But I want to know all of you. You and me? Mind-blowing. But I don't want it to be the only reason we see each other. You're captivating and I ache to know everything about you. Not just your body. I made a mistake signing up at Alias; that lifestyle, it isn't me. This right here, this is me. I need to know your desires, fears, pet peeves, the way you look when you wake up, the last thing you do before you go to bed at night. How you like your eggs. Everything. Anything less than all of you will never be enough for me."

Words failed me, and I smiled. Could this be real? Was he real? A man who wanted to know me when I lost all sense of myself as I tumbled deeper into the abyss. If there ever was a time to fight back, to get out of the dark, it was now.

Did I not deserve a normal life? A life filled with hope, laughter, ambition, and maybe even love? Perhaps with him. My Walker.

"What do you want to know, Mister Walker?" I pulled away from him, tucking my legs under me, stroking the rawness of my chin.

We spent the rest of the evening playing a game. We had to guess each other's favourite things and fears. We shared our dreams for our futures and for the first time I had to put thought into what my future held, consider that there was a life to live ahead of me.

"I think I want to go back to school and do my doctorates in both Criminology and Psychology. What do you want to do?"

"I want to finish my residency and specialise as an Obstetrician and Gynaecologist."

"Is that a line you use on women? Has it ever worked for you?"

"It's not a line. Would that even work on any self-respecting woman? I saw so much death and destruction during the war, I want to believe there is still beauty in this world. To bring new life into this world is a gift and we should cherish it." His fingers played with mine.

"To answer your question, no, not one with a drop of self-respect. You were in active duty?"

"Yes. I did three tours and then I couldn't take it anymore. I realised I wanted to save lives, not take them."

"How old you are, Doctor Walker?"

"I enlisted straight out of school, doubt we served at the same time." That boyish grin of his and I wished he didn't want to know all of me, but rather know my body – right there and then.

"How do you know I served?"

"The way you walk, talk, and not a lot of women carry a gun holstered at her ankle to go to a bar."

He was good. He was bad. I wanted to know everything about this incredible man.

This man who saved lives.

We watched a movie. Well, we kissed through a movie and went to bed. Aidan kissed me good night, and then he fell asleep. His bare chest against my back, his arms around me. My whole body tingled as I waited for sleep to come.

Being with him was exhilarating. In that moment I felt hopeful of my future being the Finley I was before I walked into war, before war followed me home.

His calm breathing lulled me into a peaceful sleep.

The next morning, Aidan found me on the patio and brought me a coffee. He had remembered how I drink it. Perhaps there was something to his game.

"I was worried when I woke up and you weren't next to me."

"I couldn't sleep and didn't want to wake you." Taking my coffee from him. Something splashed in my stomach as our fingers touched.

"It's a beautiful day, isn't it?" He looked out across the ocean, his shirtless back seducing me. He had the body of a runner or a surfer. Lean, strong and every muscle perfection. What I wouldn't give to trace the outline of each with my tongue. Even through his jeans his gluteus maximus were magnificent. I ogled a doctor, I had to remember the correct anatomical terminology.

"When you are done undressing me, come here. There are orcas in the bay."

Black and white figures played in the calmness of the ocean, there were two calves with them. Carefree, the pod splashed with their tail fins, leaping out and crashing into the dark water below. It's a comforting thought knowing you're the apex predator.

His hand found mine as I held on to the banister to steady my legs as his shoulder brushed against mine. "The pool is heated."

"I didn't think to pack my bikini to go cancel my membership at Alias."

"Who said anything about clothing? Come on, I won't look. Much." Naughtiness in the daylight.

I removed my robe, letting it fall at my feet, my eyes on his as I removed my underwear and glided into the pool, grateful it was heated. Not once did his eyes leave mine.

"Turn around. I don't trust you not to take a peek." I obliged. The anticipation electric. Electricity and water don't go together. *Dangerous. I do like danger.*

"Look at me." His arms slid around me. I never even heard him get in the pool. "Cancel all your plans for the weekend; we're staying here. I'm not letting you go." His mouth found mine, and I wrapped my legs around his waist. Feeling what the moment did to him sent my heart into a frenzy, and for the first time there was nothing between us. He lifted me higher as I teased against him. *He was good.* We stayed in the pool for close to an hour, playing Marco Polo and kissing whenever we found each other.

Aidan again instructed me to turn around before he got out of the pool and found us towels, holding one out for me, his eyes never left mine.

"Phone whoever you need to and ask them to bring you a weekend bag with everything you need to stay here. Tell them to leave it at reception, we can have a porter bring it up for us. You're not going anywhere."

I phoned Lizzie.

"You want me to do what?" I don't know whether she was confused or intrigued. I explained as much as possible with Aidan in the next room, not conveying the fullness of the dream I found myself in.

"Please. I will explain everything when I see you."

"I will drive past there on my way to the lake house. I hope you don't mind but I need to get out of the city and Wild Bay is too far a drive for the night."

"Lizzie, please don't go alone. I will come with you."

"No, you won't. You'll stay there and let this man get to know you. I mean it. You need to live again. Eli is going with me, it's time. I can't expect him to keep waiting for me." He would've, he saw in her what I started to see in Aidan.

Lizzie dropped my things off at The Marcella and whoever Aidan phoned brought his.

"I'm going to take a shower. You stay right here." I seductively walked away, his gaze followed me.

Warm water enveloped me. For the first time, I smiled the

giddy smile of a teenager after she had kissed her crush for the first time. It had tried to escape since I saw him in Alias. I didn't hear him open the shower door.

His hand wrapped around my neck as his other grabbed around my waist. *My gun?* In the dresser drawer where I had put it the night before.

My elbow found his ribs, and he groaned, I spun around, hands up and ready to punch my way out and away from him.

"Wait, I didn't mean to startle you." He held on to his bruised and maybe cracked ribs. "I," trying to catch his breath, "I just had to know."

"What?" My fists raised in front of my face, my elbows pulled in. My breath came out hard.

"If you're a natural blonde." His eyes found their way down my body as did the hand not holding his side; his mouth lifted to the side and his eyes screamed desire. "I guess I'll never know."

He pushed me against the cold wetness of the tiles, his mouth hard on mine, his hand teasing, exploring. Strong.

"I thought you wanted to wait." Towel drying my hair, still trembling from what happened in the shower.

"If you remember, I said to wait with sex. That wasn't sex. Well, not exactly."

I couldn't remember the last time I was with a man and it hadn't led to sex. Second base, as we called it at UM.

Aidan wrapped his arms around me and nuzzled my neck. "Maybe it's time for a new game. How about we flip a coin? Heads, second base, tails, third base. When we can't stop at kissing and first base, that must always be included. I can't get enough of either of them." Aidan turned me around and his eyes fixated on first base. *Money well spent.*

"Do you have any idea how beautiful you are? I lose myself in your eyes every time you look at me, I have never seen a blue so blue. You make me sound like an idiot; I can't find the right words with you still so wet." He tugged at my robe.

He was bad.
"Find me a coin."
Aidan did. It landed on tails. *Wow.*

I had been oblivious to the rhythmic beeping of my mobile phone. After we got dressed, I saw Lizzie's car had gone past the cameras and she had deactivated the alarm at the lake house. She was safe, with Eli. Aidan and I spent the rest of the weekend getting to know each other even better, watching movies, cuddling on the bed or sofa, ordering room service. There was no place I would rather be than with that man and his grin. Not once did we have an uncomfortable silence. Comfortable, yet thrilling.

I awoke to the rhythmic beeping of my mobile phone; the tone I had chosen for the motion detection cameras. To others it would simply sound like a message tone; to me it was an alert tone. The time displayed on the screen – 03:30 a.m. Lizzie wouldn't have left that early for the city. She had texted me on Sunday saying she would only leave on Monday around midday, and Eli planned to stay with her.

Confusion settled as I lay next to Aidan waiting for the image to be displayed on the screen. His breathing calm.

Mine stopped.

Staring straight into the camera, his hideous grin provoking me.

He found me.

Twenty-four

Without making a sound, I collected my things. I couldn't tell Aidan why I was leaving when we had made plans to spend the morning together. He worked the night shift the following week. I opened the dresser's top drawer as softly as I could, taking out my Glock. My SIG was at Lizzie's house, the Remington in the safe at my penthouse. I wished I had access to all the toys in the back of Ari's SUV; Pandora's trunk. There was no time to stop for either of my weapons and the rest of my father's guns were still in storage as the estate still wasn't sorted out. My Glock, training, and the hunting knife in my SUV would have to do. I couldn't waste time if id had Lizzie. Id wouldn't think twice about killing her. If id broke into the house, id might think she was me, we look so much alike and in the dark... *Oh, Lizzie, what have I done.*

I left Aidan a note:
I'm sorry, Aidan.
Maybe in a different life.
Remember the orcas.
Finley.

The elevator couldn't descend fast enough, and the notion stirred as I stood watching the floor numbers counting down, powerless to do anything but watch. I, too, descended, back into the abyss, back into shark-infested waters. *'Remember the orcas,'* I reminded myself. I would find Tony Andretti and kill id, even if it costs me my life. I ran out of the hotel, down the street, my SUV still parked in Alias' parking lot. My erratic breathing and the ocean were the only sounds at this hour.

Only one camera detected id. Id's movements weren't picked up by any of the other cameras. It was possible id deactivated it; saw it before it saw id. A million thoughts crashed like storm waves through my mind. One made me scream out loud as anger and frustration collided.

I broke every traffic law to reach my sister in time. I had to be in time. Eli was with her, I reminded myself; but Tony Andretti saw Ari with me, and id would expect two people, would be prepared for two. Id would kill both of them. I stepped on the accelerator, wishing I had rather taken my SLS AMG when I left the lake house. Hindsight is a bitch.

Out of utter fear for my sister's safety, I wished Aidan was with me; he had been a soldier once. No. He could never see this world, he's too good for it.

"I'm sorry, Aidan!" I screamed at my windshield. Clenching my steering wheel, my knuckles turned the grey-white of a corpse, not that I could see my hands in the darkness, I didn't have to.

"Tony Andretti, today you die." My windshield remained unfazed by my outbursts.

The early morning was quiet as I got out of the SUV, except for a few early rising birds. I doubt worms were awake at this hour, but the one I hunted was.

I hunched down in case id was watching me and made my way around the house. All the windows and doors were still locked. I phoned Eli, perhaps phoning him as a last desperate attempt to shield Lizzie from this world. *Oh Lizzie, what have I done?*

Eli's sleepy voice answered after the second ring, "Finley, what's wrong?"

"Is Lizzie with you?" My heart pounded in my head.

"Yes, she's next to me. Why? What's going on?" They found their way to each other and for a split second, I smiled.

"He found me, Eli. Get Lizzie into the wine cellar, she knows how to get in. Stay there until I come for you." Hushed-yelling at my phone. *I removed all the toys, good.* "Do you have your gun with you?"

"Always. I will take Lizzie to the wine cellar but I'm coming with you. You can't take him on, not on your own." I wasn't in the mood to negotiate with my sister's lover or one of my best friends.

"This isn't a negotiation. Take Lizzie, take your gun and hers if she has it. Get to the wine cellar. Now."

Lizzie woke up; confusion in her voice. Before ending the call, I heard her voice. "Finley?"

I ran into the dark woods, no night vision goggles to help at this crescent moon hour. Where was he? I ran towards where I had last seen him. The very place I saved his angel.

I crouched next to the last row of trees, the last line of defence before I'd be out and in the clear. My gun drawn, I scanned for movement. The remains of the night felt unnaturally still and silent under the dim moon that hung low in the sky. I listened for movement, sniffed at the air – nothing but the woody smell of trees and moist foliage. Ari's voice was a sweet, deadly guidance in my memory.

A twig snapped, and I leapt for the nearest tree. I pushed my back against the old elm.

I shouldn't be here, not alone. Blood drumming, deafening in my ears, I forced my breathing to slow. A faint rustle on the other side of the elm protecting my six.

I rolled left and turned, sighted down the gun's barrel.

A startled rabbit bolted for the underbrush. I lowered the pistol just a little, with a shaky sigh.

Something slammed into the back of my head. Pain stabbed through my skull, darkness, I collapsed to the ground.

"So, the little Finley thinks she's a saviour." Angel Taker's cackled voice stabbing me.

I felt the back of my head, wetness matting my hair. My eyes regained focus as I concentrated on his vile voice. *My gun! Where is it?*

Id found it first, id's face beaming with pride. I fought back the bile pushing up inside me.

Then I noticed – the empty sleeve where id's left arm used to be. I smiled. The stump a reminder of the night Riley lived, the night I put an end to id's hunting.

My jaw locked. I leapt up and pulverised id's face until my knuckles bled. Blinded by rage, I didn't notice the barrel of the Glock heading towards me. I fell. Blood ran along where the scar had been. Id towered over me and I stared down the barrel of my own gun.

"The police are looking for you. They will figure out you're the Hangman."

My foot met id's groin, I leapt to my feet as id staggered back and fell to the ground. I kept kicking, holding the elm for balance. Combat-boot to id's face, teeth shattered, obliterating that sickening smile.

"You think you scare me? I'm not a little girl! I will end you!" My boot stomped on id's face. Rage shrouded my logic, I didn't see id raise id's leg. My ribs cracked against the pressure of id's size twelve shoe. My head struck the ground. Darkness.

I came to, struggling for air with id's hand around my throat. *Breathe.*

Id's full body weight was on me. *Breathe.* I grabbed at the dirt and my hand found the knife from the night Ari had trained me for this moment.

The blade penetrated id's left lung, and I twisted. I yanked the knife out, ready to plunge it into id again. Stunned eyes met death in mine. The knife plunged into id's neck. A gunshot echoed. Warm liquid dripped onto my face.

I pushed id's unmoving carcass off me and breathed deeply. In the early morning light, I saw a portion of the back of id's head, gone. I turned onto my stomach found my gun, barrel facing in the direction where the sound originated from.

Movement in the distance. Something or someone moved at great speed. Sidestepping trees, getting smaller with each step. Something or someone was running away from me.

Without haste I pushed myself to my feet; oxygen had not yet reached all my extremities.

I stared down at Tony Andretti, self-proclaimed Angel Taker. Id. Bullets ripped into id's carcass which made small jerking movements. I emptied my magazine.

This monster would never come back, not like they do in the movies even when their heads had been severed in an earlier instalment.

In a daze of pain and the loss of my precious blood, I stumbled back to the house. I found Lizzie and Eli in the wine cellar. They were safe.

The Angel Taker finally dead.

Sirens wailed towards us and Uncle Tom burst through the front door. He wrapped his arms around me without a word. Who had phoned the police, I couldn't say. After I had opened the doors for Lizzie and Eli, I walked to the couch and collapsed. I lay motionless as confusion and gratitude played tug of war inside me.

Lizzie was unharmed and Riley could sleep. The last time we spoke her parents had told me she had terrible nightmares. I had to make sure she was surviving the fallout of what that monster did to her. 'The dead monster' I thought, and laughed as Uncle Tom held me. In the distance, I heard Lizzie cry. *It doesn't matter, he didn't get to her.*

The police found the carcass where I had left id. A bullet hole for every little girl the ocean gave back. The kill shot a gift from someone else. Whoever fired it stood approximately fifty metres away from us I had estimated as Uncle Tom and Captain Taylor took my statement. He stood that close, and I didn't realise someone was there, blinded by pain, rage, and my need to survive.

"Why didn't you call us, Finley? I warned you not to go rogue." Captain Taylor ignored the implication of Uncle Tom's words.

"No time. I kept thinking about Lizzie, I couldn't let him get to her. He could've thought she was me. He didn't see my face, and he knew there were two people that night and Eli was here with her. Sorry." I lied. I wanted to kill him.

"Who shot him?"

"I don't know. I saw a figure in the distance and as soon as I saw it, it vanished."

"We need to take a look at the camera footage, maybe we can see his face. I want to see if my suspicions are confirmed."

"It wasn't Eli. He was with Lizzie and he wouldn't run from me. He would've told you when you got here."

"I will wait for ballistics, but it won't surprise me if it matches the calibre of bullet used by the sniper. You seem to draw them to you."

"You better tell me." My head rested in my hands.

"Tell you what?"

"If the sniper saved my life. I deserve to know." I had no doubt it was him.

The intriguing figure who dressed as I did, saved my life, even when he could've taken it twice before. A small part of me didn't want him to be caught. *He saved me.*

How do you say thank you to someone you can't reach? A 'thank you' card or a gift basket, neither were viable options. Where would I have had it delivered? Serial sniper headquarters? Spraying THANK YOU in big bold letters across a building in the middle of his hunting ground seemed desperate. Like those marriage proposals spray-painted onto bridges. It's graffiti and tacky. Finley D. Williams is many things, but tacky I'm not.

"You need to get to the hospital." Lizzie touched my shoulder and my head found my palms again. *Aidan works there.*

"I'm fine. Just give me a handful of painkillers and a Walker." I meant the drinking kind.

"Finley, it's seven in the morning. You're going to hospital. Even if I need to drive you myself and drag you in by your feet." Lizzie stopped crying. It made the pounding in my head worse every time she gasped for air.

I reluctantly agreed, only because Aidan was supposed to be working the night shift. I could be in and out before he gets there. I never asked which hospital he worked at. He thought my name was Victoria, he wouldn't make the connection.

Remember the orcas. Finley. In my haste, I had signed my name. The perfect time never presented itself to tell him I wasn't my mother.

Uncle Tom drove me to the hospital; Lizzie had been in no state to drive. I refused to get in the ambulance, I didn't want extra paperwork where Aidan might see my name. Finley isn't an uncommon name, but to my knowledge, I'm the only female Finley in the city. The doctor on duty wasn't Aidan, a mixture of relief and regret mixed inside me into a vile gut-wrenching pot. I wanted nothing more than to explain to him why I left, leaving only a note. An hour later, the doctor discharged me, and I asked Uncle Tom to head straight to The Marcella.

"What do you mean he left?" My head ached at the sound of my irritated voice.

"I'm sorry. Doctor Walker just left, he didn't sign out."

A sense of forlorn overcame me. To phone all five hospitals in the city to track him down; too stalker for me. If this non-stalker would find her Walker, it would have to be an act of fate, just like we had found each other at Alias.

I closed my eyes, thankful Uncle Tom wasn't in the mood for small talk as he drove me to the penthouse. Both my cars stood in the driveway at the lake house, and I didn't want to explain the Ducati Monster I had added to my collection of charcoal-coloured modes of transport. Eyes closed against the stabs of the sun's rays. *A light!* Not the end of the tunnel light. I recalled seeing a light in my rear-view mirror as I raced to save Lizzie from that shark. My focus had been on the road ahead, and it didn't occur to me to look in my rear-view mirror, not once. There were no other cars on the road so early in the morning. The notion stirred. A glimpse of headlights seconds before I screamed in a fit of rage. *Was he following me?*

How could the sniper have known where I was or what vehicle I, Finley, drove? Why would he be following me? He saw me getting rid of the first id, the first night we met. Perhaps stared at each other is a better description, as no formal introductions were made. Just me talking to him, asking him why he did the same thing I did. Killing. Well, in my defence I killed none of them except for the vile thing that touched my sister. The very thing that led me to Aidan. *Will I ever see him again? Pick up where we left off?*

Perhaps I would go all stalker on his beautifully sculpted ass. For him it was worth it, putting myself out there, hoping he would understand that I needed to protect my sister.

"The beautiful thing about orcas, and in my opinion it's what makes them so deadly, is that they are capable of emotion. Look how they're playing with each other, protecting each other. They're like us. We need to be protected and protect those we love." I smiled remembering his words, the perfect fit of our bodies as he held me while we watched the orcas. I didn't want to stalk him, I wanted to walk up to him and kiss that boyish grin right off his face. Not lurk in the shadows only to watch him. No, I wanted to be with him more than anything, protect him and be protected by him. This man who showed me a different life to the only one I had ever known before being with him.

I only wanted one Walker, and this one didn't come from a bottle. Aidan chose life over death and I wanted to choose that, too.

The decision was yanked from me by Uncle Tom's words as we sat down in my penthouse with our much-needed coffees.

Twenty-five

"Finley, do you remember the girl we thought ran away from Tabula Rasa?"

I did. Megan had come to us about two months earlier. Local police found her in the back of a car during a routine roadblock, being taken somewhere to have unspeakable things done to her. Maybe not worse than what she had already been through.

"We found her. Well, part of her."

"What do you mean, part of her?" The notion again scurried towards the pit.

"They only found her torso." Uncle Tom no longer hid his exhaustion as he put his feet on the coffee table.

"Where is the rest of her?"

"I don't, we don't..." His eyes wouldn't meet mine. My stomach turned on itself; he had come to me for a reason. He wasn't talking to the protector of Tabula Rasa, he was talking to the person he had seen months before in Lizzie's home office.

"Tell me everything – and I mean everything. I willl help you find whoever did this to her." The notion couldn't reach the pit in time.

"We have seen some awful things over the years, and you know more than I want to believe you do about the murder of Damian Prescott." *Well, his surname I didn't know nor why he gave me his real name.*

"But this, Fin, this is sick. There is no other way to describe it." Uncle Tom told me everything. When he finished, my stomach emptied itself on my beautiful Persian carpet. Maybe due to my mild concussion, but this was worse than anything I had seen up to that point in any corner of the abyss, except for what they did to all those poor children. I had to find him. My future had to remain just that, a one day, not a today.

"Show me so I can get a better understanding of what I need to look out for." The notion tried to scream, but it had no voice.

"You can't un-see things, Fin. I promise you this is far worse than anything you have ever seen. It's one thing to hear what I tell you, but seeing...I wouldn't be asking for your help if we stood a chance of catching him through conventional methods. But this is not the first and it won't be the last."

"Why am I only hearing about this now? Something like this, the media will be all over it." He didn't have to tell me, things like this are only withheld from the public when it's horrendous, violent, and sick.

"This is the third one they found, the other two were outside Wild Bay. He is making his way up the coast and we can only estimate how long before he moves on from here."

"His hunting ground is larger in Marcel. Easier to hide around here, too. He will stick around for a while unless we can turn up the heat and flush him out. I don't want him to move on, out of our reach. We must stop him. He needs to pay for what he did to Megan and the others."

Id was mobile and not territorial. I was racing against time. I had to pull out the big guns if I was going to catch him. This was personal. Megan had tried her best to put the nightmare behind her, she even considered going back to school the last time we had spoken.

"Show me the file. I'm ready." I wasn't, further destroying my beautiful rug seconds after opening the first file.

Uncle Tom fetched me a washcloth without uttering a single word. He wanted me take out the mask and help no matter the personal cost.

Lizzie was on her way to bring me dinner. I had no appetite, my head still throbbed to a monotonous drum from where the rock had broken my skin, my breathing shallow against my cracked, not broken, ribs. The Angel Taker was dead. One less monster, but another had taken id's place. Something equally, if not more, evil. A destroyer of young women. Id took only what id needed. Not knowing what id did with the rest of them made my skin crawl.

"What do you do with the rest of them? Do you bury them, burn them or dump them in the ocean? Do you eat them?" Again, speaking to the non-present id. If id was sitting next to me, I had ways of making id talk, and not the cookies and milk kind of way.

Cannibalism wasn't something I had even considered when Uncle Tom and I were going over the case files. He had brought me copies of the other two cases in Wild Bay to review. Actually, it was eight cases from the Wild Bay cases, plus our four. *Twelve*. The best profilers in the country had already been consulted on the case, but Uncle Tom trusted my judgement more when it came to serial killers. *Judgement or capabilities?*

"You have a way of knowing Fin, you understand them. Not following a checklist, you get inside their minds and see what they see, feel what they feel. You understand their darkness, their need to kill, the thing that fuels their desires. At first you scared me, but now I realise it's a gift." He left and I wondered if Uncle Tom knew the thing once known as Damian Prescott had died at my hand.

Lizzie threw her arms around me as I opened the door. "I'm so glad you're okay! How is your head?"

"Please lower your voice, I have a mild concussion. I'm not deaf."

"I was worried sick about you. Eli just told me to rush down to the wine cellar and wait for you to come and let us out. It looks different down there."

"I'm thinking of making it into a home theatre or something, the soundproofing will be great for acoustics." Screams sounded better down there; the acoustics were fantastic. "I don't want to talk about it. You're safe and very much in love."

Eli wrapped her in his arms, his touch calming her. "Thank you for whatever you did, Finley, your sister came to her senses." He kissed the top of her head. He said nothing, but I suspected he had known what that thing did to her. Ari didn't find the footage by himself. I often wondered why he sent the links to me and not Eli. Perhaps he did because I would take care of it, my hands weren't tied like Eli's were, helping the city with unofficial, yet official enough, work.

"I will pour you a Walker and then you need to tell me why I had to bring you clothes at The Marcella when you live five blocks away." Lizzie opened the door to what must have been driving her insane. She is as inquisitive as she is brilliant.

"I met someone. This is awkward, I can't tell you about him when Ari is Eli's best friend."

"You deserve to be happy. Ari wanted it for you," Eli, my friend, said. My dark life wasn't a secret I kept from him, yet he didn't know the details of what I did in the dark.

"We met at Alias and before you say anything, Liz," I gave her a stern look and she pursed her lips, "Friday night I went there to cancel our memberships and he was there, his first night. His name is Doctor Aidan Walker and—"

"I know him." I grabbed my pounding head. "Sorry, Fin, but I do. He trains with me."

"What?" My jaw reached for the floor, fighting against the muscles and tendons holding it in place.

"Yes, he trains with me. Man, can that guy fight. He used to be in the army, years ago. I'm not sure what division, it doesn't matter, that guy can give a mean uppercut. Lucky for me, he's a doctor, he instinctively checked me after he almost took my head off."

"What?" My head started spinning. Eli knew Aidan; I didn't have to go all stalker on him. I refrained from thinking about his magnificent ass in case it clouded my judgement and I throttled Eli until he gave me his number. I couldn't. Not until this one had been stopped, and I found my way back into what's deemed the normal world. *Finley's normal, yet still badass, life.* I wonder if anyone would follow me around with cameras, giving me a script to guide the normalcy of my new-found, no longer in the abyss, having dreams for myself and my future, life. No longer starring as Cerberus in others' nightmares.

"Do you have his number? Phone him, tell him to come over and join us for dinner," Lizzie said in a restrained yell.

"He's working tonight, and I don't have his number."

"Do you want his number? I'm sure he will call you tomorrow if he doesn't tonight. He strikes me as a gentleman and not into that three day rule crap." Eli spoke like one of the girls.

"He doesn't have it. I left him a note when I rushed out to get to the lake. Before you say anything else, I will kill you if you give him my number. Something happened and I need to give it my full attention. Promise me, Eli. Even if for some strange reason he tells you about me, you are not to say a word to him. Are we clear?"

"Yes, ma'am. If he figures it out some other way, can I then give him your number or address?"

"If by some act of fate that doesn't involve your meddling hand, then, yes you can give it to him. Hell, send him straight to my house if that's the case." I reckoned the odds of this happening were slim and Eli wouldn't stop, he was, after all, my friend. Friends want to see friends happy. I couldn't be happier for him and Lizzie and just a little jealous as another shark had made its way into my waters and kept me from happiness.

I didn't care that Aidan was an ex-soldier, impressor of Eli with his hand-to-hand combat skills, he didn't deserve to be part of this world. It had no claim on him; he chose life.

"Just because Eli can't intervene, doesn't mean you can't tell me what happened. You need to tell me everything, right now. Eli, honey, would you mind setting the table? I'm sure you don't want to hear all about my sister's sex-escapades." Lizzie pushed me towards the deck even before I had a chance to say there were no sex-escapades, just a lot of base coverage.

I told her everything, and I expected her to explode when I told her about the coin flipping.

"Why are you still here? Go to him."

I didn't want to tell her about the predator which had found his way into our midst, devouring one of the girls desperate for a new life while she stayed at Tabula Rasa. Lizzie deserved no part of this world either.

"I can't Liz, something happened and I need to give Tabula Rasa all my attention. I will not tell you about it, just trust me."

"The chronicles of the self-sabotaging Williams sisters continue." She shook her head and left to help Eli with dinner.

I politely asked them to leave after dinner. In truth, my head did hurt, as per the excuse I gave them, but I needed to get hunting and find id so that this could be over, perhaps even sleep that night. A tired warrior is not a strong warrior. I didn't care if there were more after this one, there always would be. I was done. Aidan had shown me what life can be, that there is a way of fighting without putting yourself in danger, and I, too, would find my way.

Long before the sun appeared on the first day of my last hunt for the man the police were referring to as Scarecrow, I stood on the deck, watching the orcas as they greeted the morning with enthusiastic play before they would set out on their own hunt. *Kill their own shark.* I smiled as the image played itself out in my mind. It was time.

I walked inside, leaving the light for one last rendezvous with the abyss. The notion came out of slumber, arising from much needed rest.

What is he doing with the rest of them? I had my work cut out for me; finding Scarecrow wouldn't be easy and for the first time, I hoped to find id on the dark web. Swimming in plain sight, ready for me to attack. My phone vibrated, still on silent from the previous night's attempt to catch up on sleep. The weekend had not been spent sleeping. Much.

A news report flashed on my phone's screen. The sniper

had struck the day before, claiming three lives, a pastor, a banker, and a teacher. Not one of my dark humoured jokes. There was no discernible pattern, no way for me to tell who would be next. But he wasn't choosing them at random.

I pushed the memory of the man who had saved me deep down into a place the darkness didn't reach. Uncle Tom hadn't called me with the ballistics report, he didn't have to. The sniper had my back. *Why kill three people after saving me? Why protect me?*

The dark web is like a medieval fortress. Many buildings within its walls, each building made up of various rooms. The rooms each hold an array of corners; corners of perversion. To find the fortress is easy enough; the right building, not so much, and finding the correct room even less so. If you are lucky enough to find the room you are looking for, and there might be thousands of the same room in the totality of the fortress, you still need to find the exact corner where the id you seek hides. Not as easy as doing a simple Google search, no SEO's used in the abyss. You need to know what you're looking for and if by some act of pure luck, not that anything in the abyss must ever be associated with luck, you may find it.

It took me a week to get close and then I had to search again until I thought I found it. Or what would bring me closest to finding the hideous thing called Scarecrow. During my week-long hunt I spent every day at Tabula Rasa and I even asked Eli to train all the guests in self-defence, even the toddlers. I hated myself for not thinking of it before.

How is one to survive without being able to protect yourself?

The following Wednesday morning, Ashley called me into her office.

"How are you doing, Fin?" The weight of regret and perhaps a sense of failure weighed on her shoulders like a Challenger 2 tank.

"I should ask you the same question?"

"How did I not do more to protect Megan? How did he get to her? She was in my care."

"Our care, Ash. Our protection." I hated how she internalised everything. We had learned that word the same day.

"You don't have to remind me." Ashley tried to hide the wetness on her face by looking at her hands. "But how did he get her?"

"The police don't know. They won't tell me what they saw on the closed-circuit television footage outside her work. Maybe Uncle Tom will when I see him again." *He should have, it would have changed everything.*

"And the other victims; do they know where they went missing? Names, anything?" Her relentless babble pulled the horrific details from me.

I studied Psychology too, but she always used our friendship against me when she needed information, and I adored her for it. Ashley is a brilliant psychiatrist in her gentle and understanding way. Loved by all who met her and most loved by Hope.

I could never be a psychiatrist, I'm too empathetic. Perhaps my empathy is the reason I understand the darkness of monsters; I absorb all their emotions and experience them as if they are my own. The Scarecrow's hatred touched me when I saw the destruction and creation of id's hand. *Creation?* Perhaps id considered it art. Whatever id called it, it came from something horrific I struggled to understand. Id's rage roared through me the more time I spent trying to get inside id's mind. I kept wondering what id did with the parts id didn't use. For a moment, I considered asking Ashley for her professional opinion, ask her if she thought cannibalism played any role in this.

"Not the majority, no. They have been able to identify a few using DNA samples brought in by family or friends."

"What are we going to do, Finley? How are we going to

keep everyone safe?"

I didn't tell her I was working on it, not sleeping and vomiting so often I considered getting veneers.

"We can tell them the basics. Walk in groups, phone either you or me to fetch them if it's late. Don't talk to strangers no matter how trusting they look. They know these things. Our guests aren't oblivious to what's out there in this world. Perhaps they believe because they have already been through it, it can't happen again."

I often caught myself thinking the same thing when I touched the area on my face which used to be scarred. Even though no longer visible, a slight ridge remained, and I was desperate to forget. You never do. It creeps out of the dark and jumps on top of you when you least expect it. A song, a smell, the colour peach; you never forget. Monsters do the second they are finished with you and then move on to the next, leaving you to carry the burden of what they have done. Time does not heal everything. You can only hope to get knocked so hard in the head that the impact will destroy the memory, not even that worked. The only way to get through anything is to get through it. You grow stronger carrying the weight. Resilience isn't for sale in any store, over the counter or with a prescription. You earn it, the same way I would earn my doctorates and pursue a dream I had long since forgotten I once had. 'Dreams are not allowed in the dark', the sign reads at the gate.

"I'm grateful Eli is training everyone. If not only for self-defence, it shows them the power of their own bodies, their own physical strength. It will do wonders for their mental well-being. Thank you again for carrying the cost. Although I guess with you two being friends, you get the friends and family discount." Ashley smiled for the first time since I had informed her about Megan.

"Eli is a wonderful person and a good friend."

"Do you miss him?" Ashley got up to make us coffee.

"Who? Eli?"

"No, Ari. Do you miss him?"

"I do some days. He came into my life at a time I needed to be reminded that not all men want to hurt me physically."

I hated saying the word rape in front of her, I always felt like a hypocrite as she had gone through much worse than I ever did. Once I mentioned this to her, she smiled and said, 'We can't measure it, Fin. Rape is not something to compare. Just because you were older doesn't make it less horrific. I don't see you as any less of a victim and neither should you.'

"Are you waiting for him?"

"No. I realised I need to focus on what's ahead of me – only me – not with anyone. I don't want to be with someone as a crutch, it isn't fair to him or me. Two halves don't make a whole. Ash, I want to be happy with myself and want what I want."

"So, you're not going to give Aidan a call?"

I hated when Lizzie invited Ashley for lunch. She asked to spend time with Hope, but she only wanted an excuse to see Ashley and use her as her own personal bazooka against me.

Sneaky Liz may be, but tactful, not so much. For all her faults, she loves me, and only wanted me to be happy. In her mind I needed to be in a relationship to be whole, which might have stemmed from her need for adoration by someone when her employees referred to her as a tyrant. Williams Pharmaceuticals prospered under her leadership and I was proud of her when she told me they were exploring a 'vaccine' for GHB and other date-rape drugs, and it would be produced for over-the-counter sales. We even discussed ways to get sponsors on board and hand it out at the free clinics, schools, and universities. She had contacted international partners. Something good was coming from the horror that befell her. That's what survivors do.

Perhaps Lizzie needed someone as she was whole, but frightful of losing me and being alone. I often forgot what it must have been like to lose our parents, knowing what I had to endure, not knowing where I was and powerless to save me.

"No, not now. First, I need to sort myself out. He deserves to be with a whole person. I'm considering starting parkour training."

"You want to do what?" Ashley looked comical in her confusion. "You're changing the subject, Finley. You and your games."

For the first time, I thought of Aidan's games. My ears ached for the warmth of his breath when he whispered in that husky voice of his first thing in the morning. Just the thought sent shock waves through me. Perhaps we could be friends? *No, no, no.* There are few people in this life we meet who we want as lovers, well, in mine at least, and Aidan owns the lover category. I could never be friends with him and I had Eli to be my bro, never doing bro-hugs though, Liz would kill me. Try to at least, although she was getting good at Krav Maga.

"Parkour, Ashley, parkour. You use the city as one big obstacle course, jumping from building to building, climbing stuff or running up against some other stuff."

"Do what you need to do for yourself, Finley. I'm proud of you for how far you have come since you got back. You're no longer carrying your anger as a shield."

Eviscerating the thing that touched my sister was a great outlet for all my pent-up anger, I didn't say it out loud.

We had similar discussions every day, and I felt more at ease to leave the darkness behind me and carve a new destiny out of the concrete block of a future in front of me. I had to finish one thing before I would put it all behind me. Would that even be possible, knowing what I had done about the abyss?

Finding them wasn't easy; this group are not open about their desires. I wish paedophiles were less open about the depravities, not proudly sharing their vileness in newspapers with the full support of their spouses. The devotees hid in a corner reserved for them, but I had found them. They shared one thing: Acrotomophilia. For them, sexual arousal comes from body parts, not only amputees. If I was going to find him on the dark web, this was the place to start. Can't call it a good place. I found the interaction and comments interesting from a psychological perspective. Most of them didn't kill for parts, they bought them.

Who better to contact when you need to get rid of the parts you don't need? If this was what Scarecrow did, I underestimated id's intelligence. It took a week to find this specific group of devotees and from what I gathered they were local or at least in the country. I played the newbie card, asking questions, expressing my inexperienced desires, and they were all eager to teach me their ways. People who hide enjoy company. I ventured into their corner a little at a time, easing into it until I had spent enough time earning their trust to tell them what I wanted, *needed,* to be precise.

I whimsically chose Tisiphone as my pseudonym as a devotee. Mostly because the ones I thought of were already in use and people don't overanalyse the meaning of a pseudonym. Those who wanted to remain unseen did just that. I became Tisiphone, one of the Furies in Greek Mythology. She was the punisher of those who committed homicide, fratricide, and parricide. I should've perhaps considered it during my time spent as Cerberus.

Tisiphone: *Hello, fellow devotees. I'm new to this group and I was wondering, do any of you know where I might find arms or legs that have been ripped off? I don't like the clean, surgical cut, it has to be torn or ripped. If I can tell you a secret: I need to trace the ragged edges with my fingers. Hmmm...thank you.*

I waited almost two weeks before someone responded. A devotee, Appendagebeau, knew someone and would send me details on how I could reach his or her contact. I laughed at 'Appendagebeau' the first time I saw the name. Well, it wouldn't shock me if there were people out there who are aroused by appendixes; at that point, nothing shocked me anymore. Not even my growing desire to drive around the city at night to find the sniper and thank him personally for saving my life. Something drew me to him, and sorrow overwhelmed me each time he killed, not only for the victim but for him. To be honest, mostly him.

I slept well, no longer dreaming of wet, white hair sinking into the abyss; that monster was dead. There were a few nights I woke up screaming and immediately thought of him. "You don't need to do this," I said to him, in the darkness of my bedroom. Was he doing what I had done? None of his victims had criminal records, neither did most of mine. What compelled him to kill? I hadn't been back to the lake house but had to go prepare the room for one last visitor who would arrive soon.

I left in the early evening for the lake house. I wanted to spend time training by myself in the woods. I had not yet received the contact details for Appendagebeau's contact. Why I left at night and not the following morning will forever be a mystery to me. I wanted to get to the lake, perhaps to analyse what had happened with Tony Andretti. For all my training and years of combat, I saw myself as a failure for not killing him.

I was angry at the sniper for taking him out, but grateful he had saved my life. Had he not, I'm not sure I would've walked away from that fight. Even with one arm Tony Andretti was strong; he had been since I first met him. Getting him off Ashley hadn't been easy.

I drove into the night, comforted as always by the size of my G-Class; powerful and dark. Deep in thought, I didn't realise I turned towards the inner city.

Nobody stopped killing, maiming, or raping as news spread and more carcasses dangled across the city. The death penalty isn't an effective deterrent but ensures that that specific beast will no longer reign terror on unsuspecting victims. It's cheaper than keeping someone alive confined to a life in prison and I'm all about living in a world where money is allocated to those who need it, not keeping monsters alive only to let them free again. No matter the length of any sentence, it's never long enough. Death is the closest to enough there is.

I parked where I had left the first id hanging. My form of indirect public execution, id was dead long before id got to id's final hanging place.

As I parked my G I wondered what brought me there. Many thoughts rushed through my mind as I sat in the stillness of the decrepit parking structure, in the safety of my big vehicle.

Movement to my right.

I reached for my SIG, not wanting to give away my position, forgetting the windows were tinted and he couldn't see me.

He walked closer, tilting his masked face ever so slightly to the right, the same way he had during our first encounter. I opened my door and climbed out, showed him my hands.

He stood motionless, staring at my uncovered face. No point in hiding what he saw when he had saved my life.

"Thank you." The words fell out of my mouth and he tilted his head to the other side, still staring at me.

"Thank you for saving my life. Do you know who you killed?"

He nodded.

"Do you realise you don't have to do this?"

He shook his head, standing so close I saw his chest move as he sighed, then nodded.

"I will stop, you can too."

The ghost kept his gaze on me.

"I need to take care of one more and then I'm done. This is not worth losing ourselves for, there are other ways of fighting. Do you realise you can have a happy and full life?" Empathetic Fin having her own talk show, audience of one.

He nodded again and closed the distance between us, positioning his rifle over his shoulder.

"This makes no sense and don't ask me why I'm telling you this, but I met someone who showed me we don't have to choose war. You served your country once, I have known since your first kill."

He nodded and kept closing the space between us. I didn't fear him, but my heart pounded.

"I'm choosing life, after this last one. Please do the same. Let go of what haunts you and live."

He looked down at me and raised a gloved finger to the ghost's gapping mouth. I obeyed.

He covered my eyes with his hand, my hands trembled as I reached for him, clawing for calm against his waist. His heat and fevered breathing made it worse.

My SIG made a thunk sound as he pressed me into the metal behind me. The tension between us grew with every turbulent beat of our hearts.

I pulled him closer, lifting my head to show him I wanted it.

His lips brushed against mine, testing me. I don't know whether I failed or passed, I couldn't think straight.

I grabbed his face and pulled his mouth hard onto mine.

A wildfire ignited, scorching every part of me.

I left the parking structure heading for the lake house, but ended up at the penthouse. The moon watched me with great judgement as I stared over the ocean. *He kissed me.* Why did he kiss me and why did I want him to? How could I be drawn to a serial killer? Had I turned into one of those despicable and sad women who fall in love with murderers, even after they had been sentenced?

I knew what he was, and he knew what I was. Perhaps I was also just a killer, although I didn't kill, except for the last one. I wanted to kill them, reigning in my anger as I recorded their tales of grotesque acts of violence when they could've chosen much earlier to just take their own lives. They all chose in the end. Not one chose the special bowl of pasta. *Who doesn't like a dollop of razor blades?*

The tumbler was cool in my hand as I stood at the railing still trembling. I rested my arms on the railing for composure.

His kiss had left me mesmerized. *Who is he and why on earth is his kiss the best I have ever had?* If not for the stubble brushing against my face, the strong hand gripping my ass and another responsive part of him, he could've been a she.

I only opened my eyes when I heard the door to the staircase close. Our kiss had been brief; too brief, but intense. A shared hunger exploded between us.

I hoped it served as a thank you, it felt like it did.

Who are you? He didn't answer; the moon my only company.

Twenty-six

The police found another – I don't know what to call it – left by Scarecrow. The news reporter informed me as I drove to the lake house the next morning, this time staying on course. *Sixteen.* Uncle Tom phoned as I reached the dirt road that leads to the lake.

"Not a good morning."

"No, Finley, not a good morning." He always sounded tired. Perhaps tired from years and years of being in the darkness had caught up with him, or losing his wife and his best friends.

"Any new information that can help me?"

"Yes. I will see you in an hour. Do you mind if I stay the weekend?" He had his own house by the lake, on the south side, but he didn't like being there alone. It was where he missed Aunt Kelly the most.

Uncle Tom arrived fifty-five minutes later; he had packed before I had said yes. He took his bags straight to the room he always stayed in when he visited and came back down. I made us breakfast and kept the coffee flowing, his black, no sugar. We ate in silence.

The memory of the previous night's kiss consumed my mind. The warmth of his touch as his thumbs had brushed along my jaw. How he wrapped his arms around me and pulled me closer before he removed his mouth from mine. It felt like a hug. *Why would he hug me?* The hug bothered me more than the kiss. A hug is personal, intimate, a way to say hello or goodbye. Was he saying goodbye? Were our nocturnal encounters over? Was he leaving? Giving up the ghost, so to speak.

"Finley, did you hear me?" *Clearly not, Uncle Tom.*

"Sorry, Uncle Tom, I'm thinking." I couldn't tell him, not

198

that anything I could say at that point in our relationship would shock him. "About the girls. These killings, not that we have proof he is killing them."

"What do you mean? How the hell is he getting parts? From a butchery?" Not only tired, but in one of his sarcastic moods, the only thing I didn't like about him. As well as his truth-detection-superhero-abilities of course.

"I found something. Again, we're not talking about this in any official capacity, but you can ask a few questions."

He wanted me to take care of the problem, not oblivious to what that entailed. He was Commissioner Gordon to my Batman.

"Finley, just tell me." Tiredness won the battle against sarcasm; I rooted for the winning team.

I told him what I had found. He was disgusted, confused, and curious; he had never heard of Acrotomophilia. I explained the meaning to him in layman's terms.

"They get sexually aroused either by seeing or being with a person who has had a limb removed or the amputated limb itself."

"So, let me get this straight, you think he is buying parts to do what he does?"

"No. I believe he is selling what he doesn't need. Lucrative business, it would surprise you how expensive parts are on the black market. It will cost you an arm and a leg." It slipped out.

"Finley Duncan Williams, that's disgusting!" Him using my full names was a clear indication I had gone too far.

"I'm sorry, Uncle Tom." For the sake of us still needing to spend the weekend together I conceded, forced a sigh, apologised again, and gave him more caffeine. He had no appreciation for my dark sense of humour.

As I brought the mug to my mouth I continued. "Something has been bugging me. Did you bring the forensic pathologist's report? We are past you not sharing information with me."

"I did." He fetched the file from his room and placed it in front of me on the coffee table. I read through everything twice and did online searches for words I no longer remembered, perhaps never even knew.

"Did you see this? This will make catching him even more difficult." I showed him the section I was referring to with an unsteady finger. The notion scurried around. *Freezer burn.*

"So, he freezes their bodies; it's not uncommon for killers to do that. What are you getting at?"

"Yes, but that indicates he's meticulous in what he wants for his creation. He finds the perfect legs from one, perfect arms from another, perfect torso, and the perfect face. If you consider all four scarecrows, for lack of a better word, they look the same. See past the decomposition and what the animals did. The four heads were of brunette women; he cut their hair in the same style. Do you have photos of how they looked in life?" I waited as he sifted through the growing pile of documents, evidence of what this predator was doing, and I tried to understand, desperate to do so. As he placed the photos of the four victims in front of me, the notion pointed. *That's it.*

"He's killing the same woman over and over. I wonder if he's already killed her or if he's building up to it?" The women identified so far were close to thirty years old.

"No signs of sexual trauma, sperm or spermicide from a condom. Am I missing something? Something about this doesn't add up. For him to show this level of violence, torture even, they were alive when he ripped them apart. It has to have a sexual component." I hated myself for deviating from my dream of being a profiler, more so in that moment than ever before. *What am I missing?*

I reread the offender profiles created by the qualified profilers. They were nowhere closer to understanding this than I was. Doctors Gavel and Truman had surmised he fell within the organised dichotomy and was between twenty-five and forty-five, and white, as serial murder is, in general, an intraracial occurrence. He lives alone, as he needs privacy and the space to kill and freeze the bodies. Not territorial, as he moved his hunting ground from Wild Bay to Marcel. They also wondered whether cannibalism played a part in his fantasy, but there were no bite marks on any of the extremities found so far. Not that it meant we were wrong.

I went back to the forensic pathologist's report. The women were malnourished. The stomachs were empty in the torsos that had been found.

"He keeps them, tortures them physically and psychologically, inflicting his rage, perhaps, on the parts he doesn't plan on using for his scarecrows. Anything significant about the poles he uses?" The photos showed a crude crucifix once the parts had been removed.

"Anything from the nails he uses to hold the parts in place? How is it possible that he's not leaving any shoe prints? He has to either drag it in assembled or do it there. Under cover of darkness? That takes time and someone could catch him. We aren't going to stop him, are we?" I was on the verge of shooting something as frustration rose to dangerous levels inside me.

"We will catch him, just like Gary Ridgway, Dennis Rader, and countless other killers across the world were brought to justice years after their last kill. Maybe not us, but someone will."

"I have to; for Megan. For the other women who he has used as pieces in his…I don't know if he sees it as art or if he is just posing them. That's it!" I leapt to my feet. The rage did a one-eighty, and I realised something. My instinct kicked in, I had his scent and was eager for the hunt.

"You have that horrible look on your face, the same one you had that morning…" He didn't finish his sentence.

"Sorry. I need to do this and the world will be a better place for it."

"You're not sorry." He wiped his eyes, hoping I wouldn't see.

"You promised to never ask questions. You promised." Anger steered me back on course.

"And I won't, but that doesn't mean I don't know. You grew up in front of me. For years I have seen the darkness that festers inside you; it has always been a storm gaining strength as it makes its way towards land. A part of me always worried one day you would seek vengeance."

"We're not discussing this. If it makes you sleep better at night, I haven't killed anyone. I don't have blood on my hands." My eyes bore into the side of his head.

"Not for the most part, Fin, but Damian Prescott and that boy you left in that thing..."

The boy he referred to I had tried to forget. I never expected a child to come to a transfer. Never in my darkest moments did I once consider a child could talk like that, know those things that no one ever should. The things he had already done and would have continued doing if no one stopped him. I didn't have a choice.

A child got out of the car as I waited for a buyer, hoping it would be the Angel Taker on that specific night as the buyer had been adamant id wanted a little blonde girl. He couldn't have been much older than seventeen.

Seventeen and he had already fallen face first into the abyss devouring children when he himself was still one. I couldn't let him kill himself, no matter what he was. I cried every time I left the room, not vomiting like I had done with the others. Society has failed when children kill children. When a boy is that proud of what he had done, perhaps in his youthful arrogance not realising that there would be reactions to his actions. *It's a basic Newtonian law.* To let him walk away wasn't an option, not after what he had said. Not after what he had done to three little girls.

It never occurred to me that there might be more, so proud and boastful in his confession. So arrogant I didn't need my toys. I kept him for five days, deprived of food and water – my form of punishment – and I wondered, and still do, whether he became a predator because of no form of punishment in his formative years, or if perhaps he had endured too much.

I didn't want to have empathy for him, I still don't.

The police found him hanging, just as they did with the others, but for him I built a gibbet. His first prison, and he would never see the outside of a prison again. His confession to the detective together with the one I had sent was enough for him to be tried as an adult and sentenced to life imprisonment, the maximum for each of the little girls he had killed, to run consecutively. At most, he would be out in time for his ninety-second birthday. He didn't make it to his twenty-first birthday. There is always something worse than you in any environment you enter; he learned that the hard way.

"I'm not confessing to the murder of Damian Prescott, but it's time you heard what he did. His death was a blessing to too many women that didn't even know what he did to them."

I told Uncle Tom what I had received, and said I was grateful someone else had gotten to him before I did. He knew my statement was a lie, but after I told him what that thing did to my sister, his goddaughter, he never spoke of it again.

"Does Lizzie know?" he screamed, no longer hiding his anguish. Perhaps the same tears he cried for me when my captors sent videos, vividly describing what they were doing to me and the others and on some recordings, showing my broken and bleeding body.

"I had to tell her." I have regretted few things in my life as much as I regretted Lizzie seeing what he had done to her. Uncle Tom paced the length of the living area, cussing with every step.

"Is she okay?" His red eyes were too much to bare and I cried too, for my sister, for him, for myself, and for all the women torn to pieces by a predator I doubted I was capable of stopping.

"Yes, she is." We always underestimated Lizzie's strength because she was the softer, gentler one of the two of us. Over the preceding months, my sister showed me sides of herself I never knew she had. I admired her more than ever.

"It's not fair, Finley. That both of you endured so much,

yet you are both such remarkable women. Strong and resilient. Your parents would be proud of you, for the most part." *For the most part* cut into my stomach like barbwire.

"Life isn't fair, Uncle Tom. If it were, we wouldn't be sitting here with those images staring back at us. Our loved ones buried. We wouldn't need to hunt predators to try and better this world, but we do. You remember what you told me years ago when I first came to you with the idea of being a profiler and again when I told you I wanted to join the army?"

"It feels like a lifetime ago," he sighed.

"It is. You said something to me I have lived my life by. That first time you turned to me and quoted John Stuart Mill, 'Bad men need nothing more to compass their ends, than that good men should look on and do nothing.' I have always looked up to you, long before you became state prosecutor, because you never looked away from evil. You looked straight at it and took it by the horns. You're as much a warrior as I am."

"I am not the man I used to be. Kelly's death, your parents', what happened to you and now to Lizzie. I didn't protect any of you and that is something I need to carry with me to my death. I protected none of you. I didn't even know what happened to Ashley at UM."

"Stop this pity party right this minute or I will punch you, old man."

The corners of his mouth lifted.

"You have saved countless others and you know what? We *will* find this one and we will put an end to his killing." I hugged him. We both needed it more than either of us realised.

"Now that that's behind us, how about we catch us a killer?" Fire returned to his eyes, and he listened as I explained my plan to him.

I reminded him we were never to talk about it again.

Twenty-seven

Appendagebeau's contact made contact with me and we arranged a transfer. My plan remained the same as with the others, but I needed information. Something that would lead me to Scarecrow before id packed up and moved again. Nomadic predators are the pits.

It took five sellers for me to get a usable lead on Scarecrow. The five dangled above isolated city streets. Their gibbets weren't the work of art of the first, but I didn't have time to care whether it was less than perfect. The perfectionist in me got used to being smothered.

They were all sentenced for the desecration of a corpse and they didn't have it easy in prison. If you want a good time in prison, be a gang-banger, affiliated with the most prolific gang, of course. Life is full of choices; make the right one.

My morning runs remained an outlet for me and I often ended up where the sniper had saved my life. Sitting in the quiet and comfort of the woods, I allowed myself to think of him. He was killing less, perhaps coming to terms with whatever haunted him.

That morning had been like any other. I ran until my lungs and legs failed me and I ended up in the same spot. Something caught my eye, and I walked closer, too out of breath for any physical reaction. A black envelope hung from a tree, I opened it and removed a note typed on white paper.

Everything has to end, but will you be standing? I hope so. I need to kiss you again.

Tired butterflies fluttered with the little energy they had. *I want to kiss you, too.*

He often filled my mind when I closed my laptop, tired and worn-out from hours leading nowhere. Was I wrong for feeling this way about a killer, or was it because I, too, am a killer, I saw him in a different way? Not that I ever saw him.

A ghost face often stood watch in the corner of my tortured dreams. He stood holding his rifle, his eyes always on me, seeing what I did. My dream-hands always covered in blood, the place where I didn't hold back. No restraint in my subconscious and the memories of those explicit scenes left me nauseous for hours after I woke. The only thing that helped: running.

I had another transfer arranged for that night and I wasn't looking forward to it. Scarecrow remained elusive; no way to set it up for him to find me. Id took from the streets, the abyss, wherever id pleased, took only what id needed, frozen until it was time to create or sell, maybe eat. The element of cannibalism kept plaguing me, even in my dreams where I often took part in the feast id set before me, id's face obscured by darkness.

Running never helped, I couldn't eat meat for days. Only hurting Eli helped; the repulsion had to be released. My friend the unlucky recipient. In his defence, he gave as good as he took.

Headlights came around the corner. Id had followed my instructions, just as the others had. The same as all the other evenings. I sighed, eager to get it over and done with; another dead end. Well not dead, just hanging in a gibbet until they were removed by the police, awaiting the taped confession to be delivered. Same-day delivery, under the sun's warm gaze. Truth always comes to light. Poetic.

A slight drizzle started just as the first camera captured id's passing. I shivered as the cold water penetrated my clothes; I had not expected rain. Id climbed out of its soon-to-be vanishing car, I couldn't make out the model but it was white or light in colour from where I stood, clenching the tranquiliser gun in my right hand hidden from id's view.

"May I have a piece?" Id walked towards me.

"Help yourself." I pointed towards the boot of my transfer vehicle with my free hand.

Id walked over to the car and with id's back facing me, I shot the dart into the unsuspecting neck. Lucky for me, id wore a golf shirt, the collar not turned up against the drenching water now coming down with enthusiasm.

The dart entered.

Everything went dark.

Voices in the distance were barely distinguishable as raindrops created a melancholic symphony. An odour stung my nostrils, a mixture of dirt, hay and a familiar metallic smell. *Dried blood.*

My head and neck throbbed. No pain where you would expect pain, where I had had excruciating pain for four months. I kept my eyes closed until I had taken in my surroundings. *What happened? Where am I? How did he get me? Who is he?*

"She should've woken up by now." A man's voice became louder. My legs burned as he kicked me. *Play possum.*

"Don't worry about her, come help me with this one." Another male voice followed by footsteps moving away from me. A terrified scream. My stomach emptied itself.

I turned my head in the direction of the screams. Dark red spurts of fluid from where her legs should've been, and she kept screaming until her body bled out. Minutes feel like days.

Horror filled me as I saw what I had been trying to understand for weeks.

"Put her in the freezer, then help me clean. This smell is disgusting."

The human body does strange things when confronted with death; when you have seen beforehand how yours would come.

"What do you want from this one?" Unblinking eyes stared at me. One walked over to me and covered my face in a spray of spit.

"You really thought I wouldn't figure out what you were doing to my buyers?" I couldn't make out his expression, blinded by his saliva, unable to use my hands to clear my eyes.

"To think we were the ones to find her, we make the best team, E," the other one said. The one who must have sucker-struck me with something that left a goose egg on the back of my head; I didn't need my hands to feel it.

The cameras didn't show two, but under the cover of darkness he could've hidden in the back of the car, waiting for the perfect moment.

"You will pay for what you did, bitch. I'm going to take my time with you." E kicked me and I felt my ribs bend inwards in a way ribs should never bend. A snap sound followed.

"We need to get moving, E, the sun will be up soon. Leave her, she isn't going anywhere. Not until we have had our fun with her." They laughed as they walked away. *Off to leave another scarecrow.*

As I heard their car drive off, my body trembled uncontrollably. No one knew where I was. No one knew I had set up a transfer. *No one will look for me.*

Uncle Tom would realise something was wrong when he wouldn't find me at the lake house, as he was supposed to come over later the following day. With effort I pushed myself into a semi-seated position, my ribs ached and I struggled for breath.

I scanned my surroundings. From my position I could see unpainted walls, a rusty corrugated iron roof and two big sliding doors. *I'm in a barn.*

Their device stood as a grave reminder of what my future held.

It looked similar to the ones depicted in history books, but this one was constructed to also rip a head off. The notion stirred, and I wondered what they would take from me. Which part of me would play a part in their creation? Which part of me would be found and compared to Lizzie's DNA, or perhaps my toothbrush, or whatever she took to identify my part or parts. I had to get out. *But how?*

My legs were tied with a heavy chain to the axle of a rusty

blue tractor, my only companion. Well, the notion was there, scared, hiding in a corner, not even making an attempt to get back into the pit. If they moved on and took me with them, it would be even harder for anyone to find me. They have done it before.

I prayed. I begged God to help me and forgive me for what I had done, for what I had become. In the distance I heard the faint sound of a train passing, enjoying its freedom to go wherever the tracks lead. *A train*. Not too far from the lake house, further inland, was an old rail track infrequently used to transport whatever had to be moved. I had never given it much thought before.

My will to survive came rushing back. *I will not be held captive and tortured again.* I would not die by the twisting of mechanisms, ripping me apart. Not by their hands. The desire to survive is ignorant. In that moment I had hope; I looked around, scanning for anything I could use to get out, there was nothing. Just more chains and the same big lock that weighed on my feet. The one restraining my hands felt smaller, I tugged at it in desperation. The ground stained where the other chains lay, no longer holding whoever they had held before. *In a freezer somewhere.*

A car pulled up outside. Idling, the doors opened, showing sunlight and freedom beyond my reach. *Soon Uncle Tom will realise I'm missing, but will it be soon enough?*

"You're going to have to wait a little longer." E sneered as he got out of the car and the other closed the barn doors. Sunlight and hope shut out.

"Nothing you do can be worse than what I've gone through before!" I shouted, although my throat felt as dry as the dirt I sat on. Desperate for someone to hear my screams, yet pointless as no one had heard the dying screams of the woman murdered in front of me.

"Doubt it." The other shook with excitement. "Ed is so good at this. He really is."

"Shut up you moron." E punched the other. "Why did you say my name?" E kept punching until the other fell backwards, clutching id's bleeding nose.

"Sorry. It's not like she will tell anyone." Id whimpered.

"I shouldn't hurt you, B. Please forgive me." E pulled B up and into an embrace, the way lovers do.

"You're right, she isn't going anywhere." Their laughter punched me in the gut as they walked away.

Not once did it occur to me that Scarecrow might be Scarecrows. Team killers are not unheard of but remain rare. This gave me an angle, even if just to buy me time until someone came to rescue me. *Please, God, let them find me in time.*

From where I sat chained to the tractor, I could see sunlight above me, golden rays of hope streamed through a crevice where the cement washed wall met the rusty roof. There were more crevices in my body than any visible around the barn. My body had become an object on which they perfected their craft. Cutting, ripping, slashing and punching. B brought me food once a day. It must have been early in the morning as I heard a rooster call the sun shortly before B arrived. I lost the will to track the days.

"Please let me go." My voice hoarse from lack of fluids, apart from the blood dripping down my throat, gifted by a fist to my nose hours before.

"He isn't done with you yet and we don't want you to die, now do we? Not before he decides it's time."

"You don't have to do this." The tear in my lip bled as I pushed through the pain to talk. B was my best chance at surviving. I had lost hope of being found. Poor Lizzie, having to go through this again.

"Stupid cow, I want to. It makes him happy, and a happy E makes me happy." A gap-toothed grin spread over B's face as he said 'E', the way you say the name of the person you love.

"Why is he doing this? Why are you helping him? You're not a killer." To reason with a serial killer when you are at his mercy is like negotiating bedtime with a toddler.

"He enjoys it, you dumb slut." E pointed at the device as he walked towards me. "This? His idea. He's brilliant."

I may have tried to hitch my wagon to the wrong shark.

Horses are such majestic and noble creatures. For a moment, I forgot where I was and thought back to the days when my mother had taught me how to ride. *You're a natural, honey. The horse can sense your spirit and that's why he obeys your commands. As long as you respect him and take care of him, he will be your friend.* My mother had treated animals with the same respect she did people. The memory of her as I sat chained, covered in my own filth, kept me sane.

I had to get between them. Their bond must have formed years ago, the reason why they held on to each other and repeatedly indulged in their fantasies. Insight hit me like a freak wave.

"Who was it?" The wave knocked my will to survive out of me. I died a little more each day I remained chained in that stench. There is only so much the human body can take and even mine, which was accustomed to torture, gave up.

"Who was who?" B stood and walked over to E.

"B and E." A strained laugh echoed into the darkness. "How many times were you boys mocked about that? B and E, breaking women, entering none." I became dizzy as my body fought against exhaustion to laugh.

"Who molested you? No. Who raped you?" Perhaps my slice of stale bread for the day was stabilizing my blood sugar.

"You know nothing." Fists struck my face. After weeks, I estimated, I had found it. The trigger to their rage.

"She raped you. To avoid her smiling face, you turned your head and stared out the window. It stood watching, day after day, not doing anything to help you. Did you beg it? Did you plead with the scarecrow? It didn't help you when you first fought her, later submitting to just have her finish and gone. How old were you? Nine, ten, eleven, twelve?"

"You don't know anything." A fist plunged into my stomach leaving me gasping for air.

If I were to die, it would be when I decided to; I still held that power.

"I know what she did to you. Who was she? Your mother, sister, grandmother, aunt? No, she was your foster mother, caretaker—" My face again bore the consequences of speaking the truth.

Fury spilled out of my mouth. Anger at being held captive again, at not being rescued, watching as they ripped two more women apart. Two women I had spent time with, women I was desperate to save even though there was nothing I could do. Not while I was chained to a tractor which wouldn't budge no matter how hard I yanked on the chains. Two women whose frightened faces haunted me every single day. Their faces riddled with fear as they were dragged to that device. Screams. Their screams, my only companions in the dark, and their eyes – bewildered and frightened at knowing how they would die.

"Have you killed her or are you building up the courage, practising on all the others until you find the nerve to kill the one person you want to kill more than anyone else? Did she make you watch when she did it to the other one? She took turns with you and you were powerless to stop her, or protect each other because you were scared little boys and no one believed you. Or were you too afraid to tell anyone?"

Four feet took turns, relentless until they were out of breath and everything went dark. *Play possum.*

"How does she know?" One asked the other.

"She doesn't know shit. Let's end her and put her in the freezer. We still need a head. We can dye her hair."

"It's not the same."

"I don't want to hear this anymore; we have come too far. It's coming back again."

"Stop it. Don't let her get in your head. The bitch knows nothing."

I couldn't open my eyes, no matter how hard I tried.

"She does, she knows everything. I can smell her. The

tobacco that followed her everywhere, that clung to me long after she was done."

"We took care of her, E, she can't hurt you anymore. Don't you remember? You pushed that pole right through her, she looked like a finger puppet but on a stick. We both laughed and then we…right there next to her."

"I remember. How can I forget? We were free."

Motionless I lay, listening to them confirm what I already knew. Knowing what would follow. *I'm sorry, Lizzie.*

I cried with no tears. Cried for my sister who would one day hear what had happened during my last days, and Uncle Tom would see the photos when they found a part or parts of me. Crying for the future I wouldn't have, just like all the millions of others who had their lives stolen from them, the millions who would still be robbed. I cried for all of them. No one came to save me, not Uncle Tom or the police, not Ari, not the sniper.

I tried to open my eyes again, but couldn't and I didn't want to be there anymore. It was time.

My strained moans got their attention. I still had power over my death.

"Let's take her legs, I can see she's a runner."

"I don't like any part of her."

Strange to find comfort in the fact that a serial killer found no part of me fulfilled his fantasy, but not comforted enough to forget how they would kill me.

"What do you want to do then?"

"Let's see what we can sell. We need the money."

One of them opened the lock and removed the chains from my ankles. I didn't fight; my strength failed me. The small amount of food they had given me earlier I gave back when they trampled me. The chains around my wrists were used to drag me to the end.

I took comfort in not being able to see poetic justice awaiting me.

I hung suspended, my wrists and ankles bound by that

horrible rope. The familiar sound stabbed into me as they twisted the mechanisms. *Don't scream. They will not relish in my fear.*

I welcomed death. I deserved to die by a similar sword to the one I wielded. Excruciating pain in my shoulders as I felt both pop out of their sockets.

For the last time I embraced darkness.

Twenty-eight

"Finley, can you hear me?" His Israeli accent pulled me out of darkness' grip. "She's over here. Hurry."

Gunshots, raised voices. Strained, pointless attempts to open my eyes.

"Ari?"

"It's me, Eli, you're safe. Anderson, I have her. Get a paramedic now, she doesn't look good."

I remember little after that; only screams, sirens and a constant beeping sound.

A hand held the broken bones of mine. A whisper. Warm lips brushing against mine. *A dream?*

"I'm here." I couldn't place the voice.

Darkness reclaimed me.

"Fin, can you hear me? Please open your eyes." Uncle Tom. It was Uncle Tom's voice. *He is here.* They found me. *Thank you, God, they found me.*

I willed my eyes open and saw nothing but a blur. 'Blink. Focus. Open your eyes,' I commanded my tired body to respond. It did; my everything ached.

"You're safe, Fin, we found you in time. The doctor who took care of you said if we had arrived a minute later you would have died from your wounds if they..." He cried, gripping my hand, releasing the pressure when I flinched.

"I'm sorry, Finley." His sobs relentless.

"Did you get them?" I whispered.

"Yes, both were killed trying to run away. I'm so sorry we didn't get to you sooner."

"It's okay." I don't know if I meant it, I had been ready to die.

"Lizzie shouldn't see you like this; it's bad, Fin." He cried, releasing my hand.

Darkness reclaimed me.

Waking up in a hospital is confusing to say the least. It's bright and noisy and if only I had my gun to shoot the culprit behind that irritating beeping sound. I took it in, savouring all of it, except the beep. I had survived. Again. God answered my prayers.

A nurse came to check up on me, startled at seeing my eyes as she looked up from the chart at the foot of the bed.

"Doctor, she's awake!" The nurse screamed down the corridor. Her kind face brought comfort as she smiled at me when she rushed back, taking hold of my good hand. I took in the sight of her, far from retirement age, but she had a few hard years on her face.

"Welcome back, Miss Williams." I expected a hug.

A man came into my room, a smile took up half of his face. *Why is everyone smiling?*

"Miss Williams, I'm Doctor Stuart. You were placed under my care after you were transferred from ICU. What's the last thing you remember?" His voice was kind, with a hint of professionalism. You have to appreciate a doctor who has good bedside manner.

"I can't remember. Shouts, gunshots; Uncle Tom, I don't know." I fought the urge to ask if someone had kissed me.

"Uncle Tom being Mr Anderson?"

I nodded. My body fought my attempts to sit up straight.

"Hold on Miss Williams, you've been through hell. Take it slow. Nurse, please adjust Miss Williams' bed and make sure she's comfortable. You can phone her family." He turned his smiling face towards me. "I'm sure you would love to see them."

"Please. And thank you, doctor." I watched him leave and found the nurse's hand, desperate for more kindness, some human warmth.

She looked at me and gave me the hug I needed.

"How long?" I couldn't believe I had to ask that question again. The nurse gave me a sip of water, then another.

"A week, but we kept you sedated so that the swelling in your brain could subside. You will be fine, Miss Williams. I'm so proud of you." She hugged me again and tears wet my cheek, but not my own.

I asked again, I had to know. "No, how long did they have me?"

"Close to three weeks is what I heard."

"Has my sister been here?" I hoped they had kept her away, knowing she wouldn't allow anything or anyone to stop her.

"Yes, we tried to warn her, but she wouldn't hear it."

"That's Lizzie, too stubborn for her own good." Uncle Tom could've identified our parents, but Lizzie had to put herself through it.

"Anyone else?" I asked without knowing what I hoped the answer would be.

"Only your sister's friend, the handsome man, I think his name is Eli. Some doctors and nurses kept on visiting you. You're the first to regain consciousness."

"The first?"

"The others the police found, they're in hospitals across the city."

"What others? I was alone, they killed both the women held with me." My memory returned and I couldn't do anything to repress it. I cried, savouring the human contact the nurse offered me as she stroked my hair and held me against her. She only got up once to close the door so I could cry without everyone in the hospital hearing my anger, my pain, the horrible words coming from my mouth. She waited until I had finished crying then pulled away from me, and with a stern look, told me what I never expected to hear.

"You were never alone, Miss Williams. There were three young men there, too. The paper said they were held in the house on that farm. The police found DNA and wallets, something about trophies or something like that. Someone mentioned the bodies they found had bite marks. They ate pieces of them."

"Not possible, they killed women, not men." I didn't want to discuss eating people on an empty stomach, so I avoided the subject. *You only ate bread.*

"I don't know what to tell you, Miss Williams."

"Finley, please call me Finley. What's your name?"

"Okay, Finley. My name is Victoria, but you can call me Vicky." She had more than my mother's name, she had her warm brown eyes.

I heard Lizzie long before I saw her. The sound of her high heel shoes echoing through the corridors. She fell on the bed next to me crying, and I stroked her hair the same way I had when she broke down at the airport when I came home. So much had happened since I returned to Marcel.

"I'm fine, Lizzie. Should be out in a day or two." The doctor never indicated how long I was to remain in hospital.

"Eli." He leaned against the doorframe, not wanting to intrude. "Come here." I held my other hand out to him. "Thank you, Eli." I didn't want to say more, uncertain as to what Lizzie had been told. He blinked once and kissed my cheek.

Lizzie pulled herself together. "What happened? How did they get you? What happened?"

"I can't remember." But I did, every word, every sight, every second in that hell.

"The doctor said you might have memory loss because of what they did to you." She cried so loud Eli closed the door, not that it spared any of the other patients or staff.

"Lizzie, look at me. Look at me." I waited for her to meet my eyes. "I'm fine. I'm *going* to be fine. It's just a few bumps and bruises, I'll be out of here and kicking Eli's ass in no time." Eli gently wrapped his arms around me and kissed my cheek again.

"I want to talk to your doctor, hear for myself that you'll be okay now that you're awake." She steadied her feet and walked towards the door, turning back to give Eli her death stare.

"I will stay with Finley, you go talk to the doctor."

Lizzie nodded and headed out the door. The poor doctor had no idea a freight train headed straight for him.

"How did you find me?" I jumped right in; it was only a matter of time before the Lizzie Express headed in our direction.

"I'm sorry I didn't find you sooner." Tears welled up in his eyes, my strong friend on the verge of tears. I cried with him.

"You found me and I'm alive." Words jumped out in between the jerking movements of my sore chest.

"Getting into your laptop was the easy part, but it took weeks to find where you kept the backup files of the footage of the cameras and there was a lot to go through. Under different circumstances I would've said good job with the algorithm you used to scramble date stamps. Three days before we found you, I found a blurry shot of a number plate, pixilated, but we figured it out. The car came back as stolen so we combed through CCTV footage from across the city, trying to see if we could pick it up anywhere else, to see if we could get an image of a driver. The day before we found you, we got a face and tracked him down through facial recognition software. It came back as Ben Adams. He had priors for solicitation, possession, the usual. Tom got his juvenile record unsealed, and we found the address where he had stayed as a boy, a foster home. That's where he met Edward Harper. The address for the foster home was listed in the records, we had an address, somewhere to start. The farm is mid-way between Marcel and Wild Bay, geographically it made sense."

"She raped them."

"Who raped who?"

"The foster mother raped them, that's the reason they did this." Anger appeared on my face and neck. Anger towards them and her.

"That doesn't explain why they killed all those men. Listen, Fin, we can discuss it later. For now, you need to rest and heal. I know you will be here much longer than a few days, by now Lizzie should too."

I stayed in the hospital for a month. A week is a long time to be in any one place, a month bordered on torture. I kept that thought to myself. As soon as I could, I tried to move every day, desperate to return to the outside world. Not to return to my previous life, but a new life.

I did research and applied for my doctorates at UM. The courses started in five months, giving me enough time to get back on my feet and focus on Tabula Rasa and whatever else I wanted. It was freeing to sit and dream of the future. I spent the majority of my time reading and everyday Lizzie, Eli, and Uncle Tom came to visit. Lizzie had come to terms with what had happened to her, putting more effort into the research for the 'vaccine'. Her mission was to protect as many women, men and adolescents against the predators who drug their victims.

Eli bought me a new laptop, 'one for only good things,' he said when he came to visit me one day on his own.

Uncle Tom did what he does best; he put criminals behind bars – the right way. Not as effective, but the right way.

After being discharged from the hospital I stayed with Lizzie for a month, and it drove me insane to be out but not in my own space. I did online shopping and redecorated the whole lake house from the comfort of Lizzie's sofa.

Ashley drove me out to oversee deliveries; I recreated my world into what I wanted. Everything I no longer needed we used either for Tabula Rasa or the farm. Ashley and Kyle postponed their wedding, as she refused to get married without me as her bridesmaid. She did agree to getting married in front of a judge to speed up their adoption of Hope.

***

"Lizzie, I'm going to the lake house tomorrow morning; I need to pick up my guns on the way." Healed enough to drive myself and the first thing I had bought was a new SIG and a new Glock. Mine now evidence and I never wanted it back. B and E took it for themselves and used it for destruction, killing innocent men after doing unspeakable things to them. It baffled me that they killed men and women, but monsters are also diverse and no one fits a specific profile.

"No, you're not." Lizzie sounded like my father when I had said I wanted a motorcycle for my sixteenth birthday.

"I'm fine. I have to do this; I can't stay here forever. What happened is nothing more than bad luck; I thought I was stopping to help someone." We had lied to her; told her I had been a good Samaritan that night. She would never know the truth; Eli, Uncle Tom, and I swore to protect her.

"Please don't leave me." Her back towards me, she stood looking out on to her perfect garden, the palm tree's leaves swaying in the breeze.

"I have to go, for me. I need to be in control and you need your space. We both need to move on with our lives."

"I can't go through this again."

"You don't need to, Liz. I won't get abducted again. You need to move on with your life, with Eli. He loves you."

Eli planned to propose to her, and they would leave for Israel to introduce her to his family after Ashley and Kyle's wedding. He had asked me for my blessing.

I loved training again. It made me feel strong and free. No longer training for the hunt, but for me.

"I know. It's time; go pack your stuff while I make dinner. Do you want a Walker?"

A Walker? Did I want the drinking kind?

"No, thank you. Just coffee if you don't mind." I had been thinking of the other kind of Walker. So much time had passed since our weekend together and he hadn't come looking for me.

I went into the guest room which had become my bedroom

during the time spent at Lizzie's and removed it from where I kept it hidden. For the umpteenth time, I opened it and smiled as I read the lines that had been ingrained in my heart.

I never stopped looking for you. You're safe, that's all that matters.

I'm done and I hope you're too. I can still feel your lips against mine.

He had risked seeing me, standing next to me. Without his mask, he had walked into my world and out of his own darkness.

The sniper and I were both free.

I never asked Eli to hack the hospitals security cameras; to me he would remain faceless.

As long as he was free, it didn't matter.

Twenty-nine

The lake house, on the outside at least, looked as I had left it. It took a week to tile the floor and walls of the *room*. I filled the holes left from where the hooks once hung and repainted the ceiling. That room would never be used for torture or death again, but a panic room is crucial in this world. To close those doors for the last time was my last act of putting the darkness behind me. I hung an ornate wrought iron mirror over the door, a visual reminder of how far I had come every time I saw my reflection. To everyone else, it was just another of the many changes I had made. The lake house was finally decorated the way I had always envisioned. My mother didn't share my minimalist taste, no matter how many times I had tried to persuade her when they did their own remodelling.

Warmed by the fire, I sat on the dark leather couch looking out over the lake, my favourite place to await the start of a new day. There was something comforting in the plush cushions of my couch; bear hugs. My new morning ritual: get up, run, then wait for the sun to make its appearance. I relished in the tranquillity; peace had settled in the emptiness left by darkness' final disappearance.

My phone rang, and my hand reached for my Glock before the other hand found the thing that made me question my new-found calm.

"Hello, Uncle Tom, miss me already?"

"When can you be at my office?" In all my years never once had he asked me to his office. Ashley and I had taken him lunch occasionally as teenagers, but this was my first time being summoned.

"What's wrong?" I steadied the Glock against the other side of my head.

"A package addressed to you got delivered here this morning. Well, not addressed by name. We can open it, but you will never forgive me if we do. The bomb techs scanned the parcel. Fin, you need to get over here."

"On my way." I didn't want to leave the lake house; déjà vu. *I'm out of the darkness, let me go.* Before I headed to my bedroom, I cocked my Glock; my life not as quaint as a Dr Seuss story.

I got dressed; not battle-ready in low-cut dark jeans and my black leather jacket. Not dressing in full black as I did most days, my attempt at reminding myself I no longer fought any wars.

Maybe the sniper sent me something and doesn't have my home addresses, both unlisted, I thought as I pulled the helmet over my face and drove off to open a surprise I doubted I would enjoy or want if not from the sniper.

To find parking proved easier with the Ducati Monster, and I considered making it my main means of transport. *New Fin, new wheels.* I removed the helmet and shook my hair out. I must have been a sight, because I felt stares and saw a few people turn their heads. Adrenaline still pumped through me; I drove to Uncle Tom's office in less than half an hour, but steady enough for my palms to itch. Beady eyes watched me as I entered the building.

The inside of the building looked like any other government building – old. As a child I had thought it smelled like justice, but as an adult, I knew the building smelled old and justice like the decomposing carcass of a human shark.

I found Uncle Tom in his office, his tie loose around his red neck. A clear sign of his anger. He stood with his back to the door, staring at the box on his desk.

"Uncle Tom, what is it? Did the bomb techs x-ray the box or use a puffer machine?"

"X-ray. Not a bomb. If you want, I will open it." His back still turned to the door.

"It's mine to open." I removed the Smith and Wesson

Border Guard folding knife from my pocket and nudged Uncle Tom out of the way.

"Wait. Captain Taylor needs to be here." He turned and pulled me into his arms.

Captain Taylor found us holding each other, both staring at the box.

"Good morning, Captain. Thank you for the flowers. They were lovely, and the fruit basket even more so." The strange things people send to those who survived horrors.

"A small gesture, Finley. I wish we could've gotten to you sooner."

"You got there in time. May I open the box now?" *What's in the box?*

"Please do, but you don't have to. We can open it."

"Whoever sent this addressed it to me. I will open it."

Captain Taylor handed me a pair of blue latex gloves, which I dutifully pulled over my hands. I picked up the knife, which now lay next to the box, cut through the tape at the top and sides, steadied my hands and opened it. Bubble wrap popped as I pulled the contents out, placing it on the desk. I peeled back the layers until I saw the surprise. An envelope addressed to 'The woman survivor of the farm of horrors', typed in Times New Roman.

I slid open the envelope and took out a letter, typed in the same font, steadying it on the desk. It read: *bitch, you will die worse than the others. E.*

I stepped to my left for the two men breathing down my neck to read and removed the rest of the bubble wrap. A disfigured doll stared at me with no eyes. The doll's head, arms and legs were removed and dipped in something that had a faint copper smell. Her hair blonde, like mine. The pieces put together to resemble a scarecrow.

"Who is E?" Uncle Tom's hands gripped his desk, his knuckles white.

"Get me the file. Now." I stepped back, away from animated me.

"You can't see it, Finley, there are photos of you. You can't."

"I don't need photos to remind me of what they did, I remember every single time I see my wrist, my whole bloody body is one big reminder. Now show me the file." Something stirred in me; an emotion that had become a companion, although not a trusty one. Rage.

"Finley, I—" Captain Taylor tried, but I held up my hand.

"Now, both of you listen. I'm not some victim of what they did. Something has been bothering me since I heard about the male victims and you will show me the file, right now, or I will tear this place apart and anyone in my way."

Reluctantly, Uncle Tom gave me the file, and I asked them to leave me alone, but they protested. I slammed my fist into the wall next to the window and they obliged. Luckily for me, my less dominant hand was broken when I took that final beating.

I read the file twice, forcing myself to read as if I didn't know. The second time I ignored my name and read about what had happened to another Finley Williams and found the courage to look at the photos. *Impossible!*

"It's not him, it isn't E." I crossed my arms over my chest.

"What do you mean it isn't him?" Both men rushed back into the room.

"This is B or Ben Adams." I pointed at what remained of a face in the photo. "But this here, this isn't E." An unscathed face I didn't know.

"That's Edward Harper, we got him, Finley. Eli shot him. Why do you keep calling them B and E?"

"That might be Edward Harper, but that isn't E. They referred to each other as B and E; at first I thought they didn't want me to hear their names, but they were going to kill me so I realised it was their pet names for each other. You do realise they were lovers? That's why he's coming after me, he blames me for B's death, as if I had anything to do with it." My blood refused to thaw.

"Who is E?" Captain Taylor asked.

"E was with B the whole time. They did that to me." I pointed to where the photos of my mangled body lay. "E is still out there, and he's coming after me."

My life had become a bad horror movie, and I wanted to strangle the script writer and perhaps the director too.

"Let me look at the list of the other boys' names again, the ones who were in foster care the same time they were." Captain Taylor handed me the list and I sat, ran my index finger down the list and found Eddie Mitchell.

"Can you get me a photo of Eddie Mitchell? How he looks now?" I finished two cups of disgusting percolated coffee before Captain Taylor returned and handed me a printout.

He looked several kills younger, but there was no mistaking it; Eddie Mitchell and E were the same id.

"That's E. Did you find Ben's DNA on any of the men?"

"No," they both said.

"Well, gentlemen, Edward Harper killed the men. Ben Adams and Eddie Mitchell made scarecrows. E, Eddie Mitchell, is coming for me." I walked over to the window, seeing nothing but a dark wave closing in.

"We will put a surveillance team on you, you need to come back to the city and stay at the penthouse."

"You will do no such thing, I will not be his prisoner again."

"Finley, you don't have a choice." Uncle Tom placed his hands on my stiff shoulders.

"I do have a choice. I will not miss Ashley's wedding because of this thing, not again. This isn't a negotiation, Uncle Tom. I can take care of myself, even if you don't think so. Has the fact that I've been held captive twice somehow diminished my capabilities to protect myself? It doesn't erase the long list of times I saved my squad and everything else I have done." I hoped Captain Taylor wouldn't see the way I looked at Uncle Tom when I said 'everything else'.

"There is no reasoning with you when you're this angry. Please think about it. I don't want you up there by yourself. If Tony Andretti could get to you, then so can this E person." A mixture of anger and fear swirled in his eyes. I realised I kept putting Uncle Tom through hell.

"You need to reconsider, your life is more important." Captain Taylor waded into the storm.

"No, the lives of everyone I love are most important. I have an idea and you will both agree to it." I told them my idea; they both agreed.

Uncle Tom brought us more vile coffee, and we went over the plan one more time. They had work to do and not a lot of time to do it.

I drove back to the lake house, much slower than I wanted to, but the marked police car had to keep up. You can't get arrested by the officers assigned to protect you; well, I could, but that would be a waste of time.

I walked into the lake house and waited. My plan set.

How could I be captured twice?

Thirty

I hated that Ashley had to postpone her wedding on account of me being missing. They got married in front of a judge, but it still weighed heavily on me. To make up for what was beyond my control, I paid for their second honeymoon. I knew she would love Dubai as much as I do.

Lizzie, Eli, and I headed to Wild Bay a few days before Ashley's bigger-big day. It was my first time back there since our parents had died. There was never time, but now time was all I had. I looked forward to spending time there with Lizzie. Our days were filled with time spent at the beach, dinners the three of us prepared together, and laughter. Stomach-ache laughter. It was perfect.

The morning of the wedding, Lizzie and Eli went to the grocery store. For the first time since we had arrived four days earlier, I found myself alone. I sat on the deck and missed my parents. The house was still as they had left it; Lizzie shared my mother's taste for whites and blues. It was homely and safe. Just as they were.

I made the most of my time and worked on my tan. The dress I bought for the reception was backless and I didn't want visible tan lines, and a healthy glow would make the white scars less visible. Tan lines and scar tissue look so tacky with an elegant dress. I took off my bikini top and lay down, no longer thinking of my parents. The sound of the waves lulled me into content. I had always lived close to the ocean, but being there had a vacation vibe. I couldn't remember when last I had been on a vacation.

The surroundings of the lake house stood in contrast to the ocean views I grew up with and the darkness of the woods spoke to me from a young age. My parents knew Lizzie and

I so well, leaving us each the perfect part of their purchased world. Memories of Lizzie and my wild days of youth spent at Wild Bay filled me with nostalgia. Being there cleared my mind, it reminded me of who I once was, before war. Both kinds.

Voices. I must have fallen asleep on the lounger.

"Wait! Give me a minute before you come out here." I wriggled around like a beached whale trying to fasten my top. Silence. I lifted my bum still wriggling and won the battle.

As I stood up, a hand grabbed hold of my heart, clenching the air from my lungs. My heart broke free and beat louder than the crashing waves.

I couldn't read his expression. A reflection of my own.

"I'm sorry if I startled you, but I'm not sorry for seeing you like this." His eyes stroked me. All of semi-naked me.

"I have eyes. If you don't mind." *How did he find me? Here, of all places?*

"You can't blame me for admiring the view." He didn't know facial anatomy. His eyes everywhere but on mine.

"If that's your best line you better keep working on it."

"I told you before I can't think straight around you." His body reacted to what he saw. The same reaction stirred in me.

"Did you come here to stare?" My heart beat the only thing I heard. That, and his sexy, husky voice.

He looked even more like the doppelgänger of the movie star whose name I can't remember. Their names or surnames the same. I couldn't think straight seeing him like that. Dressed in swim shorts and a T-shirt, the sight of him was captivating. I forgot how to breathe.

"Marco." Dimples appeared under his faint stubble.

"Polo," I said, and he closed the distance between us. His hands glided around my waist and as he found my back, he pulled me against him. A soft moan slipped from my mouth. His Nordic-blue eyes finally found mine, our mouths the same perfect fit.

We kissed until my head spun, until all of me did. My heart rate increased with each hungry touch of our tongues. Teasing, hinting, reminding me of how it felt to be with him. The constant anticipation. His naughty games. Oh, how I missed his games. *I ached for you.*

My legs failed me, he held me tighter. I needed to breathe, give my poor heart time to calm itself.

My heart won the battle for calm and forced my mouth from his. "How did you find me?"

He traced my bottom lip with his thumb. A smile followed, and I almost kissed him again.

"I bumped into Eli and Lizzie at the store. Eli told me you were here."

"You can't blame me for meddling, Fin." Eli stepped out onto the deck, carrying his victory on his face.

"I won't. But that still doesn't explain what you're doing here." Curiosity tried to take another of my nine lives. Not that I had many left.

"I'm in town for a wedding, staying at my parents' house. They will retire one day and plan on moving down here."

"Ashley and Kyle's wedding?" Impossible. *Has my life turned into a range of different movie genres all in one lifetime?*

"Yes." His hand reached for mine. "Please tell me you don't have a date."

"I don't."

"You do now." He lifted my hand to his mouth, his lips warm on my warm skin. I was sure my heart detonated an IED.

"What makes you think I wasn't planning on sleeping with the best man?"

"John is married. And I would prefer if you go home with me."

Eli shifted and headed back into the house; his stride reminded me of a race horse out of the gates.

"Who said anything about going home with him?"

"Woman, you're making this harder than it has to be. Just

say you will be my date for the wedding."

Anticipation would kill me long before curiosity had the chance to claim my last life. "Doctor Walker, I made it hard long before you kissed me." I forgot how naughty I was around him, a side of me reserved only for him.

Aidan laughed, took my other hand, spun me around and danced with me. No music, just us.

The wedding was everything Ashley dreamed it would be. As far as beach weddings go, it was perfect. Clear skies and a gentle breeze to ward off the heat. Ashley looked beautiful in Aunt Kelly's wedding dress. A few alterations to make it more modern. Uncle Tom cried when he gave her away, oblivious to the fact he had done it before in the courthouse.

Aidan couldn't tell me enough how beautiful I looked when Lizzie and I came out of the room before the four of us headed to the wedding. He sent me a text message while I stood next to Ashley to remind me. I read it long after he sent it, rereading it every chance I got. He didn't have to send it; I felt his eyes on me throughout the ceremony.

The bridal party had a wardrobe change before we headed to the reception. Our dresses and suits were wet from the photos taken in the ocean. Hope cried every time the waves crashed around her, but there were enough willing arms to keep her dry.

Aidan waited for me at the bar, turning to watch me long before I reached him. No matter how much fun I had playing with Hope on the beach, I was desperate to get back to him.

"You can't do this." He could've passed for James Bond leaning against the bar in his black suit, if it wasn't for the whiskey in his hand. The sight of Aidan in a suit left me shaken and stirred.

"Can't do what? I just got here."

"You're upstaging the bride. We need to get you home and out of that dress."

"Did you bring your coin?"

"That's not what I meant and you know it." His eyes said something else.

"Well, we have a problem then. I like this dress and I'm not taking it off. If you want me out of it, you need to take it off." Finley the porn star crashed the wedding. I'm not proud of her, but she has the tendency to show up around him. And, I liked the dress, the only one I have ever enjoyed wearing. An elegant floor-length silk dress. I loved the way the material stroked the hollow of my back. True to my taste, it was black. It made me feel feminine yet dangerous. *Something a spy would wear to a cocktail party.*

Uncle Tom walked over to us and kissed my cheek without taking his eyes off Aidan.

"Doctor Walker, I didn't know you would be here." He didn't sound like the father of the bride.

"Mister Anderson, nice to see you again. Kyle and I go way back." Aidan held his hand out to Uncle Tom, who took it, but his grip was much harder than necessary. Aidan didn't flinch.

"How do you know Finley? I thought you had left for India." Not the voice of my godfather.

"How we first met is a long story. You know I treated her when she came into the emergency room after she was rescued."

This, I didn't know. I turned to face him. Aidan answered my confusion with a wink. "We can talk about it later." I didn't push the matter.

"Congratulations on your daughter's wedding. If you don't mind, I would like to go give them both my best and see my beautiful Hope." Aidan excused himself.

The way Uncle Tom watched him leave left me more confused. *Why did he refer to Hope as his Hope? India?*

"What's wrong, Uncle Tom?" I didn't know him to act so strangely.

"Finley, be careful. I have a feeling that man is hiding something."

"You've been on the job for too long. With everything that

Lizzie and I have been through, I can understand if you're apprehensive of new people in our lives."

"What do you know about him?" He wore his interrogation face.

"I know enough to know I want to see where this relationship goes." Aidan and I hadn't discussed that it was a relationship, but I knew there was something real between us. I was in no mood to have my new-found happiness spoiled by my over-protective godfather. In an attempt to diffuse the situation, I offered what I knew.

"I know he served in the military, he's a medical doctor, brilliant, and is an honest and real person. His willpower is off the charts." I didn't offer the reason for the latter observation.

"Be careful with him. Don't let your guard down." Uncle Tom waved at the bartender who brought him a brandy.

"I don't need a guard with Aidan. Get to know him and you'll see for yourself what a remarkable person he is. Trust me."

"I trust you. I don't trust him." He was relentless.

"Where is all of this coming from? When Ari and I were, let's say, seeing each other, you had no reservations, not for the most part." My spine went rigid. I wasn't some schoolgirl who needed to be warned against the bad boy.

"Don't allow whatever issues you have to become a problem between us. I love you, and you need to love me enough to let me make my own decisions. I will continue seeing Aidan and that's the end of this discussion. This is your daughter's wedding, focus on her."

"You're right. I just don't want you to get hurt, you have been through enough." Meaningless words; I knew when he lied.

Uncle Tom kissed my cheek again and left. I ordered myself a double of my no-longer favourite Walker and emptied the tumbler before I went looking for Aidan.

***

The rest of the evening was filled with speeches leaving everyone in tears and fits of laughter, delicious meals and matrimonial bliss. The only part of it which wasn't normal was the way something else, unknown to me before, awoke when I saw Aidan with Hope. She couldn't get enough of him, and his infatuation with her was visible from the stratosphere. They danced, her gleeful squeals drew everyone's attention to them. She came looking for him time after time when he finished dancing with her and returned her to Ashley and Kyle. Hope's wobbly legs made determined strides towards him, arms up, begging for another dance. She fell asleep in his arms, and his face radiated warmth and love. Seeing him with Hope, I knew without a doubt I was in love. Not in a silly love-at-first-sight kind of way, but deeply in love with him.

"May I have a turn to dance with you?"

"I don't know if I can throw you in the air. But if it makes you laugh like it did Hope, I will try." His boyish grin. For the first time in my life, Uncle Tom was wrong.

"Dance with me, Aidan." I pulled him to his feet. His scent filled the room. *Deep in love.*

His free hand trailed the length of my spine as he whispered in my ear. "Do you know why I couldn't say anything this morning?"

"Because you were kissing me?"

"No, before you even saw me." He stopped moving.

"Why?" The roundness of his shoulder under my free hand. I craved the feeling of his muscles twitching under my mouth.

"It took restraint I didn't know I have not to make love to you right there on that lounger. In front of your sister and Eli. The way your body moved as you tried to fasten your top." His eyes tried to tell me something. "I'm in love with you, Finley. I have been ever since our first night together. You might not realise it, but you're mine now. I'm never letting you go. Nothing will ever take you away from me, I won't let it." We were the only two people in the room.

"Make love? No one's first time is making love."

"Ours will be. I know you."

"You don't know me; spending one weekend and one day together isn't long enough to get to know someone."

"If I don't know you, how do I know you love Eggs Benedict for breakfast? Only after your second cup of coffee – milk no sugar – do you feel ready to take on the world. Your favourite colour is black, which for the record isn't a true colour. You hate slow drivers, slow walkers – slow everything – so this must be torture for you. Sorry, I didn't mean that."

I brushed my lips against his and asked him to continue. "Your favourite bands are Metallica, Five Finger Death Punch, and U2. You don't tell people this because you're such a badass, but you enjoy country music."

He winked, sending my heart running for the coolness of the ocean. "You love it when I bite your neck and I remember the way your body responds when I touch you, kiss you, and the way you taste."

Aidan pulled his lower lip between his teeth sending shock waves through me. "You never told me, but I know you want to be a mother. The way you couldn't take your eyes off Hope and me as we danced. Don't worry, I won't tell. Every part of you, every secret, is safe with me."

I wanted him to know me even more. And I realised he paid attention when we played his little game that night, so long ago, but the memories so vivid it could've been the previous night. Aidan was right, seeing him with Hope reminded me I wanted to be a mother. A desire I hadn't entertained in years.

"What more is there you can learn about me? But I have an idea with you I will discover sides of myself I never knew. Aidan, nothing will ever take me from you. But I need to know something. Let's go down to the beach."

We walked in silence, our fingers intertwined for the duration of the way. I found the spot where Hope and I had tried to build sandcastles. Sand heaps more than castles as she had crushed whatever I tried to build for her.

"Aidan, what's this about you taking care of me when I was

brought into the hospital?" Curiosity aimed for another life. He refused to give me his eyes, and I focused on what he gave them to. White streaks on the water. Moonlight illuminated the dark surface. We sat in silence; my other hand found his face. He pressed his lips to my palm, and I doubted whether I wanted answers; I would much rather feel his lips on mine.

"You need to understand I had no way of knowing it was you. The way you looked, what they did to you." Emotion filled his voice, and I leaned my head on his shoulder. I didn't recognise myself.

"The paramedics rushed you in and I did what I had to do to keep you alive. Did they tell you? You flatlined twice. You died in front of me, twice."

"You saved my life?" The nurse told me I had died but never told me the name of the doctor who saved me.

"I left the following day for training in India and then went on sabbatical. If I had known it was you I would've stayed and never left your side." Strained emotion in his voice.

"You saved my life. You're here now. It's all I need. Thank you."

"For what?" His eyes met mine.

"For not giving up, for saving my life, for finding me. All of whatever this is." His face was warm in my hands and stubble tickled my palms.

Our lips met; tears mixed.

"How do you know Kyle?" I had more questions, avoiding the one I needed to be answered the most.

"We attended the same high school, but lost contact over the years. Life. One night he and Ashley rushed into the ER with Hope, she had a fever. We recognised each other and remained in contact, became friends again. I love that little girl, maybe more so because Ashley told me how she came into their lives."

"She is remarkable. You have a way with her." My heart survived the earlier detonation and raced away from the scene. *Deep in love.*

"I love children. It's part of why I won't specialise as a paediatrician. I can't bear to see children sick or hurt."

"You, Aidan Walker, are an amazing person. I'm captivated by you." My lips found his. It was the perfect moment and my body moved itself over his. We kissed until I couldn't keep myself from tugging at his clothes.

Aidan pulled away. "Patience. Our first time will not be on a beach. You deserve more than a lust filled moment. I want to dance with you, in front of people. I don't trust you and for the first time in my life, I don't trust myself."

I wished he had less self-control, but he was worth knowing. The best chance for our relationship to be real and to last. I wanted nothing more. "So, I take it you are not coming home with me?"

"Did you not see the overnight bag on the backseat of my SUV?" I had, but I was more intrigued because he had the same G-Class I did, but his was palladium silver.

"Yes, but—" He put a finger to my mouth.

"Did you not hear me earlier? You're mine. There's nothing I want more than to fall asleep with you in my arms. Kiss your beautiful face even before I open my eyes. Just don't run away again."

I wondered when he would bring it up. "I'm sorry, I can't tell you why I had to leave. When I got back to the hotel you had already left. I wasn't sure you wanted me to contact you." I made myself look vulnerable. Desperate to change the subject of me leaving him. Forget the horrible reason, I didn't want to open the abyss to him.

"It surprised me, too. The way we were together, it was too good to be true. I assumed you didn't want me to contact you, Finley – or should I call you Victoria?"

I laughed and kissed him; the conversation needed to end. It didn't matter anymore.

Aidan spent the following day with us at what was now Lizzie's beach house. It felt even more like a vacation with him there.

Even though E still hadn't made an appearance, I didn't care about the darkness, it couldn't penetrate the walls of our happiness. I felt safe, surrounded by the people I held most dear, their laughter crushed reminders of the danger that still lurked. Circling me, bumping me, waiting to breach and devour me.

If E went looking, id would find me at the lake house. I was there. A clever ruse to draw E out. I hoped id would take the bait. That this nightmare would end while I lived my life. Far away from the abyss. My life had turned into what I had learned to be normal.

Being with Aidan was not normal in any form, and I've never experienced such intensity with anyone before. It was real, yet surreal. Lizzie accepted him, they bonded over their shared interest in medicine and for the first time she met someone by far her intellectual superior. Eli knew him from their training together, but I didn't know they sometimes went out for a beer. They told me how Aidan had run into them at the store. Aidan was startled at the sight of Lizzie, and for a moment he thought he was looking at me. He asked Eli if Lizzie had a sister as she headed to the cashier. Eli could finally say what he had wanted to since I had threatened him into silence. My friend; he only wanted me to be happy, and he knew Aidan would make me happy. Ari was and always would be his friend, but he left. We all needed to move on. We had a long time ago. Life has a funny way of working out even when you can't see it.

"When do you need to be back at work?" I asked as Aidan loaded my luggage into his SUV.

"Only next week. Do you mind if we spend the rest of the week together? I'm not ready to wake up yet." His fingers pushed my hair away from my face and kept it in place at the back of my head.

"Let's go to the lake. I have a house up there and it's the perfect place to keep dreaming." My lips teased his.

"If you don't feed me, I will go to my place there." The teasing ceased. I don't know who surrendered first.

Eli and Lizzie left the same day. I talked to Eli about our plans while Lizzie showered. She still had no idea about the threat to my life.

"Eli, we're going to the lake house for the week."

"Go home Finley, you can go back once the police find him." Eli ran his hands down his face and sighed.

"That's my home and he can find me anywhere. I won't let him control my life."

"Stop being so stubborn. Do you want to die? If you said this weeks ago, I wouldn't have been shocked. But now, you're putting Aidan in danger too. You know what he will do to you. He has been planning this for months. Don't do this."

"What's going on?" I didn't hear Aidan walk up behind us. The ocean was louder than usual and a storm formed on the horizon. Eli and I kept staring at each other. I didn't want to drag Aidan into this, but by going to the lake I would do exactly that.

"The guys who held me, one got away." My focus was still on Eli.

"And he's making threats against her. Please, Aidan, talk her out of this. For both her and your safety." For the first time I heard desperate concern in Eli's voice.

Aidan took both my hands in his. "Do you want to go?"

"Yes, but I can't put you in danger. I don't want to go back to the city and be back in reality. Not yet."

"Fin, the reality is, he wants to kill you. You know how he plans to do it. Why the hell do you want to give him the chance to get to you?" I had no answer for Eli.

"The police are still there. They won't leave and as much as the body double looks like me, he will know it's not me." I don't know why I wanted to go back. Maybe I wanted him to come after me so it could end, by my hand. I didn't want to live in constant fear.

"I will keep her safe, Eli." Aidan wrapped his arms around

me and drew my head to his chest. "You know I won't let anyone take her away from me."

"You don't know what you're up against. Not with him. The woods are dense around her house."

"If Finley wants to go, we will go. Arguing with her will only make her more determined."

Why do men have this way of talking about me as if I'm not even here?

"I'm standing right here. Eli, you know I can take care of myself."

"Like you did the night they took you? Or the night Tony Andretti almost killed you?" He was having none of it.

"That's not fair, you know what happened. The fact is he can get me anywhere, I will not live in fear of him. This discussion is over."

"Promise me you won't go out by yourself and you will keep your guns on you at all times."

"Does she ever not carry at least one? So do I." Aidan's hand patted the SIG holstered at his back.

Lizzie walked out to join us, ending the conversation without knowing it.

We said goodbye and left. Eli hugged me a little longer than usual before he closed the passenger door. I looked forward to having him for a brother. In-law or not, he had become part of the family. He was taking Lizzie to meet his parents the following day. To ask her to marry him. He had my blessing; I had helped pick out her ring. An exquisite princess cut set in titanium; to him, it was the perfect symbol of their relationship.

Thirty-one

Aidan drove us to the lake house, our first road trip. We laughed most of the way, reminiscing about all the drunk guests and their antics at the wedding. Lizzie, to my surprise, not the drunkest guest.

"Are you up for one of my crazy ideas?" His ideas were always good.

"Yes, let's do it." I do hate slow anything.

"No, you sex-crazed woman, I think we need to go away together. Have our own adventure, just you and me." The way he looked that day, who could blame me. The blue of his shirt played with the blue in his eyes, dark jeans a perfect fit for his masculine ass.

"Only if you pack the coin and don't book yourself a separate room."

"I don't care where I lay my head as long as I get to hold you and not sleep."

I unfastened my seatbelt, pressed my lips to his neck, and tried to climb on top of him. Aidan pushed me off with one arm, lifting my hand to his mouth in one fluid motion.

"Finley, I'm driving. How are we going to be together for the rest of our lives if we're in the ground?"

"Forever?" My thumb brushed over my wrist.

"Yes, forever. You're my orca. Is that why you got the tattoo?"

"Are you saying I'm as big as a whale?"

"Pregnant Finley might be." He laughed, I punched his leg, and the beautiful sound ceased.

"We need to have sex to get pregnant, Doctor; you're going to suck as an OBGYN."

"Why the orca?" He reached for my arm and pressed his

lips against the black ink.

"To an extent, because of the conversation we had. To remind me I'm not a victim, but a survivor. Not just once, but twice. If you only count the times I was held hostage and not factor in all the other times my life has been in danger. And to cover the horrible scar which I'm pretty sure you stitched. Am I right?"

"Even without knowing it was you, I wouldn't allow anyone else to touch you. I cleaned and stitched all your wounds. My hand cramped up you had so many wounds. I can't believe it healed so well."

"So that's why you took your time last night, you were playing doctor?"

"No and yes. Of course I want to make sure you're okay, needing to take care of you seems to be instinctive for me. But more than anything, I wanted to see every part of you, saviour the site of what's mine. I missed you."

"Who wouldn't?"

He pulled me closer and brushed his lips against mine, returning his focus to the road ahead just as fast. "Are you afraid? Of this E person coming after you?"

"Yes and no. Yes, I don't want to die, maybe in my sleep when I'm a hundred years old, but not the way he kills. No, because I embraced death once before. It isn't bad to die, letting go is easier than you would expect."

"You had nothing to hold on to, to fight for."

"No, I did, but I couldn't anymore. It felt right." I didn't want to tell him I thought it had been my punishment for everything I had done. "No, I'm not afraid of him, he's only human, he bleeds like the rest of us. And Eli tells me you are quite the marksmen. I will show you where the safe is, my Remington is in there if you ever need to use it. I hope you don't."

Aidan and I settled into the lake house as if we had lived together for years. It was exhilarating and comfortable, being with him made me feel sheltered. There is something to be said about a relationship filled with so much laughter and honesty. I looked forward to the adventure we discussed on the drive from Wild Bay. Aidan said he wanted to take me somewhere, I only needed to give him my passport and trust him. I trusted him, more than I had ever trusted anyone, ridiculous if you considered how short our time together had been. But when you know, you know.

He slept so peacefully that morning I didn't want to wake him. As much as I enjoyed having him with me, I wanted to spend half an hour alone just to let it all settle within me. I needed to release the giddy laughter I held in around him and jump up and down and do all the things a girl crazy in love does when the boy can't see her. Aidan hadn't been a boy in several years, he was very much a man, which made me even crazier about him.

I left him a note saying I had gone for my morning run and would be back soon if not before he wakes. Pointless to add to the note, but I own my silliness. Aidan had no idea that day was my birthday.

Setting my watch as I left the house it displayed the time as 05:00 a.m. On the deck, I nodded as I tied my bright turquoise running shoes, my signal to whoever watched me, waiting for E. Hidden under camouflage I didn't know where they were, but they were familiar with my routine, the same the body double had followed each morning she was me while I had been in Wild Bay.

Golden streaks streamed through the trees on the other side of the lake. I ran the same route every morning, always aware of the Glock by my side. After I received the box, I stopped running with earphones as I needed to hear if something or someone approached. *When will this movie end? End with: They lived happily ever after.* The movie of my life had terrible writing and the lighting wasn't that great either as the sun rose with little haste. In dense areas of the woods, darkness remained.

I couldn't stop smiling, rushing to get back to Aidan whom I hoped to find still in bed.

Id came out of nowhere.

No time to think about horror movies as my blood froze. Memories of id's grin as id hammered the spike through my wrist. The tobacco stench of id's spit on my face.

E stood in front of me. The barrel of id's gun greeted me. *Happy death day to me.*

No time to reach for my gun. Id stood motionless, except for id's finger squeezing the trigger. Three rapid punches to my chest.

I staggered back, collided with the dirt, gasping for air.

Breathe. My head was heavy as I tried to push myself up. My chest burned as I struggled for breath.

"No!" A voice in the distance. The barrel of E's gun shifted in the direction of the voice.

Movement in the distance, something or someone moved at great speed. Sidestepping trees, getting bigger with each stride. I found my Glock and stared down the sight.

I stopped trying to breathe as I watched him running towards me, E's gun followed his every move. *Not today, not him.*

I squeezed the trigger until the magazine was spent; E never saw death close in.

I fell back still struggling for air, staring at the green canopy. *Now that is how you thank someone for saving your life.*

"No. I can't lose you." His voice and hands frantic as he fell by my side and lifted my shirt. The sight of the Kevlar vest calmed him. I may have been getting older, but I wasn't stupid.

"You? It was you?" I struggled to fill my lungs with air.

"If you tell me you're okay, I will leave and never come back." Tears streamed down his face; the sight broke my heart.

"Where are the officers stationed outside my house?"

He pulled me into a seated position, and I buried my face in his chest. "Dead. He slit their throats."

***

The police arrived an hour after I phoned Uncle Tom. No need to rush when the monster is dead. My injuries were nothing more than three red and painful spots which turned blue, purple, yellow, the entire rainbow before they faded completely two weeks later.

Captain Taylor took my statement and then that of the person who had run towards me. I watched the police leave, watched as two bodies were driven away followed by a carcass in a separate vehicle.

For the first time I dreaded walking into my house. I headed straight to the coffee machine and made two coffees. As I carried them to the living room, he was still standing in the door, sunlight forming a halo behind him. He waited for me to invite him in.

"Sit, I made coffee. You need to start talking and no, I will not put my gun down." My Glock had been taken as evidence and I felt comforted by the size of the SIG in my right hand, pointed at him, my finger not yet on the trigger. My dark guardian angel sat to my left on a dark leather wingback chair. *Irony.*

"Talk," I growled.

"I'm done with it. After seeing you like that, I couldn't do it anymore." His eyes wouldn't meet mine.

"Why did you kill those people?"

"For the same reasons you did. To make the world a better place." He glanced at me.

"You and I are nothing alike." I officially hated my birthday; first Ari had left and now this.

"We are. The people I killed were monsters. Two years before my first kill, a fourteen-year-old girl was brought into the ER. Her name was Jessie, and she died of sepsis under my care. The sepsis was caused by the decomposing foetus still in her uterus. I held the pieces of a murdered foetus in my hands. In my *hands*, Finley. If her sister had brought her in earlier, I… she could've been saved."

He struggled to control his trembling hands. "I cornered

the sister and demanded answers. She started talking the moment I threatened to report her to the police. She admitted to taking Jessie to a back-street clinic for an abortion and admitted to pimping Jessie out. Her own sister, a child. The teacher I killed ran the clinic. He was once a surgeon but had his license revoked due to malpractice and ended up teaching biology at a high school. I got the names of all the men who had raped Jessie; the sister had kept a detailed client list and tried to calm me by telling me she only allowed those specific clients to touch Jessie. They weren't clients, they were rapists and paedophiles. Finley, Jessie was only fourteen. Fourteen. You can't understand what I lost that night."

The pain I had spent months trying to understand spilled out of him. His pained screams echoed through the house. He released the pain he had carried for too long. I wanted to hold him but pushed myself into the couch.

"Who did you lose?" My voice almost inaudible, I didn't expect him to answer.

His whole being cried, shaking as he let go of the anguish that had been torturing him. I couldn't bear seeing his pain and walked over to where he sat hunched over and put my arms around him. He held onto me and cried until he no longer had any tears.

Intelligent. Beautiful. Broken. My Aidan.

"Who did you lose?" I don't know why I asked again, but I had to know the root of his pain, which drove this remarkable man to commit murder.

"My wife and my son."

No words seemed right, so I held him, waited for him to talk, plead his case, convince me to stay with him, beg me not to turn him into the police. *I can't.* We were alike. How could I judge him after what I had done? I waited for him to find his way back to me.

"It's my fault they died. I was supposed to leave after my shift and take my wife to her parents for dinner, but I asked her to meet me there so I had more time to interrogate Jessie's sister. A truck skipped a red light and T-boned her car, impact was on the driver's side. My wife died and so did my son. She was eight months pregnant. I should've been home; I should've driven them to my in-laws. But because of Jessie's sister's actions, I wasn't there when my family needed me. I should've died that night with them. I never got to hold my son, only held his coffin the day of their funeral. That day I lost the one thing I wanted more than I wanted to breathe – my child."

His hair was soft under my lips. "I'm sorry, Aidan." I waited for him to meet my eyes.

"If I didn't stop them, they would have just raped another child. I couldn't let Jessie's sister live after what she had done to her own sister, her own blood. Then you and I met that night in the parking lot, and the way you spoke to me...I knew if there was one person who would understand it would be you. I saw you dump the first one; well, not you, I only realised the woman I spent that amazing weekend with had been you when I saw you in the parking structure again. In case you wondered, the night you torched the car I couldn't get a clear view of your face. Then you were abducted, and I tried everything to find you, but I failed. Your beautiful face, what they did to you. You died twice, but you came back and I knew you were worth putting all of this behind me for, to have a normal life, a happy life. And I hope a future with you."

"Why did you leave?" Senseless questions because I dreaded the one he would ask me.

"I was scheduled to go to the symposium, that part is true. I stayed on to give myself time to deal with everything and to make sure once I came back, I would stop. I won't kill again no matter what; they're all dead now. You were safe and I couldn't do anything for you. I sat next to your bed, watched you sleep and kissed you before I left. You needed time to heal and I had to ensure I would stop, not go out and search for more perverts, before I could be with you. I want to give you the life you deserve."

"Can you stop?"

"Yes. I have. I know I will still see horrible things, but I don't want to be that person anymore, I want to be the person I am when I'm with you. Can you give it up?" I expected him to ask, but it wasn't the question I dreaded the most

"Yes. I have. I have enrolled for my doctorates and start in a few months. Going forward, I will fight this the right way."

"Do we have a future?"

There it was.

I freed myself from his arms and got myself a Walker, the drinking kind, and poured him one for the irony of it. Aidan prefers Jameson. I took my position on the couch, away from him, looking out over the lake. The sun high on a beautiful grim day. I downed my glass of Walker, hoping the bottom held the answer.

"We have both done things, Aidan. To us maybe not terrible things, but necessary. We can't judge each other." I still didn't know what to say. I inhaled as deep as my bruised sternum would allow. I needed time to think, but before I reached the door, I looked at him. His gorgeous face was tormented.

"I'm in love with you, Aidan Walker. More than I ever thought possible for any person to be in love. Maybe more so now than when I woke up this morning. We have seen each other's dark sides and still, we want this. For the right reasons, not because we relish in each other's darkness but because we see each other's light and the future we could have. It will do us both good to get professional help, perhaps even together."

My eyes bore into him. "If you ever kill anyone again, I will turn you in. No matter how much I love you, no matter whether we have children. We make a promise right here, right now, and if you break that promise I will hunt you myself."

He pushed to his feet, his boyish grin returning to his face. "You want to have children with me?" His wet eyes glistened as he stepped into the sunlight.

"Yes, one day I want to have your babies. Our secrets are ours; not yours or mine. Ours."

As his mouth met mine, I knew I made the right decision. I wanted nothing more than to keep him safe and be kept safe by him.

"So, what are your plans with my sister?" We weren't even through Lizzie's front door. She refused to have dinner in a restaurant; a birthday is intimate, she had said, and invited us for dinner instead. My birthday, but I knew it would end up being her engagement party.

"Elizabeth Williams!" I shouted at her as I made my way to give her a hug, opting for a childish punch to her shoulder.

"I'm engaged." Her head bobbed as she jumped and pulled me into her arms to force me to jump with her. *Joy.*

"I know, who do you think helped choose your ring?" I pee'd on her parade.

"Thank you, Finley, I love it." She shook my pee off.

"Congratulations to both of you." Aidan shook Eli's hand and when he held his hand out to Lizzie, she pulled him into an embrace.

"He does smell good, Fin. Damn."

"He's mine. Hands off." Eli pushed Lizzie off Aidan and hugged him. That's how Uncle Tom found them.

The look in Uncle Tom's eyes made my stomach turn. We had agreed earlier to not talk about the morning's events during dinner. No point in upsetting Liz, it was over. I had already told Eli earlier when they phoned me to wish me a happy birthday.

It ended up being a better day than I expected. Considering the year and a half before, it couldn't have been better. It could've, but Aidan remained adamant about sticking to the rules of the coin. I considered begging, but even after everything that had happened, I still had my self-respect.

Aidan walked over to Uncle Tom to greet him; Uncle Tom pulled him onto the porch and closed the door. I ran out onto the patio, around to the front of the house and hid behind the bushes like a nosy teenager.

"You're not going away, are you?" Uncle Tom asked.

"No, I'm not. I will not leave her no matter how many times you threaten me. This is the last time I will say this, I'm not the sniper. Just because I can hit a target at a distance of two kilometres does not mean I'm the person you're looking for. You have my military records. Stop this or you will force me to lay a charge of harassment against you."

"You wouldn't dare. All I have to do is walk into that house and tell Finley you are a suspect."

"I told her. We don't have secrets. You don't have a shred of evidence and you're wasting my time."

"I know it's you, I will find proof. And I will see to it you end up where you belong."

"The only place I belong is in Finley's bed." Uncle Tom's fist headed for Aidan's face. Aidan grabbed it and twisted it fast, Uncle Tom winced. Still twisting, Aidan breathed hard. "I'm never letting her go. I love her." Aidan let go of Uncle Tom's fist and walked back into the house.

I emerged from the darkness like the Grim Reaper and walked up to Uncle Tom, his hands still shaking. "Let this go, I beg you."

"That man is a killer. I won't allow him to be a part of your life."

I straightened my shoulders. "For the last time, let this go. If you want to be a part of my life, you will let this go and look for the real killer. If you don't...come on, Uncle Tom don't you think I would know if Aidan is a killer? My palms don't itch around him. And I love him."

"You and your palms." He shook his head, rubbing his injured wrist. "Do you love him more than you loved Ari?"

"Yes," I said without hesitation. "What Ari and I had doesn't compare to this. Yes, he was good for me at that time in my life, but what I have with Aidan is what you had with Aunt Kelly."

"Don't you dare compare your silly infatuation with the love we shared." His breathing became louder, but his voice remained low.

"Are you going to try to punch me as well? You let me be, turned a blind eye to what I did, even had the balls to ask for my help. And look where that got me." I played the card I had held close to my chest since the wedding. "You need to go explain to my sister why you won't be here tonight. Call me when you're ready to apologise." I turned and walked into the house, bumping the door into Aidan's back. I didn't care if he had heard, I took his hand and walked towards the kitchen. It would take both my Walkers to ease the pressure in my shoulders.

Uncle Tom excused himself, claiming a work emergency. I didn't see him for months after that night.

The following morning Aidan and I left for the lake house to spend the last two days of our dream together. Come Monday, Aidan would start work again and we would find ourselves in uncharted territory – normal everyday life. Aidan and normal are not synonymous.

We stayed at the penthouse the night of Lizzie's impromptu engagement party; party of four. Aidan loved the penthouse and woke me up early to watch the sunrise. 'The first day of the rest of our life.' It sounded super corny but coming from him it was sweet and true.

He drove us to the lake house after breakfast and I enjoyed simply driving and not rushing anywhere, finding out we didn't have the same taste in music. I could get used to alternative rock as long as it wasn't pop.

Aidan headed straight to the fireplace and built a fire. I watched him and snuggled into his arms on the couch. It rained as we turned onto the road leading to the lake. The alarm tone on my phone sounded from the cameras, thirty minutes after where we had passed. I ignored it, keeping my focus on Aidan as he drove, teasing him, kissing his face, laughing with him.

"Want to hear something crazy?" His fingers intertwined with mine.

"Always. As long as it involves tossing the coin into the lake."

"I hate when you do that, I'm trying to tell you something. Won't mention it being hard to tell you something ever again. That naughty mouth of yours—"

"I love you, Aidan Walker." I won; I said it first.

"Woman, you stole my thunder. Finley Duncan Williams, I love you the most."

I would make Lizzie pay for blurting out Duncan after her fifth glass of French champagne.

He kissed me with a hunger he had never shown before. His hands made their way down my body, pulling and lifting clothes in the right directions. I pulled and lifted at his clothes, our breathing rushed and uncontrolled.

Aidan looked at me, leaving my body aching for his touch. I bent down and kissed him. He stood up with me in his arms and laid me down on the couch. "There's one thing I need to know right now."

"Which is?" I drowned in the want in his eyes.

"Where on this beautiful body of yours are you ticklish?" His hands went wild as he tried to make me laugh. I tickled him back, and he lost his balance. *Wow!*

"Sorry, I didn't..."

I wrapped my legs around him and pulled him closer. "Forget the coin. I want you, only you, for the rest of my life. All of you."

Aidan brushed his lips against mine, took my hands in his and stretched my arms above my head. He was right. *Mindblowing. Love.*

Epilogue

Two years later, Aidan played me a recording of a telephone conversation he acquired through a black-ops group who were tracking the movements of the individuals involved in the conversation. It was recorded the day I ignored the alerts of the motion detection cameras.

"Hello."

"It's me. I want back in."

"What happened? Did you talk to her?"

"She was busy."

"What do you mean she was busy?"

"I had to watch another man make love to my Ley. She was supposed to be mine, and it was your idea for me to leave and make her believe I'm some kind of hero."

"Your Ley? Oh, that's precious. I warned you not to fall in love with her. Maybe you weren't the right man for the job after all."

"And maybe you should've been a real godfather to her. Let's not forget the reason you hired me, and Eli, to infiltrate the lives of the Williams sisters."

"Don't you forget what's at stake. You had no qualms to insert yourself in her life and make her fall in love with you. You and Eli both knew what you were getting into."

"Who is the guy? Can we take him out?"

"Doctor Aidan Walker. I don't have any evidence yet, but I know he's the Marcel Sniper. She refuses to believe me. Finley has gone into protector mode with him and you know what a hard-ass she is when she does that."

"If she's in danger, I will rip his throat out."

"That is not the way to get him away from her. He will shred you to pieces if he suspects you're a threat. Ari, he's one of the best in the world, I have seen his records. You won't even know he's in the same city before his bullet rips through your skull."

"Is she in danger?"

"No, he won't hurt her. But Ari, I mean it. Whoever gets in his way is in danger. Where are you?"

"On my way back to the city."

"Come stay with me until we come up with a new plan. There's another case I can put you on so you can get over your pathetic crush. You fit the victim profile to a tee. But I have no idea what we're up against. So far we know of three men who have vanished from their homes."

"Thank you, Tom, you're a great handler and an even better friend. See you soon."

Acknowledgements

This book is dedicated to my family and friends - for their unwavering support and belief in my imagination and ambition.

To my first pass readers - Andrea, Annelize, Benita, Jean, Mariaan, Maricka, Marie, Naomi, Nicolina, and Tania. Thank you for loving Finley as much as I do.

Marcel, thank you for allowing me use of your name.

To my editor, Megan Pereira. You do so much more for me than only better my writing.

To my husband for listening when I plot scenes and still sleeping next to me no matter how dark my thoughts, or questionable my internet search history.

Most of all, to God. All I can offer in gratitude is my life.

All mistakes are my own.

About the author

Mariëtte Whitcomb studied Criminology and Psychology at the University of Pretoria. Writing allows her to pursue her childhood dream to hunt criminals, albeit fictional and born in the darkest corners of her imagination.

When Mariëtte isn't writing, she loves reading psychological thrillers and true crime books or spends time with her family, friends, and two miniature schnauzers.

Connect with Mariëtte:
Sign up for her newsletter on her website:
https://mariettewhitcomb.com
Email: mariette@mariettewhitcomb.com
Facebook: @mariettewhitcombauthor
Instagram: @mariettewhitcomb
Goodreads: https://www.goodreads.com/
goodsreadscommariettewhitcomb
Bookbub: https://www.bookbub.com/authors/mariette-whitcomb

Also by Mariëtte Whitcomb

FINLEY SERIES

Orca / Book One

Deception / Book Two

Binding Lies / Book Three

Fortius / Book Four

STANDALONE THRILLERS

The Skull Keeper

DEATH TRILOGY

Death Isn't Enough / Book One

Silent Death / Book Two

Even in Death / Book Three

www.ingramcontent.com/pod-product-compliance
Lightning Source LLC
Chambersburg PA
CBHW020054180626
46812CB00006B/2327